TWICE WE MAKE MAGIC

First published in Great Britain 2022 by Farshore

An imprint of HarperCollins*Publishers*
1 London Bridge Street, London SE1 9GF

farshore.co.uk

HarperCollins*Publishers*
1st Floor, Watermarque Building,
Ringsend Road, Dublin 4, Ireland

Text copyright © 2022 Sarah Driver
Illustrations copyright © 2022 Fabi Santiago

The moral rights of the author and illustrator have been asserted

ISBN 978 1 4052 9556 7
Printed and bound in the UK using 100% renewable electricity
at CPI Group (UK) Ltd
1

A CIP catalogue record for this title is available
from the British Library

Stay safe online. Any website addresses listed in this book are
correct at the time of going to print. However, Farshore is
not responsible for content hosted by third parties. Please be
aware that online content can be subject to change and websites
can contain content that is unsuitable for children. We advise
that all children are supervised when using the internet.

TWICE WE MAKE MAGIC

SARAH DRIVER

Illustrated by Fabi Santiago

For Ruth, a true adventurer.

And for Lil, one of life's great teachers.

The Ring

The Funeral
Parlour

Arundel

Knuckerhole
Village

PART ONE:

THE BARROW

Ingredients for a spell

A coven of girls once Wicked,

Hiding in a funeral home.

A missing undertaker,

A trainee in residence,

A cat who seems to know.

Heirloom tapestries,

Infused with stolen magic.

A tree whose roots taste every realm.

Ghosts demanding ice-cream,

A Rookery sheltering a Hangman.

Bone broth and rook eggs.

Barrows,

Thirteen moons.

A Shadow-Born girl, dwelling

above a tomb.

December 2021
As told by a local storyteller
at the Red Lion Inn, Arundel

On a hill overlooking Knuckerhole village stands a circle of trees. People call it the Ring. The Ring has stood for as long as anyone can remember, and as long as their long-dead ancestors could. And for as long as the Ring has stood, a funeral parlour has hunched in its shadow. A house for the dead.

At least, that's what the old stories say.

Now, the Ring is shrouded in an eternal, foul fog. Only the trees remain. There is no funeral parlour there.

Prologue

Flux often wondered whether their afterlife had been better before the Hangman had found them playing hide-and-seek in his Rookery; the lumpen mounds of greasy feathers forming avenues like those of a twisted amusement maze.

Undoubtedly, they should never have been there. As a traveller Flux liked to take the odd detour, but even they didn't expect to cheat true death for much longer.

The Hangman had proposed a deal that would help Flux evade death for far, far longer. Coveted books in exchange for a home, and the honing of the craft that had been sacred in their lifetime. Life, of sorts, clinging by a thread.

'Transfer to me the power of your Book of Shadows,' the Hangman had intoned, clawlike nails stroking the cover of the book that had been in Flux's bloodline for generations. 'And assist me in my task of gathering up all the other witches' books. Do it, and I will gift you the power of ever-walking. Prevailing upon this world, defying the shadow path.'

Flux wept, thinking of the ancient barrow where their

bones slept alongside those of their clan, bejewelled with grave trinkets. After death, Flux had begun to follow the paintings left as a guide to the afterlife, but realised they still had the talent of unrestricted travel. They had strayed from the path, into temptation.

Flux considered the Hangman's bargain, and agreed. The book transferred into his possession, cutting the last link to Flux's past. A thread began to grow between their shoulder blades.

Flux never had another moment empty of the Hangman. If they tried to free their mind of him, the tether twanged, thickened, pulled. Pain pooled between their shoulder blades, deep and wide as a killing wound.

The rain thickened, blown hard by the wind. It thumped and smeared across the windows. The world was a bog.

Flux stood underneath the tapestry, stared into its mouth, and shivered.

The Hangman had been very clear.

'This time, you will bring me the book I seek,' he had rasped. 'For threads can be snipped.'

Imagined pain bloomed like an omen between Flux's shoulder blades. It would be pain like bone marrow scooped out by the fistfuls. They could not fail. For time untold Flux had done the Hangman's bidding, hunting witches' Books of Shadow and searching for the most fabled book – a skull-smooth grimoire, old as the bones of the earth.

Worlds travelled courtesy of the slightest clue, whispers fizzing in the dark like arrows. Meetings in rain-soaked alleyways, warnings, portents, thunderstones exchanged for the barest information. Agile aircraft sculpted from bone, launched through portals to hunt for witch-books. Flux forever aware of the tether in their back; a pull, an ache, a duty and a reminder of their false freedom. Though wasn't that a better fate than death?

The grimoire did not reveal itself.

But this night, it happened, sudden as anything attempted for centuries and no longer expected – they spied it, the fabled grimoire. The tapestry began to perspire, feverish in anticipation. Its threads twitched and danced, sketching the ghostly trees of a felled great forest, and the shadows of creatures that once dwelled in that wild place.

Crouched in a gap between worlds, Flux saw a child sitting in bed, face pressed close to the pages of her witch's book. A bald child, with a faraway quality about her. A magic distance.

The veil was there, but it was thin. Flux regretted not consulting a moon.

The child glanced up, quizzing the atmosphere with soft but knowing brown eyes. Eyes that thinned the magic veil between them even further.

Flux gasped. Stumbled. Fell backwards under the power of the girl's stare.

Running didn't feel so much like running as like being spat out by the book.

1
Elspeth Wrythe,
Undertaker in Residence

January 2022
Funeral parlour of the Ring, Knuckerhole,
Old Kingdom of Sussex

'Ghosts can't eat ice cream!' I shout. I must have told the spirit the same thing a hundred times by now, because that's how many times he's asked me for ice cream. I've fought all afternoon to keep the edge of frustration from my voice, and I needn't have bothered. My patience has officially snapped.

The ghost – in the image of the tall, middle-aged man he was until recently – shoots away from me and swipes at the freezer. Annie Turner, our mentor, swears loudly. 'Girls! Can you please try and get that spirit under control? I'm brewing a very important spell here.'

A steady *plink, plink, plink* distracts me for a moment. There's another leak in the roof, and someone's put a bucket under it. The rain has fallen in sheets for weeks, turning the Ring into a bog and bloating the stream at the bottom of the hill. The funeral parlour has been half sucked into the earth. Annie tells us the people around here have fifty words for mud. I can believe it.

'He wants *ice cream*?' asks Mariam, abandoning the obituary she's been typing to help me keep the freezer from toppling under the force of the ghost's desperate rattling. Vines grow from the plants on the windowsill and stretch across the floor to help her. 'I thought he wanted to freak us out!'

'They usually want whatever you or I would want,' I tell the former Mouldheels' School head of dorm. 'Wouldn't you want ice cream if you were in denial about your own death?'

The ghost stops rattling the freezer and there's a break in the tension of the air as he rushes away in another direction. I stumble after him into the threadbare, faded floral sitting room. A pot plant crashes on to its side, spilling soil across the worn carpet.

'Oh, has he given in?' enquires Layla, pushing her glasses higher up her nose. She's been poring over a spellbook, looking for ways to disarm a poltergeist.

'Um, no, not really!' I yell, scurrying after the ghost.

'He will soon, don't worry, Spel!' Layla calls back. Her powers involve prediction and premonition, so I suppose I should trust her on that.

I'm the only one that can actually see him, but no one can miss the trail of destruction he's leaving around the funeral parlour. All of this is my responsibility, ultimately, but so far

I'm not doing a great job of it. The undertaker, Shranken Putch, left a scrappy note for me that I think about so many times a day it's giving me a permanent headache.

The Ring is in want of an undertaker, small Wrythe. The boots are yours to fill until Putch returns. The living and the dead have need of you. Help the spirits through – or you'll be overrun by ditchlings.

When I replay the words in my head, they're in his grumbly voice. I picture his tangled eyebrows furrowed together as he wrote it, his cap of wild hair quivering. When we first came here, I thought I'd never met a stranger person. But it didn't take long to realise he was the kindest grown-up we'd ever known, and the best hot-chocolate maker ever. And that odd people are the best people, anyway.

The ghost starts trying to tear a heavy black drape off the mirror in the sitting room, but I grab hold of the other end of the material and yank it back into place. 'You really don't want to do that! Spirits can be sucked into mirrors, that's why we cover them!'

Isla looks up from the catalogue where she's been marking how many shrouds and urns we need to order. 'Ooh, can they?' she says, pale face glowing with feverish excitement. She flings the catalogue aside and crouches near the mirror, eyes fruitlessly searching the air. A flame pops into life on the end of her fingertip, as though she thinks the glow will help her see the dead.

'Don't get any ideas,' I tell her. 'The mirrors stay covered.'

The ghost falters for a moment, dark eyes flashing and wet, like two pools of paint. He's just projecting the impression of eyes. But his feelings are very real. He gives the drape one last yank and flits away, skimming across the floor and spotting the sofa in globs of green slime.

I've learned that ghosts' emotions are shed in various messy ways. For some of them, that means slime. Unfortunately, the sofa is where Jameela's been curled up, revising her driving theory. More unfortunately, the slime falls directly on to her upturned face.

'Urgh!' she screeches, jolting upright. 'Elspeth, what are you up to now?'

'Nothing!' I pant, despair rising as the ghost pings around the room.

'That's what you get for refusing to help, Jam,' sing-songs Egg, poking out her tongue.

'Refusing to help? That's what you call learning to drive the hearse, and spending the past two days dealing with the council and those belligerent pallbearers Putch insisted on working with?'

'Belligerent?' replies my sister, mockingly. 'Well, *la-di-da.*'

Our tall, tack-smart coven-mate rolls her eyes and gets back to her reading.

Clouds of ash filter through the air. The ghost scrabbles around at the mouth of the fireplace, scattering old coals and ashes across the room.

'What are you doing?' I yell, darting over to him. Briefly, it crosses my mind that I have an incredibly long night ahead of me. The evening is already blending into night.

The long night of the soul, as Shranken Putch liked to call it.

There might be a fair amount of drama, but I'm actually really impressed with my former dorm-mates – and current coven-mates – for the way they've taken death, ghosts and funeral arranging into their stride. Annie Turner is our adult in charge, and she's doing pretty well at that, too. She used to be our Mistress at Mouldheels' School for Wicked Girls, but we didn't know she was an undercover witch.

Since Putch left, we've had to think on our feet. We discovered where he ordered coffins from, and we order them one by one according to need. A plain, lined coffin is included in the cost of a basic pauper funeral.

We instruct the bereaved in the death customs, and we observe them here as well, out of respect. I've already stopped all the clocks to prevent bad luck, and turned down the photographs so the people in them won't be possessed by the spirits of the dead. Egg has covered the mirrors.

I can't even begin to hold the wake – sitting with the body while the spirit passes through into the Shadow Way, the world of the dead – until I've convinced this spirit that he is really dead and managed to get him back into the basement. I'm already *so* tired.

The living and the dead have need of you.

My eyes must have scoured the note a hundred times, searching for hidden clues that never appear. Now it's folded in my pocket. The weirdness of how Putch talks about himself in the third person hasn't eased, however many times I've read it. Something about the message just doesn't sit right.

A blistered lump of coal zooms across the room and hits me in the chest. I have an idea. 'Get the bellows,' I whisper to Mariam.

She grins, tiptoeing around the edge of the room, avoiding the places where clumps of charred ashes are flying through the air. When she has the brass and leather bellows in her hands, I direct her.

'Ready?'

She nods.

'Now!' I hiss. 'Left, right, straight ahead, keep going!'

Telling Mariam where to direct the air means that the ghost is swept across the room in a current that he wasn't expecting. If we can keep the wind strong, hopefully we can sweep him down to the basement.

But the ghost clings in the doorway.

The clews select this moment to appear, scurrying out from under the skirting board and forming themselves into an unsteady tower that whooshes towards me.

HelloElspethwouldyoulikeacupoftea?

'Bad timing,' I hiss, desperately.

Butwouldyoulikeacupoftea?

'Shhh, we're busy!' snaps Mariam.

Didweaskyou? trill the clews, staggering in their haphazard tower formation. It's dangerous to accept a cup of tea from them anyway, because you usually get scalded when they try to pass it to you.

'Charming,' mutters Mariam.

Clews are an endless spell that turns dropped cat hair into animate balls of fur that talk and do housework – not all that effectively, mind you.

Artemis, the little black undertaker's cat, loathes them. I don't know if it's anything to do with the fact that her own

shedding now has a life independent from her. As if on cue, she pounces across the floor and scoops one of them up in her mouth, making it screech in terror.

'You can't eat the clews!' I scold.

The little cat reluctantly opens her mouth and drops the poor sodden clew to the floor. It wheezes and pants, and the other clews swarm to pick it up, before carrying it off underneath the skirting board again.

If I'm not mistaken, they collectively gave off a very resentful vibe.

Still gripping the doorframe, the ghost's image pulses

frantically between a shimmering outline to a startlingly solid re-collection of flesh – a tall, heavy-set man with a piercing gaze and deep lines etched in his forehead like a grid. His memory has constructed a dark green cardigan with a missing button, and brown corduroy trousers. Fear sloughs off him as a thick black slime.

You know you're in a seriously haunted house when even the ghosts are afraid.

'Here,' Egg says. She holds out her hand and beckons, and an ancient twiggy broom flies across the room, into her grip. She passes it to me. 'Let's get this over with!'

'Thanks!' I sweep the ghost through the doorway, and Mariam redoubles her efforts with the bellows, sweat beginning to trickle down the sides of her face.

The rest of our coven – Isla, Egg, Layla, even Jameela, still furious about the ghost slime – follow us, yelling, stamping, flapping their hands, clapping, singing out nonsense which you'd think wouldn't help, but weirdly does.

When we get him into the hall, he swishes off to the right and darts into the laying-out room.

This is where we keep the coffins, and the bodies while we're preparing them for funeral, and things like shrouds and make-up and the trolley we take to collect the dead. It's also where a neat little brass whorl sits in the floor, like an ear, for what Shranken Putch called 'drainage'. Originally, everything went to plan with this ghost. He did what all the others do, slipping through the whorl into the basement, ready to cross into the world of the dead. But then he broke out and started rampaging around the parlour.

The ghost flickers defiantly, skimming closer to where his former body is laid out. Most of the day that's where he's been hiding, curled inside an ear or nostril.

'Oops, got to finish the face. Layla?' Egg calls. The two of them bathed and dressed the body earlier. Now Layla grabs the make-up kit and they set to work again, brandishing brushes and palettes. The ghost leans close to the coffin, watching the girls work and making irritated noises.

'Please don't disappear up the nose again,' I beg, voice hoarse with exhaustion. His emotions are flying around the room like poisoned arrows, and I can feel the sting of each and every one. Seeing the spirits of the dead and absorbing their feelings makes this so much more tiring than a normal job. The others don't understand that part of it – witnessing the unravelling of a human life, the trauma of struggling to let go. 'You can't come back from death, and it'll all take so much longer if you resist. It's easier if you can accept what's happened.'

The wake is going to take way too long. The council is going to need us to book the funeral, and there are so many more souls waiting to pass through. I know because I've seen all the ghosts hunched in the trees of the Ring like tattered crows. Sometimes they drift into the parlour and follow me around, singing sad songs.

15

The spirit's streaky memory of a face watches mine, sullenly. With renewed determination, I seize the broom handle, and uttering a battle cry, sweep the ghost towards the drainage whorl.

He shrieks, stumbles, falls and is inhaled into the basement below our feet.

Heart thrashing, I tear out of the laying-out room and along the hallway, before plunging into the darkness of the stairwell that leads to the basement. Artemis skitters down the stairs behind me. Cats have always presided over wakes. Together, we rush into the basement room. The footsteps of the coven drum the stairs behind us.

Here's what you need to know about this room. It's fairly creepy, even by *isolated funeral parlour in the middle of the countryside* standards. Not to mention the fact that Annie says the hill underneath us is an ancient burial mound, full of centuries-old graves.

The space is dominated by a huge stone well in the middle of the floor. Egg and I were originally forbidden from going in here, because at that time we didn't know that Shranken Putch had a pudding-addicted water dragon – a knucker – living in a well underneath the parlour. The knucker guards the portals to the Other Ways: worlds that are parallel to our own. I happen to have been born in one – the Shadow Way. Or the world of the dead, if you like to call a spade a spade.

At the back of the room, underneath the shelves crammed with old books and bottles, a dank brown growth has pushed up through the floor. It's domed and hairy and about the size of a large mixing bowl, and it stinks. We have no idea what it is or what to do about it, so Annie has just suggested that I *keep an eye* on it, which is the last thing I feel like doing because it is gross. It is also, I am certain, growing.

I sense the presence of the coven as they squeeze through the door. My part in all this is now the most important, and all they can do is watch.

The ghost is buzzing around in a corner like an enormous silvery-grey bluebottle.

I fumble in my pocket for the smooth silver watch that was once my mother's. I'm so used to working with the timepiece now that I flick open the casing with my thumb and push the tiny hands backwards – the Other way – all in one practised movement.

I'm the only one that can make a timepiece tick the Other way. When I do it, the boundaries between the realms grows thin. Reality is no longer what it's been pretending to be.

The moment that time starts moving backwards, the ghost's face appears more clearly to me. Freckles have bloomed across his face as they did in life, and a tiny scar puckers his upper lip. I've fallen into the in-between.

Artemis jumps on to a shelf in the corner and stretches. Her eyes glow yellow in the gloom.

The ghost stops moving for a second and turns his wretched gaze towards me. *Will you tell that creature to stop staring?* Worldly sounds are muffled, but the ghost's voice is crystalline.

'*That creature* is here to hold your wake. You do understand that you're dead, sir?' I'm aware of how repetitive I sound. Maybe Shranken Putch would have been able to teach me ways of doing this more quickly.

He grimaces. *I am not dead!*

I take a deep breath. But before I can reply, the low hum of an engine shivers through the parlour. It's happened regularly since Egg and I returned from the Shadow Way to find Shranken Putch missing – an aircraft passes nimbly overhead, search beams bleaching the undergrowth. The craft is able to stretch in the air and turn and zip away impossibly fast. But so far its beams haven't been able to prise apart the cloaking spell in which Annie has shrouded the parlour.

My heart stamps a secret skitter-skatter rhythm in my chest. Inside my jacket, my Book of Shadows hugs my ribs. I bite the edge of my thumbnail.

The soul fizzes, watching me. *You are in danger*, he announces. I feel the power balance between us subtly shift.

I shrug, resigned. 'Maybe.' I sit down on the edge of the well. Behind my back, the well water stirs, and three bubbles pop on the surface.

Pop, pop, pop.

Grael is waiting.

I keep cookies up my sleeve for difficult cases like this one. Slowly, while the ghost goes back to flickering and wailing and generally making a fuss, I shake the slightly stale confection towards my hand and try to make it look like I'm nibbling a fingernail, when really I'm chewing off a chocolate chip. A flush of sugar makes me feel more awake.

Artemis prowls closer. She stares straight at the soul, with a look of – I must be imagining it – mockery? Maybe that's her new tactic.

The ghost glares at her. *I'm not dead. I was just minding my own business, having my elevenses, and the next thing I knew I was blundering through the wind towards this godforsaken place.*

A response pops into my head. *You choked on a bit of apple.* But it feels a bit harsh to put it like that.

A miserable look crosses his face. *I just wasn't ready.*

Finally. He accepts the truth.

I nod to the coven, waiting in the shadows. They softly begin to sing the wake dirge – old words we found copied down in Putch's accounting book, which are said to help prepare the soul for the journey ahead.

'This night, this night, every night, and all,' sings Mariam, in her low, sweet voice.

Isla takes up the tune, grinning. 'Fire and fleet and candlelight, the well receives thy soul.'

Egg lifts her chin, probably wanting to get this over with.

'When thou from hence away are past, to the Shadow Way thou come at last, this night, this night –'

'Every night, and all,' Layla sings, in a high, pure voice like a bell.

'Is anyone ever ready?' I say, surprising myself and, by the looks of things, surprising the ghost.

He glares at me. *You're about ten years old. What would you know about it?*

'Actually, I'm thirteen.'

He gives a condescending chuckle that diminishes my sympathy somewhat.

'Has he still not given up?' hisses Isla.

'Almost,' I say, out of the corner of my mouth. 'Keep singing.'

The girls lean on one another's shoulders, looking half asleep. But they're here. I'm so grateful I don't have to do this alone that, for a moment, I forget about the cold and the damp and the insanity of this situation.

'Whatever you did, wherever you went, no thorn or blade shall nick you,' warbles Mariam.

'Put off your boots and rest awhile, the sacred waters beseech you,' intones Egg, voice threaded with impatience.

Isla screeches through her line. 'We wunt be druv, you wunt be judged, no thorn nor blade beset you.'

'Lay your burdens at your feet, the needled ground becomes your seat. Beneath the boughs, the water flows,' offers Layla, more graciously.

I clear my throat. 'Fire and fleet and candlelight, the well receive thy soul!' I will it like an incantation, putting all my intent into praying that the ghost accepts his fate.

The well water stirs again. I whirl around to watch as a huge jaw breaks the surface, opening to reveal a glimpse of massive teeth. Grael rights herself, lifting her great golden eyes from the water.

Grael. Shranken Putch's funerary dragon. The last living knucker in this world. She's been summoned, which means that the ghost is almost ready to cross over.

'Do not be afraid,' I intone, the air in the room shivering with ceremony. Backwards time makes everything feel tilted. 'It is as it has always been, and will be ever after. Life and death are doubles of the same force. Your journey continues in the realm of Shadow.'

A few minutes later, the ghost whisks over the well's lip and lies gleaming on Grael's back. Then the great dragon disappears beneath the surface, trailing a seethe of bubbles.

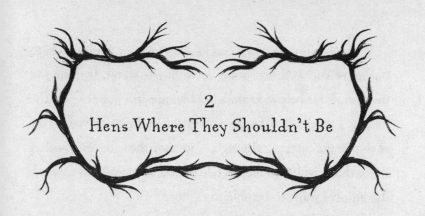

2
Hens Where They Shouldn't Be

The secret life of Spel Wrythe: daily rituals

1. There is always a pencil in my hat and a cookie up my sleeve
   – for emergencies.
2. The death phone is how people tell us when someone has died.
   We even get calls in the middle of the night.
3. We are witches. Maybe the last witches left. We are part of
   nature, like bats and owls, and we do not ride around on
   broomsticks. We each have a power and it used to show up
   as accidental Weird Things but now we're learning how to
   channel it with intention. Well, the others are. Annie doesn't
   know how to teach me.
4. Shranken Putch, the undertaker who gave me and my sister
   a home, is missing.
5. Everything that ever goes wrong is blamed on the Wicked.
   Floods, fires, crops dying in the earth. That's how it has
   always been. So we have to be very, very careful. We're
   living like foxes in a den.

A skull-splitting yawn cracks over my face. I climb on to the lip of the well and stare down at the water, thinking of the portals far below. Grael's bubbles are still popping on the surface. Little bulbs of light eddy through the deep: symptoms of the magic filtering through, now that those doors to other worlds have woken. I feel an odd little stab of jealousy towards the ghost. I want to be able to explore.

'Um, Spel?' says Mariam, warily.

'Hmm?' I turn to face the room and realise with a thump of embarrassment that I'd forgotten the others were here.

'It'd be nice if you could do that thing with the watch without going invisible,' mutters Isla.

'Oh. Right.' I jump down from the well and stare round at all the disquieted faces of my coven – all except Jameela, who keeps away from all things *ghosts and witchcraft*, as she puts it. Because she hates that stuff. 'Sorry. It just happens, though. I can't help it.'

Isla brightens. 'No wonder you were so forgettable at school,' she chirps. 'Maybe sometimes you were literally going invisible.'

Ouch. Forgettable.

'She wasn't forgettable, you oaf,' says Egg.

I love her for saying it but it's also kind of embarrassing that my big sister still has to stand up for me.

'Right. Tea, then bed,' declares Mariam. Somehow, she still looks perfectly put-together, hair neatly plaited over one shoulder, and wearing a crease-free black top and tartan skirt with polished black boots.

In contrast, everything about me is always unravelling, even without hair to deal with. With one quick glance down my front, I note the cat hair, cake crumbs, and ghost slime stuck to me.

And then I notice all the things that the ghost left behind. Sticky balls of green, blue or silver light, snagged in cobwebs or in clusters on the floor – memories, stray emotions, regrets, hopes. Fears, dreams and nightmares.

'I'll be there in a minute,' I tell her, as the others begin to traipse out of the room and up the stairs.

Artemis leaps softly down from her shelf and pads across to me. Her torn right ear has healed to make a stubbier version of the triangle on the left. She sits and blinks her great green eyes. Sometimes I feel like I know what she'd say to me if she could. *Well, wash your hands, Elspeth. Roll up your sleeves. We have to get ready to start all over again with the next one.*

I grab a broom and a duster, gathering the stray materials that the ghost shed. Ever since I survived the Shadow Way, I've kept hold of the ability to see things that shouldn't be visible. I use a fingertip to nudge each emotion or memory into a glass bottle, and write labels for what I sense them to be, which is a longer process than collecting them up. Finally, I store the bottles on the shelves, and stretch my aching muscles. Artemis pauses her vigorous washing to wink at me.

When I go to the sink in the corner to wash my hands, something is moving in the drain. I must be seriously sleep-deprived. I rinse the soap off and watch the bubbles slip down the plug.

Then my heart spasms in my chest. And, as many times as I blink and shake my head, the fact stays the same. There's a person in the drain – a miniature person, about my age, staring up at me from underneath the grey grid of the plughole.

'Urgh!'

A shudder jolts through my body. The person looks up at me, their expression closer to a glare now. I think they're saying something, because their mouth is moving, but the words are too tiny to make out.

They're draped in a long, raggedy black cloak and wearing their dark blonde hair in a bun. They're peering at me like they can't quite see my face, even though compared to them I'm a giant.

A vague sense of familiarity settles over me. I couldn't possibly say where, but I feel certain I've seen this person before.

What are you staring at?

I jump again, spinning round to face the room.

Grael has returned from escorting the soul across the membrane to the Shadow Way. Artemis leaps on to the edge of the well and bumps foreheads with the dragon.

'There's someone down there, in the plughole,' I stutter.

'A kid. A *tiny* kid – I mean my age, but miniature – looking up at me.'

Hmm, says the dragon, amusement leaking from her voice into the dank room. *Perhaps you are even more in need of pudding than I am.* She pauses. *Though a Swiss roll would be most appreciated, when you can. Family-sized.*

When I turn back to the sink and squint down the plughole, the tiny person is gone.

I find Egg standing in the kitchen, barefoot despite the freezing floor tiles. The kitchen has the jitters again. There's a shivering knife on the draining board. A trembling spoon on the table. A stack of plates in a cupboard, chattering like links in a spine.

Ever since the portals to the Other Ways opened, magic has been seeping through every brick and stone of this place. And inanimate objects have been getting nervy.

The magic of other worlds is calling me. I'm certain of it. It's not right of Annie to forbid me from going through those portals.

'It feels so weird coming back here from down there,' Egg says, without looking up at me. She taps her foot on the floor, to denote *below*. The basement. The well. The Shadow Way. A place no living person should ever know about – except the Shadow-Born, technically.

'No one else understands,' I murmur, leaning against the doorframe.

She nods. 'How could they? I feel utterly changed by it, but I could never really explain how.' She looks up at me, finally, great dark eyes shining. 'Do you know what I mean?'

'Yes.' I sigh loudly through my nose. 'I mean, *yeah*. Completely. Although, for me, it was also a bit like going home.'

The clews choose that moment to reappear. One moment they're scurrying black dots streaming out from under the skirting board, the next they're a tower weaving across the floor towards us, shrill and determined. *HelloElspeth!*

'Hello,' I say, reluctantly.

Egg bends double with laughter.

Wouldyoulikeacupoftea?

They never remember that I hate tea. 'No, thank you. Could I have hot chocolate, please? One for Egg, too.'

Egg recovers herself. 'Are you coming up to get some sleep?'

'I can't yet. I need a quick walk to clear my head first.'

A frown flickers across her face.

'I'll be fine,' I say, quickly. 'I won't go anywhere near the edge of the spell.' I feel like even with everything that's happened, she still expects me to trot around after her. 'What time is it?'

'It's – oh my god.' Egg stares at the clock on the windowsill. She smacks her forehead. 'I totally forgot I stopped them all.'

We peer through the window and study the light beginning to smudge the edges of the darkness. 'I think it's about six a.m.,' she says.

The clews reappear carrying two mugs of hot chocolate balanced on top of their furry assemblage. 'Watch out, in case they spill it,' I warn, and we make sure not to reach for a cup until both are safely on the table.

'Thank clew,' chirps Egg, over the top of her mug.

'Very funny.'

That's when Artemis decides to present herself. If it's possible for a cat to meet you hand on hip like a little mother, that's exactly what she does. She studies me, then lays a paw on my tattered sweatshirt. I can almost imagine the telling-off she'd give me if she could.

You should be in uniform, as undertaker in residence. What if someone came to call? This is a funeral parlour, not a never-ending slumber party.

Artemis unleashes a big, scratchy yowl, spiky ridges of fur showing along her back. Then she runs off, scattering muddy paw prints across the tiles that – guess what? *I'll* have to mop.

'That cat is all drama,' says Egg, distractedly. 'Spel, can you be my model later, please?' She brandishes a face palette.

'Do I have to pretend to be dead?'
'Well, duh. Yes.'

The trees have moved again. When I step into the frosty early morning, passing under secret protection spells placed years and years ago alongside horsehair and plaster, the tree nearest to the funeral parlour has pressed its lowest branches across the front door. This place is supposed to be *in the shadow* of the Ring, but now it feels like we're being absorbed into it. I think maybe the Ring is trying to protect us.

With this rare break in the rain, I want to write in my Book of Shadows outside, in the fresh air and quiet. Ideally in a tree. My Book of Shadows is a witch's diary, spellbook, and log of magical activity. I've got it tucked in my coat pocket, and there's a pencil in the brim of my beanie hat. Another cookie is wedged up my sleeve. Perfect.

Between twigs and bark is the palest moon, sinking towards the horizon. I duck under the branches, pull the door closed behind me, and gulp the frozen air. Was that person in the plughole a ghost, gatecrashing someone else's wake? It's the only possibility I can think of, though it doesn't feel right – ghosts tend to be quite self-involved, and if they were one, I'd have expected more of an attempt to talk to me, or making a nuisance of themselves.

At this time of year, the sun isn't going to get up for another hour, but the weak grey light is enough for me to pick my way past the right-hand side of the house and disappear into an ancient circle of trees known as the Ring. It crowns a hill that overlooks the sleepy little village of Knuckerhole. The cloaking spell shrouds the parlour and the Ring, and I'm careful not to step outside its shimmering perimeter.

I'm finding the hill itself more interesting since discovering that it's an ancient burial mound, called a barrow. Weird to think that beneath my feet are roots and water, bones and treasures beyond imagining. People must have lived here for hundreds of years. Maybe thousands. This has always been an important place.

It's an important place to me, too, and that's got a lot to do with Shranken Putch. He gave us a home here. It made life more dangerous for him, but he didn't turn us away. The Hunt wanted him to betray us and he fought against them. And now I have no idea what's happened to him. But I have to find out. Even though I can't go . . . well. Anywhere.

When I reach the clearing in the heart of the Ring, I try to ignore the ghosts leaning against tree trunks, hunched in branches, muttering their regrets to anyone ready to listen – magpie, or mushroom; owl, or pine cone. I used to think I didn't have a soul. Now I have so many of them it's getting ridiculous. I can't even go to the toilet any more without a ghost popping up to chat to me.

I look back at the parlour and notice how the nearest trees have laid their branches across the front and over the roof. It looks like it's being woven into a thicket.

The public never come to the parlour. We look after those who have died with no family or money. That's when the death phone rings. When Annie has to deal with the council, she disguises herself with glamour magic.

I stare down at the village for a moment, noticing one or two coils of smoke as morning fires are lit. The cold air is tinged by the smell. It strikes me how *other* we are, up here. It's not much different from being at Mistress Mouldheels' School for Wicked Girls.

My boot snaps a twig and birds scatter across the sky, stealing my breath. Owls head to bed; rooks squabble with them as they think about rising. A bramble grabs my sleeve and I pull away, tearing a thread in my red jumper. Underfoot, red yew berries are crushed with the snowdrops that have been drowned in the almost-constant rain and storms we've been having.

A ditchling pushes through the trees and staggers towards me, making a squelching noise like wet grass and drains. They're the consequence of not getting spirits through to the Shadow Way. Their soul remains, decaying forever, and never finding rest. Being overrun by ditchlings would be fairly disastrous – that's why Putch specifically warned about them in his note.

But it's too late to help this one. I dart out of its way.

Something moves in the corner of my eye. I twitch to watch as a shadow ripens on the fingertip of a tree. I grow very still, heart skittering beneath my ribs. It lengthens into the shape of a rook. I squint. Or is it just a shadow, because every moment the light is changing, and the sun and moon are crossing paths in the sky? The inky shape drops into the air, quivers, and fades from view between the branches.

An uneasy feeling settles in my stomach. Gretel – the half witch, half Hunter who tracked my sister and me both in this world and the Shadow Way – used shadow creatures that hatched from the eyes in tree trunks. They're called cahoots.

But what I just saw wasn't anything like that. I'm sure it wasn't anything at all. I pull my beanie hat further down over my ears and keep walking.

As I make my way towards the oldest, biggest tree in the Ring, I pull my Book of Shadows out of my pocket, fish the pencil out of my hat and flip through the pages. This is the Wayfaring Tree, which grows at the most easterly part of the circle, like a queen at the head of a table.

There's a sketch of this tree in my book, spanning a double page. Annie says the Wayfaring Tree shelters any witch, because there's a magic linking us that's so strong it lives forever, long after the spell-caster passed on. This tree's roots are said to have drunk the blood of witches. Anyone who has ever tried to cut it down has been struck dead themselves. Its

roots are said to reach through the burial mound, all the way into the well. I've seen Grael gnawing those roots. I've seen them snaking through into other worlds.

The needles are a deep green and the berries are poisonous red nibs, scattered across the ground. The trunk is thick and ridged, tall and full of tiny faces, if you know how to look for them. There's a ledge like a seat halfway up, and next to it a stick like a staff. It looks like a faerie throne. It looks like the perfect place to write. I imagine the world below my feet, how the roots must reach into the burial mound, maybe even miles below that.

What can I learn from you? The question rises through my mind with the sun. Annie's always talking to us about how we can learn more from plants and other creatures than we can from humans. She calls them our people. Family.

I find a foothold and am about to start climbing when a burning, burrowing sensation starts in the centre of my forehead and spreads across my skin. I put my hand out and steady myself against the Wayfaring Tree.

A great, wide eye stares from near the top of the trunk, surveying the hill, the parlour, the other trees. An eye like the ones I saw on the trees in the Shadow Way.

What if something is watching through this one?

And the pain in my head bursts, and I feel my eyes fly open – no, not my eyes. My *eye*.

The eye in my forehead. I'm aware of all the little creatures in their burrows and all the little insects crawling through the shadows in the groove of the bark and the way the light warms everything it touches and the breath of the wind on the tips of the grass and –

'Hey, Spel!' Mariam's voice jumps across the distance.

I wrench my hand away from the tree. Clean, sharp air flows into my lungs, and my vision clears. The pain fades.

Then Egg, Layla, Isla and Mariam catch up with me, with all their noise and chaos and questions and squabbles. What in the Ways just happened to me?

'Look what I found!' declares Isla merrily. She crosses the last bit of grass between us, red hair rich against her green jumper and mud already splattered up her trouser legs. She's obviously been playing with glamour magic again, because her eyes are bright purple and Egg's bobbed hair is platinum blonde, like a glossy wig.

Isla opens her palm to show us a ring. A gold band with symbols etched around the inside – I can just about see them, peering from underneath the edge. A red gem winks in the centre.

A gulf of panic erupts in me. 'Where did you get that?'

'It came out of one of those weird fruit the trees are growing,' she says. 'Would you Adam and Eve it?'

'What fruit?' I ask, making a face.

Layla points to a nearby tree. 'One's doing it now; look.'

As we watch, a shadow lengthens from the end of a branch,

just like when I tried to tell myself I was imagining it. The shadow starts off looking like a bird. Then, as it lifts away into the air, it solidifies and falls to the earth with a soft thump. Juice eases out of its ruined skin with a sound like a sigh.

It feels like time stands still as I step closer. A bruise-purple bird-shaped fruit, unseasonal and not like a thing that has ever grown in this world before.

The skin continues to soften, and hard edges begin to show through. Egg squats down, poking it with a stick. A small wooden carving throws off its fruit-skin coat – it's a tiny fox, with shining eyes made of gemstone.

'The barrow,' I whisper.

'The what?' asks Jameela.

'The burial mound,' I snap, suddenly impatient. 'What were you all doing letting Isla take that ring? We're not grave robbers.'

'Grave robbers?' repeats Mariam, incredulously. 'We thought it was pretty weird, but –'

She trails off, doubt crawling into her voice. Suddenly I see that they've all been in a daze, lulled by some force into accepting this strangeness, and I have no idea what that force is or whether it's good.

'The burial chamber under our feet is spitting out treasures,' I tell them, certainty growing in my gut as I stare down at the little carving of a fox that can't have seen the light of dawn for many, many a year.

I spin round and knock the ring out of Isla's hand. It sinks into the mud.

'What do you think you're doing?' yells Isla, skin livid.

I stare down at the gold circle. 'You found it inside a *fruit*! That can't be good, can it?'

When she stoops to pick the ring up, I cover it with my boot.

Isla fixes me with cold blue eyes. 'Okay, Elspeth Wrythe.' She rubs her fingers together, and a singed smell touches the air. Then an amber flame pops into life on the end of her finger.

'Careful!' blurts Mariam, dark eyes wild. 'We're right near the border of the cloaking spell. We can't let any magic through . . .'

'She's right,' says Egg, signalling for us all to step away from the edge of the Ring. 'And also, what are you planning to do with that poxy flame, Isla Thomas?'

'Set your sister on fire,' Isla mutters.

'I think we all need some sleep,' says Layla, calmly, wrapping an arm around Isla's shoulder and pouring magical raindrops from her own fingertips to quell the stubborn little flame. 'We'll talk to Annie about this.' She gestures vaguely to the ground littered with bizarre fruit, then presses a yawn into the collar of her jacket.

Annie's *a year and a day* rule pops into my head. It's the length of time I'm supposed to study for before I can practise my magic, because it's so unusual and dangerous, and all about blurring the boundaries of reality – seeing ghosts, turning invisible, stepping between different worlds. *I'm only half here.* No wonder I struggle to fit in. I think *a year and a day* is just a convenient way for Annie to fob me off and stop me from exploring, though.

The vows I made with Egg after we came back from the Shadow Way ring through my mind. *We will learn all we can about witchcraft, for the rest of our days. And we will protect anyone who needs us.* But I don't just want to read about magic – I want to do it.

'I wish Shranken Putch was here,' I say, miserably. 'He's the only one who knows about this place. Annie won't know anything about the burial chamber.' But – Grael might, I realise. I can ask her about it when I take her a pudding.

Isla stomps off, back towards the parlour. Jameela shakes her head at us and follows, as though we've done something wrong when really it's just that Isla is an unreasonable brat sometimes. Mariam tucks her plait over her shoulder and picks her way across the mud in their wake.

Layla and Egg turn, already deep in some private conversation, but I kneel to fish the ring out of the mud.

At first, I'd thought it was another ring come back to haunt me – the one that cursed Egg and dragged her through the portal to the Shadow Way, the one I finally managed to bind Gretel with. That was over a month ago, but the suspicion that it might have found us again set my heart thrashing and my hands sweating. Now my body calms, very slightly. The gem set in the ring is red, not green. But it's still brought back the memory of Egg being cursed. I stare around as more rook-shaped fruit ripen and fall, spilling grave trinkets on to the frozen ground. *What is making this happen?* But even as I think the question, I know I should be asking *who*, not what.

I drop the ring into my pocket, and stand. The Ring is a wild and unpredictable place. In the few minutes since the others left, the wind has risen, and now it's trying to break the trees' backs. A thunderclap rolls overhead, and the earth of the Ring trembles. It's a wonder the barrow doesn't spill dead kings as well as treasures.

By the time I get back to the parlour and shove through the weather-swollen front door, I'm windswept and skin-soaked. I'm greeted by the sight of Layla already snoring on the sofa in the sitting room, while Isla and Egg battle their powers against each other.

'What are you doing?' I hiss from the doorway, stamping my feet to get rid of the chill.

Egg's using telekinetic energy to guide a footstool closer to Isla's head. But our red-haired dorm-mate snarls, and the low fire in the grate leaps in a sudden fury, the flames licking Egg's bare ankles. My sister shrieks, and the footstool falters in the air before crashing to the floor, startling Layla awake.

I roll my eyes and start up the stairs. 'Aren't you ever going to bed?' I call down. Then the death phone rings, and I can't help but groan.

When I pick up the receiver, a load of crackling spills out. 'Who is this?' I ask. 'I can't hear you.'

The crackling keeps on, but in between the static a voice sounds like it's trying to break through. A drowning voice, coming from somewhere a very long way away.

'This is the funeral parlour of the Ring,' I state, as steadily as I can. 'Assistant – *resident* – undertaker speaking. How may I help you?'

Crackling. Fragments of a voice. Crying.

I feel a pang of sudden, sharp resentment that Shranken Putch isn't here. He's supposed to be teaching me. There's so much I should be learning about how to be an undertaker, instead of just *winging it*, as Egg says. This is too important to wing.

Has something awful happened to him? Or has he just abandoned us?

I push the thought away. 'I can't hear you properly,' I say, into the mouthpiece. The hallway floor is so January-cold that the soles of my feet are aching to the bones, even through thick socks. I press my forehead against the side of the big, wall-mounted phone, and breathe. The same fuzzy crackling spills out, mixed in with a few fractured words that sound like they're coming from the depths of a broken dream.

Eventually, I slam the receiver back in its cradle and turn away. I'm going to have to get some sleep.

I traipse up the two flights of stairs to the attic (which has become a graveyard for mould-spotted old cups of tea no one bothers to wash up). There's a pattering of paws as Artemis trots along behind me.

'I forgot to make Grael's payment pudding,' I say, around a mouthful of yawn.

Artemis yowls.

'I know, I know,' I tell her. 'I really do need to start making puddings in batches. Today she wants an entire family-sized Swiss roll.'

In our attic bedroom, I coax a small fire alive – envying Isla's powers – throw my blankets aside, and groan. Someone has put a hen in my bed, again.

As I scoop her up, Mistress Cluckerbucks issues a startled *cluck-shriek*, and her eyes goggle. 'Listen,' I tell her, putting her into Egg's bed instead. 'You should just be grateful that we brought you in from all that crazy weather in the first place.' The hens have mostly been roosting on the heaters on top of tea towels we've put there, or on top of the stove while it's cooling. But I'd prefer to draw the line at my bed. Let's see how Egg feels about it.

I slip between the covers, roll on to my front, and pass out.

Stop the clocks, cover the mirrors. Stop the clocks, cover the mirrors. Turn down the photographs. 'Stop the clocks.'

'Spel,' whines my sister, from her pillow. '*Stop.*'

'What?' I croak. '*You* stop.'

'What?' murmurs Layla, from the other side of my sister.

'Spel, please stop *babbling*,' mutters Egg darkly, turning over in bed and fixing me with eyes that glitter. 'We are trying to get some rest.'

Apparently, I've started saying the funeral customs in my sleep.

3
An Incantation for a Haunted Girl

In the bowels of the Rookery, over a cup of bone broth, the Hangman's lips quivered. 'That was a Shadow-Born, was it not.'

The not-question lingered in the air.

Flux buzzed restlessly in the corner, the yellowed knuckles of the bone mug digging painfully into their wind-bitten hands. 'Was it so? I don't know.'

'Don't know? Takes one to spy one. Thinning the edges of reality with nothing but a stare?'

Flux studied their feet. 'Shadow-Born, for sure. Another to step between the worlds, neck-breaker.'

The Hangman squirmed upon his rook throne. Bodies and bodies below where he sat, rooks were being born, and others were dying. 'But which one, and in which world?' he muttered, darkly, eyes retracting inward. 'Perhaps not even a witch world.'

'Maybe that world you told me about, where all the magic glugged away?' ventured Flux.

Not a witch world, chimed a rook: one of the largest and most aggressive, Warrior-King over his nest fellows, and with only one eye.

The Hangman twitched, full bodily. 'What was that you said?' he barked, spittle flying. 'You remember that tale, do you? Speak up, shadow child!'

'Not a witch world,' mumbled Flux, feebly, at the same time as the Rook King spoke again, more loudly.

Not a witch world, neck-breaker. Not a world of witch.

They watched in silence as the worlds revolved, visible through the pages of Flux's former Book of Shadows. The Way of Bones, the Way of Shadow, the Way of Frost, the Way of Flame, the Way of Fins. And the Drained Place, where all the wild things had become enslaved. The Hangman liked to gloat that he had had a hand in the draining.

'However would a book like that have found its way to the Drained Place?' pondered the Hangman aloud, almost pleasantly. But malice carved his face into a mask that Flux recognised all too clearly. Behind him, on the wall, the great tapestry rasped a breath into the room.

'Commune with that other Shadow-Born,' the Hangman murmured. 'Bring me the book. Five thousand years may have passed since your death, but if you fail, it is not above reason to have you wake inside a barrow. Eyelids are strong enough to open under soil.'

Inside their boots, Flux quaked.

I'm aware of everything. My roots blooming deep in the earth, the worms coiled there. Both heaviness and the feeling of my leaves shivering in the wind, high up, light. The breath of insects against my skin, bark and leaf. The way a human footfall is delicate as a moth landing on my trunk, but still the vibrations reach through me.

Fragments of past lives, buried deep beneath me in the burial barrow, forcing into my roots and travelling, trying to fruit. Fruiting.

My eye widens, pulling my forehead. Rats. Streaming across the hillside, from Petworth, and Arundel. Rats wreathed in pulsing light.

The creatures are vessels for stolen power, *creaks a voice.*

I'm falling backwards. Through rings and rings of living wood. Backwards into my bed. There's that feeling of falling that you get just before you fall asleep, but this time it's before I wake up.

My eyes snap open. My cheek is stuck to my pillow and *Hurstpier's Funereal Tome* sticks painfully into my side – I've been referring to the textbook frantically, most days. I only found out what ditchlings are from the book. *Souls so ancient and lost that they may never be lain to rest.*

Under my covers, something twines between my toes. When I reach down to investigate, my fingers return with a small pink worm. *Urgh.* The sheets are smeared with mud.

Across the room, Egg and Layla are playing a card game, their bed strewn with magazines and make-up. Layla's pyjamas are berry purple and the top has a big picture of an owl on it. My first thought, rather than *What just happened to me?*, is that I'm really envious about those pyjamas. Egg already has on her now-trademark red lips and winged- eyeliner look, even though it's barely past ten. She and Layla have been elevating their eyeliner to an art form for weeks.

'Hey,' I croak. 'It's Lay an Egg. Get it? Lay and Egg.'

'And the award for most terrible joke goes to: Spel Wrythe,' says Layla, wincing.

'Finally,' says Egg, brightly. 'It emerges.'

'Excuse you,' I snap. 'Did *you* spend all night trying to reason with wandering spirits?'

'I spent a lot of the night helping you,' she retorts.

'Sorry, Spel,' says Layla. 'I told her to keep the noise down.'

'Oi!' says my sister. 'Why does everyone always accuse me of being the noisy one? Anyway, the noise is Spel's own fault.'

She gives me a pointed look. Which is when I notice the steady *thump, thump, thump* of Grael's pudding protest, tail beating the walls of the well like a drum. Honestly, the teeth are going to fall out of that dragon's head. Her diet is pure sugar.

'Oh yeah, she wants a family-sized Swiss roll,' I say. 'It's next on my list.'

Layla bursts into a messy laugh.

I sit cross-legged and wipe the sleep from my eyes. 'I just had a Weird Thing. Maybe.'

'Ooh. You have my attention,' says Layla. Even though Weird Things are unintentional magic creeping out, everyone's still quite fascinated by them. Maybe because they're so unpredictable.

A good example of a Weird Thing is when Mariam once fell down a big flight of stairs at school, but landed lightly, without even a bruise. Annie says that's something to do with using your powers desperately in a moment of survival, even though you're untrained. Mariam slowed herself down and landed safely.

I tell them about the tree: how I felt about it yesterday, about the dream – if that's what it was. About the trees in the Shadow Way and how that's when I first learned about trees having eyes. About the feeling of ancient treasures travelling through my – *its* – roots, and rats racing towards us. Hundreds of rats. 'Something was wrong with them,' I finish, yawning. 'They were streaming here, across the countryside, and they were sort of glowing.'

'Some dreams are so odd,' says Egg. She taps Layla on the arm. 'Don't quit just because I was winning!'

But Layla looks more thoughtful. 'Spel felt like it was a Weird Thing, not just a dream.'

She opens her mouth to say more, when a determined scratching starts, somewhere in the wall to my left. I twitch away from it, rushing across the narrow room to sit on the other bed. Egg wraps me in one arm, her grey sweater with a space camp logo warming my shoulders. 'It's normal for old places like this to have rats,' she murmurs.

Layla and I exchange another look. Given what I was just talking about, it feels like way too much of a coincidence.

Then I remember the voice I heard inside the tree. 'The tree spoke to me.'

For a moment, both Lay and Egg stare at me like I'm a cracked shell. But then Layla clears her throat and says, 'Go on,' in that diplomatic way she has, while my sister snickers into her hand.

'Seriously, Egg, why would you find this unbelievable given everything else that's happened?' I squawk, crossing my arms.

'Fair point.' Egg forces her face straight. 'Do proceed.'

I huff out a breath, trying to drop my defences. 'While I was looking out across the land and noticing all the sensations felt by – um – a tree, which was a lot by the way, there was this voice that told me –'

'What?' demands Egg.

'This! *The creatures are vessels for stolen power.*' Quickly, I pull out my Book of Shadows, grab the pencil from my hat and write down everything I can remember. I put a heading at the top of the page: *What the tree told me.*

'I still can't believe you have stuff that your mum owned,' says Layla, wistfully.

We're the only ones who know anything about our family – partly because the others were all taken as babies so have no memories of anyone, and also because Annie wasn't able to grab any of their files from the school before coming here. She said she'd wanted to try, because she knew they'd want information. But alas.

'What does it mean, though?' says Egg, impatiently.

Layla's expression grows stormy. 'Well, we know that the Hunt have been making us and the whole world believe we were *Wicked* so they could lock us up and steal our magic. So maybe that's the bit about stolen power. But what's a vessel?'

'I think it's a container,' muses Egg, staring into the distance.

'So the tree meant that the rats I saw are containers for stolen power?' I say. 'But why? And why would they be scurrying across the countryside?' I glance at the walls. 'Maybe even coming here?'

'Rats run away from fires, floods and danger,' whispers Layla. 'Don't you remember when there was a fire at school? All those rats we'd never have expected to see, flowing out of the basement and across the grounds?'

I'm shocked that I could have forgotten about that. I must have been six or seven, and I remember crowding round the dining-hall windows with scores of other girls, watching a river of black fur streaking away while the Unwicked adults bellowed from the floor below, and a siren sliced through the distance.

The wind blasts down the chimney, and the grate coughs out a clump of rook feathers.

'Maybe they're trying to escape something horrific,' mutters Egg.

I think of Shranken Putch again, and his note, and I wonder for the millionth time when he's coming back.

Why would he stay away from his parlour and his dragon for so long? Annie doesn't know where he went, and there's no one I can ask. And, worst of all, no one else seems to care like I do.

'What if *Shranken Putch* is trying to escape something horrific?' I venture.

Layla shoots me a sympathetic smile. 'He left a note, Spel. He must have gone of his own accord.'

'Last time I saw him he was hurt, and he was defending me against the Witchfinder General,' I reply, a touch impatiently. 'So I'm not too comforted by that.'

'You know what, Spel?' says Egg. 'It really sucks that we can't know where everyone is and how they're doing. Think about all those other girls from school – what happened to them? Are they all soulless and in servitude to the Unwicked now? We don't know. And most days we've honestly got bigger fish to fry.'

'Egg,' says Layla. 'That's horrible.'

She shrugs. 'We have! *We're* trying to survive, too.'

'He's on his own,' I tell them, my own voice dead in my ears. 'And he gave us a home.' And I need him to teach me.

My sister's black eyes are hard as she stares through the attic window at the branches that have laced their fingers together across the glass. Sometimes I wonder if we're going to be buried alive, hidden forever under their canopy.

4
Normalitea

The wind rattles the windows, and rain leaks through the roof. 'The world is a bog,' says Jameela.

Isla sighs. 'And we are its bog children.'

'Speak for yourself,' I murmur, as I lift a tray of freshly baked sponge out of the oven.

Mariam squints at it doubtfully. There's a splotch of flour on her cheek. 'Are you sure it's risen properly?' she asks.

'It's going to be rolled up,' I reply, reaching out to dust the flour off her. She swats at my hand. 'It doesn't have to rise much.'

'You and that dragon,' scoffs Jameela. She and Isla are sitting at the kitchen table, poring over Putch's accounts book, which Annie wants us to try to keep up to date. 'She's got you properly wrapped around her claw.'

Isla chuckles. Jameela kind of has a point, though. It feels odd to be baking when I'm so anxious for Shranken Putch to come home and when we're living in hiding from people who want to drain us of our magic. But Grael deserves her reward, and I don't feel like I can quiz her for knowledge without some sort of offering.

Mariam takes an armload of washing-up to the sink while I start covering the warm sponge in a thick layer of strawberry jam. Overhead, the stairs groan under the weight of rushing footsteps.

Egg and Layla burst into the room. 'Spel, talk some sense into your sister, please,' gasps Layla, leaning against the counter beside me.

'What? Why?' I begin rolling the sponge up. Sugary gloop oozes out between the folds.

My sister swoops close, swiping a fingerful of jam from the sponge. 'I'm being smothered. I have to get out of this house.'

'Go for a walk, then,' says Jameela, nose buried in the accounts book.

Egg spins to face us. 'I want to get out of this wretched place,' she insists. 'Go somewhere else.'

'You can't,' says Layla, simply.

Mariam nods. 'The Unwicked won't hesitate to turn on us. They know about schools for the Wicked. It won't take much for them to think you've escaped from one.'

Egg snorts. 'Don't be ridiculous. We dress differently now. What's the worst that can happen?' She pulls on a fleece and a pair of boots, and scrapes her hair into a bun. 'I just want to be able to move about freely! Is that so much to ask?'

Her cheeks are glowing and her hair has starting puffing

up in that way that happens when she's getting reckless. Layla and I exchange an anxious glance. 'Where's Annie?' she asks.

'Glamoured up and bogged off to the food bank,' chimes Isla.

'A glamour!' exclaims Egg. 'If only someone were good enough at it to let us go out in disguise.' She shoots a crafty look at Isla.

I chew my tongue. Why did you have to say that, Isla Thomas? 'Now you've done it,' I mutter.

Isla's head whips up. 'I have the strongest ability with glamour magic. Except Annie, of course,' she says, smug as sunflowers.

'But we're not allowed to leave the cloaking spell,' says Mariam, firmly.

'Are you *always* just going to do as you're told?' demands my sister.

'That's not really fair, Egg,' I tell her, and she glances at me with a slightly wounded expression, like she's still surprised that these days I speak out when I have a different opinion. And sometimes that opinion will be different from hers.

'It's not really a matter of doing as we're told,' says Layla, reasonably. 'Isn't it too dangerous? Isn't that the whole point?'

'Well, nothing's really happened, has it?' says Egg. 'I mean, I don't feel unsafe right now.'

'Isn't that because of the cloaking spell?' I point out.

'I say let's go for it,' says Jameela, closing the accounts book suddenly. 'I'm sick to death of this place, too. Pun intended.'

I gape at her. She must be *really* sick of the parlour to be willing to go under a glamour spell. Everyone knows how much she loathes witchcraft.

Egg grins, triumphant.

'Where would we even go?' I ask.

'There's a little tea shop in the village,' says Egg, like she's been thinking of going there for a while. 'I remember seeing it when we used to drive past in the hearse, with Putch. Surely it can't be a problem just to go there?'

A cacophony of bickering commences.

'Please don't anyone be dramatic,' my sister begs, which is laughable because she's the most dramatic person I know. 'I simply think we should be able to go to a tea shop in the afternoon like everyone else can.'

Artemis trots into the kitchen, paws thumping the tiles. Isla leans down to scratch her between the ears. 'We're going out to tea, little cat!' she burbles. 'Yippee!' Artemis ducks away from her hand, slashing out with exposed claws. 'Ow!' yelps Isla. 'Vicious thing!'

The little black cat glares round at us with a thunderous expression. Jameela laughs. 'She doesn't think we should go.'

Artemis's fur bristles. She begins to growl like she does if she sees another cat. I frown. She really *doesn't* seem to think we should go.

'Listen!' commands Isla, putting paid to debate. 'You all

know a bit about glamour magic, right?'

We nod.

'Well,' says Isla. 'As I said, I've got the strongest ability with this, so let me lead.'

She beckons us all into a huddle in the centre of the kitchen. The she swipes a palm down each of our faces, whispering the words of a spell that paints vivid pictures in the mind – dusty books and purple potions and sea creatures turning circles in the deep. Stars and planets and the origins of a seed.

I stifle a yell as each person's face changes into that of a stranger. My sister becomes an elderly woman with blazing blue eyes. Layla is transformed into a boy with a scarred face. Mariam and Jameela and Isla herself are less distinct, like blurred images that won't quite come into focus. I put my hands to my own face and my blood jolts when features unknown press against my skin.

'Isles,' says Jameela, looking winded. 'You're really good at this.' We all know *good* is too small a word.

'Cheers,' says Isla, puffing up with pride.

We put our shoes on, and I set the Swiss roll on a cooling rack, whispering an apology to Grael.

'Perfect,' says Egg, brightly. 'Let's cut along.' She opens the back door and we all go stomping down the path at the side of the parlour, through the driving rain.

The Ring is a tangle of winter branches, echoing with

the grumbles of rooks and clogged with wispy ghosts. We hesitate at the perimeter of the cloaking spell, which takes its favourite shape – that of a great grey wolf – and leans down, showing us its teeth.

'Maybe this isn't such a good idea,' I say, but Egg reaches up to stroke the spell's muzzle. Then she leans into the spell as though against a very strong wind. Her clothes and hair stream backwards, effort strains her features. But then she pops through. Isla and Jameela push through after her. The rest of us watch as they walk down the hill beyond the spell.

'I do not always just do as I'm told,' declares Mariam, teeth gritted. Then she puts her shoulder to the spell and pushes through, plait sailing in the air behind her.

Layla and I share another fretful look. Then we follow.

It feels like being hit in the chest by a gale, like wading through a nightmare. I stumble as I leave the spell's protective edge, and its wolf shape nuzzles my clothing, trying to swat me back inside.

But we make it through, and run to catch up with the others.

By the time we reach the slippery tree-root bridge, separating the Ring from Knuckerhole, we're skin-soaked.

I twist to look back up the hill. Three rooks have followed us from the Ring, and now they hang a little way back, squabbling. There isn't a trace of our home to be seen. Annie's spell has hidden the funeral parlour entirely from view.

We reach the bottom of the hill, cross the road and the village square, and assemble under the awning of the tea shop. Somehow, I know exactly which witch is which, despite the fact that we're wearing other skins.

Mariam looks each of us in the eye. 'Don't let even a glimmer of magic show,' she instructs. 'And we'll not stay long. A cup of tea, and that's it.'

When we head into the shop, Jameela and Layla's glasses fog up. My nose fills with the smell of baking bread and hot custard and the perfume old ladies wear. Which isn't surprising since everyone else in here is over ninety years old, at least.

We've tramped a load of mud into the stuffy little shop. And row upon row of crinkled old-lady faces are staring at us disapprovingly, even though we look older with the glamour spell. We're still outsiders, after all.

'Would you mind wiping your feet?' asks a woman behind the serving counter, with hair that's been set in a series of stiff rolls, lifting off her forehead like a rearing beige slug. She's giving us such a disgusted look.

Next to the counter is a massive fridge full of posh yoghurts and fat, fancy cheeses wrapped in blood-red wax. Just one of those cheeses looks like it has more protein than we get in a week. The hens don't lay in deep winter.

'What change has anyone got?' demands my sister.

Everyone rummages in their pockets. We manage to pool £1.85 for a pot of tea for two, then we ask for six cups with extra milk. The serving lady's eyes practically pop out on stalks.

We assemble ourselves around a table, which unfortunately is in the middle of the tea shop. The serving lady approaches us uncertainly with our tea and cups, looking like some kind of wounded creature. Egg flips the lid and stares inside, doubtfully.

'Could we have some extra hot water, please?' she says.

The woman goggles again. 'It's already rather dilute, dear.' But she brings some more and we add it to the pot and we all sip tea the colour of milk, which is even more gross than normal tea but at least we feel halfway human and part of *society*. I load up my tea with sugar lumps, to make it bearable. Maybe Egg's right. Maybe this is what we needed.

I stare out of the net-curtained little window at the Ring rising above the town. The top of the hill is bare – no trees, no parlour. It's so eerie to see the effect of the cloaking spell from down here.

Egg breathes deeply and smiles. 'See? We're just like anyone else, enjoying a cup of tea,' she announces, a bit too loudly. Then we all start laughing.

Above the huge old fireplace is a plaque declaring the words *We Wunt Be Druv*.

'There's that old saying from the wake dirge,' says Mariam, pointing. 'Apparently it's an old Sussex saying, meaning *we won't be told what to do*.'

Layla speaks in a hush that is only just audible above the clanking of cutlery. 'Annie says, that's one of the reasons the Hunt had to clamp down so hard here. The people are stubborn, and the wood sheltered them. Until it was cut down.'

The wood. She means the Muddlewood, which has vanished in our world, now, except for a single ring of trees. The trees where we live.

A potted plant on the windowsill begins to lean towards Mariam as though she is the sun. Then it sends a creeping vine out towards her. She promptly taps it and it shoots back towards the pot. 'Sorry!' she whispers. Then she tops up everyone's cup with the last of the hot water.

'Oh!' yelps a voice.

We turn to look. Across the room, a woman has cupped her nose with her hands, and her fingers are threaded with ribbons of red. It takes me a moment to realise it's blood.

'Look out!' Layla pushes me to the right, and there's a crash as a picture falls from the wall above us on to the floor. Then the salt shaker falls off the table, showering the carpet in a fine white mist.

'Evil portents,' whispers someone at the table next to ours.

'All devil's signs,' their companion replies. 'And Mary two doors down says a hare crossed her path this morning.'

I'm acutely aware that everyone in the tea shop is staring.

It dawns on me – like a trickle of cold water down my

back – that we look somewhat odd. Isla is wearing a quilted waistcoat over a pink leotard and matching tutu, and her glamoured black hair is plastered to her head from the rain. Hotchpotch clothes aside, the glamour magic has made us all look unearthly – our heads are a bit too big, and our bodies are all the same stretched length like we're being propped up under our clothes by hidden creatures. Our voices are unusually deep and chiming, like old church bells.

Then it begins.

'Oh no,' whispers Isla, clutching Jameela's arm. Her face has turned whiter than porcelain. 'I think the glamour's slipping.'

No sooner has she said it aloud, than the glamour magic slides off each of us, one by one, like candle wax. It's the strangest feeling, like I'm a glass that's being emptied of water. My body shrinks and straightens and my face begins to ease back into its normal structure. All around the table, the others' faces are changing as well. Everyone's eyes shine with terror.

The muscles in my face ripple and twitch. Mariam pulls her coat over her head, Jameela puts her face in her hands. Layla's features have half switched back, but a trace of the glamour has lingered. Isla stays stock-still and it's hard to tell if she's breathing. Egg clutches her face and turns to Isla with a furious expression. 'Stop it, Isla!'

Isla snatches a breath. 'I can't,' she says, very quietly.

'I can't get a hold on the magic. It's moving too quickly.'

Dread like a heavy, cold weight falls into my stomach. Magic, moving too quickly to be caught. We're out here in the open, throwing magic around.

People are turning round in their seats to stare at us. Someone stands, pointing, their chair tips backwards on to the floor.

There's a cavernous sense of the underside of things – roots, underground caves, the maker's marks underneath plates – and patterns in nature, and things that aren't as they seem. For a sliver of time, and what also feels like an age, everything is reversed, and all the tables and chairs are on the ceiling. Then I blink, and we're back in our places.

And the world erupts.

Someone is screaming. Others point, shout, get red in the face. Everything becomes so vivid that a headache takes root behind my eyes.

We all flinch when the word fizzes into the air.

'Witches!' At first it's uttered incredulously, as though this can't be happening. Then the accusation gathers on more lips, and grows in strength as the villagers become confident in what they're seeing.

'Get up,' orders Mariam.

We do as she says, shaking.

I scrape my chair back, coat half on, and start dragging Egg by the arm. 'Hurry!'

We're about to step outside when the door opens, the little bell above it tinkling cleanly. A man steps in; short, straight red hair neatly parted, smart beige coat fastened to the chin.

He tips his head and regards us for a moment.

Then he puts his nose in the air and begins to *sniff*, with a nose that's wrinkled at the sides like a bloodhound's muzzle. A greasy black rat wriggles out of his inside pocket, thumping to the floor in a way that makes my bones squirm.

The man lifts a hand. The air puckers where his long, elegant fingers touch it. I blink, and the air settles again. But for a moment I could swear he had made an *incision*. The rat squeals, and rushes away, bumping against table legs.

Then Jameela kicks out, yelping.

The man twists his fingers against the air, the force implying an invisible resistance. A sharp sliver of light shivers from the rat's mouth to his fingers and alights on the tip of his thumb. For a whisker of time, it's a silver star. Then it sinks beneath his glove.

Egg kicks the man in the shin. He doubles over, cursing her in a voice like spat-out nails. 'Come on!' she yells to us.

We barge out of the shop, straight into a cluster of boys sheltering from the rain.

'Oi, oi!' calls out a boy, specifically to Layla, and his friends laugh.

'She's not interested in *you*,' jeers Egg.

Jameela grabs her hand and drags her away as villagers

spill out of the tea shop behind us. My heart jolts when I realise that the rat man is watching from behind a netted curtain. He is grinning like a beast.

'Run!'

We push past the boys. They follow us, until they realise where we're heading.

'You're not really going up *there*, are you?' demands one of them.

We cross the small road at the bottom of the hill, breathless, ignoring the boys. Mariam slips in the mud and I haul her up, not letting it cost us a second. Why did we let Egg convince us we could be safe in the world of the Unwicked?

'They're going up to the Ring!' a boy screams at our backs.

His words are met with jeers of derision. But when I glance over my shoulder, a crowd has swelled around the boys. A crowd with hard eyes and set mouths and accusations that jab at the air like knives. They're genuinely afraid. And if we get home, they'll see us disappear. What have we done?

We dawdle halfway up the hill with our backs together so we can keep watch all around us. We made that formation instinctively.

The man who sniffed at us casually strolls across the village square to join the crowd. He puts his hands in his pockets and rocks back on his heels, smiling pleasantly.

I feel the fingertips of my left hand beginning to tingle and thicken. When I glance down, strange shadow tendrils have gathered there. Panic sits in the back of my throat.

The boys shout rude words. Isla yells back at them.

'Shut up!' hisses Mariam, through tears.

'Enough,' says Egg. She issues a warning, pointing at the boys, and – it's not clear exactly what goes wrong. Did one of them catch his toe on a stone, and trip? Did one of his mates push him, too quickly to notice?

Either way, the boy is on the ground and rolling, clutching his knee. A thick, animal sound rattles from his throat at the same time as a clap of thunder shakes the hill.

Then a sheet of lightning illuminates the scene.

Thunder booms again, overhead. Rain drives down.

We inch further up the hill. More people gather below, far too close to us for my liking.

'What did you do?' demands Jameela. She rounds on Egg and spits more words that are eaten by the storm. Thunder rolls again but this time we all catch Jameela's words. 'Wicked Girl.'

It's like a slap.

'She's a witch!' bellows the boy who fell, standing and looking for all the world like there's nothing wrong with him. The rat man smiles. 'She struck me down!'

'They're witches!' yells another boy, and a murmur passes around the crowd like an electric pulse.

My heart starts twitching painfully in my chest, and a familiar heat pumps into my face.

Then it happens. A nub of shadow, popping out of my forefinger like a blob of ink, spiralling into the air. It grows wings above us. It's small, and soft, but the crowd sways as though enraptured, and someone screams. I snatch it out of the air and pat it between my hands to dispel it, feeling the way it soaks back into my skin where it can bide its time.

We creep higher up the hill and pause at the root bridge. 'Don't go under the spell,' cautions Mariam, voice shaking. 'If they see us disappear, we're done for.'

I can feel the way everyone's muscles are primed, desperate to run for cover. But we force ourselves to stay still.

The rat man begins to pick his way across the boggy ground towards us.

'Go across the bridge,' mutters Egg, and we do, watching with evergrowing dread as he increases his pace, his smile carving too much of his face into a raw-looking grimace.

'Those girls came out of nowhere,' incites the boy who fell. 'Down from the Ring.'

In the crowd, a collective memory seems to stir beneath all their brows. They know. But they can't quite remember that they know.

'I've seen them! They vanish up there. They reappear.'

We never, ever should have come to the village.

More people are coming out of other shops now, amassing. They all stare up at us, perched on the hillside like birds with broken wings. Uselessly waiting.

A word snakes up through the grass to nip at our ankles. *Wicked. Wicked. Wicked.*

They know.

It's all beginning again.

A sound comes that at first I think must be more thunder. It bites the air clean of threat and sends the man back to the bottom of the hill, where he stands with the others wearing a vacant expression. I can't understand how he moved like that. But as the sound fades, and my skin tingles with the aftershock, I realise it wasn't a natural sound, but a power word. An ancient, single-worded spell that must be spoken in a way that summons enough magic to weave the spell in less than a second. I've heard power words before, in the Shadow Way. The effects made the very edges of reality flicker.

Now Annie Turner has summoned one.

She comes slithering down the hill to fetch us. When I meet her eyes, they are terrified. 'Let's go. Quickly.'

We scramble across the slippery root bridge and she ushers each of us up the path ahead of her, face grimly determined. I know from that look that she wouldn't ever leave a single one of us behind. And I see in that look everything she has ever sacrificed for us, and a deep shame flares inside me.

5
The Liminal

'We must strengthen the spell, at once.' Annie marches into the kitchen and we all scuttle after her, each as wretched as the next.

A large cauldron squats on the stove like a toad, a thick dark liquid thrashing against its insides. The smell is enough to make me pause and grip the doorframe – a marshy, earthy fug.

By now we've all memorised the cloaking potion. Gleaming obsidian chips in a mixture of salted rainwater, powdered myrrh, tiny pieces of horseshoe-shaped quartz, some old nails – which apparently are good for protection, who knew – and a handful of dried creeping cinquefoil leaves. The final ingredients are exactly five drops of patchouli oil and three of frankincense.

'So, let me get this straight,' says Annie, one hand using the ancient art of craftiwork to stir the potion, the other gesticulating at us. 'Isla, apropos of nothing, decided she had a strong enough grasp of glamour magic – which you're only supposed to be learning about right now, not practising in public – to glamour *all of you* for a trip beyond the cloaking spell. And not only did that glamour wear off, but you got into a fight with some local boys and Meghan and Elspeth used magic against them –'

'*I* didn't!' bites out Egg, sulkily. She jabs her thumb in my direction. 'That was all Missus Special-Face over there.'

I stamp my foot. 'Shut up.' Her words sting. I never said I was special at all. But worse than that – much, much worse – is the terror continuing to spread all through my body, into the very tips of my fingers and toes. We've ruined everything Annie has been working so hard for. The entire village knows about us. They're calling us witches.

'What does *apopos of nothing* mean?' asks Isla.

'Be quiet when I am speaking.' Annie is all red in the face. 'You used magic against them, to the point that people were frightened and calling you witches?'

People were frightened? She sounds like she feels sorry for the Unwicked. We never used magic *against* anyone. That's totally unfair. Egg didn't use magic at all. And I – well. I chew my cheek. I'm not sure what I did.

'Did I miss anything?' demands Annie, smoke practically billowing out of her ear holes.

'Well, there was this weird nosebleed and a picture fell and –' begins Isla, but Mariam shoves into her side. Isla glares.

Remembering the mutterings of *evil portents* gives me a queasy feeling.

Artemis hunches high on a bookshelf overlooking us all, tail flicking irritably. Her eyes are narrow and her mouth is hard.

The room grows deathly silent, save for the bubbling of the cauldron. Then Annie collapses in on herself, folding her arms around her middle and fixing us all with such a pained expression that it makes me wince.

'Oh, girls,' she whispers. 'I am so, so sorry. I should have made it clearer, the situation you are in. I obviously didn't explain the dangers properly.' She sinks into a chair and presses her hand to her forehead, shutting her eyes.

'No, we're sorry!' says Layla, eyes brimming with tears. She sits on the floor at Annie's feet. We all tumble after her, surrounding Annie's chair, apologising. Exchanging glances, feeling like fools, terrified someone will breach the cloaking spell. It's only now that I notice how grey Annie's skin has become, how much her bones press against her clothes. She's wearing herself away trying to keep us hidden from the world.

When Egg gently takes Annie's hand, Annie begins to cry. It's quite a shocking thing, seeing the adult in charge lose control like that. It's all because of us. Mostly Egg. I feel the biggest stab of irritation that I've ever felt for my sister in my whole life.

Mariam is in tears. Isla picks at the table, scowling and

blinking. Jameela leans against the sink with folded arms, glaring around at us all as though she could have predicted the whole disaster. What she said before comes back to me with a sickly rush. *Wicked Girl.* So she really believes all that stuff, still.

Annie sits up straight, wiping her eyes. 'This won't do at all.' She gets up and brushes down her clothes.

'I'll make some tea,' says Jameela. She fills the kettle and sets it over a flame on the stove. Her socks are white and flashing in the dim light like rabbit tails, and when she turns to cross the room again, I see it. A spot of red brightens the sock, on her left ankle.

'Jameela,' I start, pointing, but her eyes widen and she shakes her head, just once. She tugs on her jean leg until it covers the spot. The blood. I remember her in the tea shop, yelping after the rat ran across the floor.

The Wayfaring Tree vision rushes into my head. Hundreds of rats streaming across the countryside, the message about stolen magic and creatures being vessels. I think that rat bit Jameela. And I don't really want to think about why.

'Is the potion ready?' asks Egg, scattering my thoughts. 'The spell is, um, definitely hungry.' She gestures to the window, where fog is almost pressing the pane of glass in on itself.

'But feeding the spell is just firefighting,' Isla grumbles. 'It's a short-term solution to *nothing*. They're going to find us in the end, anyway.'

'That's the spirit,' mutters Egg.

'Can someone give it a stir, please?' Annie murmurs, head inside the cupboard under the sink as she rootles around.

Mariam obliges, pulling a wooden spoon through the mixture with an expression of distaste and determination. Her usual expression.

Annie pulls a first-aid kit out of the cupboard. She opens it, movements all sharp-edged, and unearths a box of old plasters. Then she steps across to me, grabs my left hand and begins to strap plasters over my fingertips, so tightly it hurts to bend my fingers.

'Are plasters going to stop those weird shadows that came out of her?' asks Isla, apparently unable to keep a pinch of sarcasm from her voice.

'I hope so,' Annie replies, grimly. 'Remember, Elspeth. Your magic is too dangerous to practise. You must keep your powers hidden. There are people who would pay so very handsomely to steal the spark from your bones.'

The spark from my bones. I glance over at Jameela again.

'I know,' I tell Annie, misery dragging at my skin. 'I didn't mean to do anything, I really didn't.'

The kettle whistles, making us all jump. Jameela and Isla gather mugs, teabags, milk, and sugar.

'Was that man a Hunter?' says Egg, pulling at the sleeves of her fleece.

Annie nods. 'The stolen magic lay upon him like an

oily coating.' She pauses, staring into space, as though she'd like to scrub the memory out of her skull. One of Annie's gifts is seeing people's magic – and she says that the only time the Unwicked have magic is when it's been stolen from people like us. Which hardly ever happens now, because most of us are gone. 'He most likely carried a vessel to hold the magic.'

Vessel. My forehead burns with remembering all those rats again, streaming across the countryside.

Jameela and Isla carry mugs of tea to the table.

'There was a rat,' I say, my voice a small croak. 'It was in his pocket.'

I look at Jameela, and dread blossoms in her eyes.

I can feel Layla and Egg's eyes on me. 'A vessel?' asks my sister.

'Yes. That's how he will have tracked you down,' replies Annie. 'They will have been waiting for a moment like this. We just have to hope that my magic was enough to get you all out of mind – out of memory – as well as sight.'

Out of memory. The phrase makes me shudder. Witches aren't allowed to live in this world, and now we can't even exist in memory?

'Did anything else happen, before you left the tea shop?' asks Annie. 'Did any of you get hurt?'

'No,' says Jameela, too quickly, though no one else seems to notice. 'I'm going to shower.' She leaves the kitchen, footsteps thumping away down the hall.

Isla hurries after her. 'Jam?'

Annie picks up a mug of tea, cradling it to her chest. 'It's time you learned more about the world you've been born into,' she says, in a calm voice. We have to lean forward to hear her over the roiling potion. 'It's known as the Drained Place, where the populace is required by order of the Crown to report anyone they suspect of being a witch. It is particularly severe in Sussex.'

'Why?' I ask.

'Sussex was once known as the *resistant county*. There lives an old, old saying, here. The words cling to the mist rising like ragged ghosts in the morning. A sign of defiance, in a lost dialect.'

'*We wunt be druv?*' suggests Mariam. 'It means, we will not be driven to do what we're told. We will think for ourselves.'

Annie gives her a small, sad smile. 'Exactly. This county was the last pagan kingdom in Britain. It was separated from the rest of the island by a thick, wild forest to the north – the Muddlewood – and the sea to the south. But when the forest was cut down, displacing many creatures and allowing invaders through, the resistance weakened. Though the words linger on, their essence has been crushed. The Hunt established themselves in some of the great seats of Sussex – castles and manors – because the Sussex people were so stubborn and their will was harder to quash. But it happened in the end.'

'The Ring is all that's left of the Muddlewood now, isn't it?' I whisper.

Annie's sad expression is replaced by one of anger. 'Yes.' She stands up and steps over to the cauldron, whispering the words of a spell over the mixture – an old language that sounds like wind guttering a flame. Then she makes a series of movements with her fingers – more craftiwork. The potion makes a bright popping sound, and a salty breeze swoops around the kitchen, making the lampshade rock wildly.

'Get your coats and boots on, please,' she says casually, while we're all standing around gawping at her advanced magic.

We look out of the window at the driving rain, then at each other.

'Um, it's raining?' says Mariam, finally closing her awed mouth.

Annie's own lips twist with suppressed amusement. 'Our cloaking spell won't feed itself, Mariam Abdallah.'

Grumbling, everyone pulls on raincoats and wellies. The sun sinks beneath the curved edge of the Ring, plunging the parlour into late-afternoon darkness.

I'm locked in cold, grasping thoughts. If all the wild places are being destroyed, and all the witches – the ones who spoke up for the wild – are gone too, and there's nowhere safe for us, and this world is actually known as the Drained Place – then where does the hope live?

'Isla, Jameela!' calls Annie, at the bottom of the stairs.

There's a pause. 'We're on the bog!' screeches Isla, from somewhere in the depths of the parlour.

'Both of them?' queries Mariam.

'Humph,' grumbles Annie. 'Well, I haven't the energy to fight them right now.' We line up to head outside. 'Ground rules! I don't want to see even a smudge of magic being brewed. That means no secret craftiwork, no dodgy attempts at power words, no faking an *accidental* Weird Thing, no pranks. Got it?'

'*Yes*, Annie,' we chorus.

It's hard to resist a bit of sneaky craftiwork, but it can go hilariously wrong because it's such a subtle art, using intricate finger movements that will probably take years to learn. Layla tried some last week, and pulled down her own trousers with the wrong movement of her pinky finger. She laughed as hard as the rest of us.

Annie pushes the front door open, bending the encroaching tree branches back, and we step outside into a sheet of rain. Before anyone can complain, she claps her hands together in a crystalline sort of way, making a sound like a struck bell. And the rain stops.

'Is that advanced craftiwork?' whispers Layla.

All around us and across the countryside, it's raining as hard as it ever was. Except that *we* are sheltered.

'The reprieve won't last long,' Annie tells us. 'The clouds

can't hold it in forever – it's not as though as witches we can just get whatever we want. In fact, it's our job to always be in step with nature. Because?'

'We're keepers of the wise ways,' we chant, with varied enthusiasm.

Echoes of Shranken Putch's words when we first came here tingle in the back of my brain. *What it really means to be witches is to be plugged in to nature's ways. It's to be nature's voice, keeper of the old ways, of the wise ways.*

'Exactly.' Annie nods. 'Now to work. If even a small patch of the spell wears thin, we are done for – Hunters and villagers both will be able to find their way into the parlour. Who's volunteering?'

'It's Spel's turn,' says Egg.

'I know!' I snap.

Layla holds the ladder while I climb up on to the leaky, moss-covered roof. The spell swirls around me, glittery and silver, licking its teeth in anticipation of being fed.

'You're supposed to be keeping us safe, not growing teeth as long as bread knives,' I scold.

The spell-in-the-shape-of-a-wolf yawns its mouth into a grin. Layla stands below me on the ladder and passes up the cauldron. I hold it up as an offering, and the wolf dips its head inside to eat.

It almost takes the cauldron with it, so I cling on until the effort makes me sweat. The ingredients swirl up to join the fog shrouding the parlour, and the spell instantly strengthens, turning as dark as the obsidian chips I mixed in. I climb back down.

It's easier to see the boundaries of the spell now.

If we pass outside the margins again, people in the village might see witches flickering into life out of nowhere. But if we stick to the well-worn path around the parlour, and make sure we don't set a toe outside the perimeter of the Ring, we'll stay completely hidden.

Annie stands, staring at the swirling storm throwing chaos across the long grasses.

'What is it?' I ask, going to her side. In the distance, there are orange lights flickering just beyond where the root bridge crosses the threshold between here and there.

'Nothing,' she says abruptly, stepping back. 'Inside now, everyone. Dinner.'

I linger for a little longer, right at the edge of the spell, feeling the wind brushing the tip of my nose and the rain sting my eyeballs – padded by the spell, they feel like tiny needles indenting paper. 'Where are you?' I whisper, willing him to emerge from the storm. 'Where are you, Shranken Putch?'

The small orange lights glow in the distance. They move slowly closer.

The back of my coat is tugged, pulling me back from the edge. I twist to look, but there's no one near me. Everyone has gone back into the parlour, except Annie, who has one foot on the front step. But she is looking back at me. She nods.

Do not linger at the Liminal, Elspeth Wrythe.

The Liminal – that seam where the magic meets the air. What craftiwork let her hands and words reach me across a distance?

With one final look across the cold hillside, I hurry into the parlour and stamp the mud from my boots.

In the kitchen, the clews are careening around brewing tea and chattering in tiny voices too high-pitched to decipher. Isla and Jameela have come back downstairs, both looking ultra sullen.

A ghost cat twines between the table legs and a ghost man sits at the table with his head in his hands.

'What are you doing here?' I hiss at the man under the noise of the kitchen. I groan aloud when Jameela pulls out his chair and sits on him. Mariam carries a jug of orange squash to the table and steps through the ghost cat.

I go to the counter and pick up the tray with the Swiss roll I made for Grael.

'Not now, Spel,' says Annie, firmly.

'But she's been waiting ages for her pudding!'

'You eat, first.'

I sit down with a thump, knowing my protests will do no good. Isla dumps a saucepan into the middle of the table with a triumph normally reserved for those who have hunted their food by themselves. Candlelight throws shadows over the cracked and agitated crockery. Everyone crowds round the table, lifting instant noodles on to their plates. Luckily, we've all got majorly into noodles lately, and they're cheap.

I take a bite of my food. But even now, ghosts are chattering to me. From the corner of the room a ditchling stares through eyes centuries old, telling tales of hollows, bridges and swamps with just their weeping sockets. I remember when Egg and I first turned up here, and the undertaker accused us of being *a couple of skin-soaked ditchlings, sent to haunt me*. Did we really look frightful enough for him to think we were wandering ghouls?

The thought is almost enough to make me laugh, until another ghost drifts through the wall and starts singing a terribly sad song while staring determinedly at me. I put my fork down, and glare at him.

Around the table, the coven squabble, flicking threads of power under the table at each other, sneakily enough that Annie can't see. Egg makes a mistake with her craftiwork, and jolts her own chair instead of Mariam's, spilling her glass of water in the process.

I think again of what's surfacing outside: all those ancient treasures gifted to the dead. 'I need everyone to promise not to touch any of those grave trinkets hatching out at the Ring.' I stare around at each of their faces. 'Swear it.'

'Why not?' demands Isla, as Annie looks up sharply.

I tell them what happened when we were outside after the wake. Annie sags against the table, looking even more drained.

'Do you know what it means?' asks Layla.

'Not exactly,' Annie replies, hoarsely. 'But it means something is stirring – perhaps in the barrow, perhaps somewhere else. Either way, it feels malicious.' She stands abruptly and takes her bowl to the sink. 'I don't think any of you should go outside at all.'

The kitchen rings with raised voices and competing questions. A ghost begs me for noodles. I try to ignore them.

'What about funerals?' I demand, in a gap between the firing of words.

'I'll ask the pallbearers to come here first and help me transport the bodies,' Annie replies. 'Thankfully a lot of our work can be done from in here. You've already finished organising everything.'

'And what about collecting the bodies from now on?' asks Egg. Her mouth is twisted at one corner like it always is when she's descending into darkness.

Annie sighs. 'I haven't worked out all the details yet, Meghan. But I'll talk to the council. I might be able to get help to bring them here.'

'I should still be allowed out, so I can infiltrate the Hunt's ranks,' muses Egg, hair crackling with magic. She ignores the collective outrage that follows her statement. 'Why not?

It would mean we could get under their skin. Learn their secrets.'

'Don't be stupid,' says Jameela. 'Even if you actually could do that, none of us would ever trust you with anything important after that stunt you pulled today. You should have used your brain, for once.'

'Don't scold me,' snaps Egg, over the swelling rain and the clattering of cutlery.

'Try not to use the word *scold*, Meghan,' says Annie. 'It's what they used to call troublesome or unconventional women, if they spoke out against authority.' She pauses. 'They used to force them to wear a horned mask with a gag to restrain the tongue, while they paraded them around the village.'

Everyone stares at her, eyes goggling.

Isla snorts. 'So they definitely would have put one on the Wrythes, then,' she says, gleefully.

At the edge of the table, Egg flicks her thumb across the tip of her forefinger, as though striking a spark. The piece of buttered bread on Isla's side plate flies up and slaps her on the cheek.

'Very mature, Meghan,' Isla mutters, wiping butter smears off her skin.

I wish everyone would shut up for a minute so I can think.

Can I disappear along a seam?

Through a crack?

Through a chip in the teapot?

Or a gap between the floor tiles?

Hello? The voice is thick and dull and doesn't quite reach me. Even though I'm half aware of the table and my plate of food, I'm also aware of a person in a cloak of feathers, crouched underneath the floor and frowning up at me.

The thing is, I've seen them before. Down the plughole, and – the memory trickles over me, from top to toe. I was sitting on my bed, writing in my Book of Shadows, and I saw them – first on the page, then in my room. They vanished just as suddenly as they appeared.

'She's disappearing again.' A hand closes over my wrist. It stays there, warm and solid, and faintly crackling with magic. My sister's hand. A breath fills my lungs with kitchen air. I feel myself solidify.

'You gotta stop doing that, Spel.' Egg lets go and picks up her fork. 'Don't know where you go.'

Neither do I. My voice is still locked too deep so I don't say anything.

The singing ghost drifts closer to me. *Just let me have a forkful of those noodles*, he begs. *Just a taste!*

I thump the table with both hands, hard. Everyone jumps. 'How many times? Ghosts. Can't. Eat.' The ghost flickers irritably, scudding away to sulk on a corner of the ceiling.

'We need to find Shranken Putch,' I say, quickly and calmly, before the others can boil over. 'The Hunt could come for us at any moment. Today taught us that much. Then who will look for him?'

'Elspeth, we've been over this,' says Annie, softly. 'I don't have any idea where we could go. Our allies are a very long way away, if we have any left at all, and travelling together is too risky. The best thing to do is to feed the cloaking spell every day, stay in the house, and wait for Shranken Putch to return.'

'Spel's right,' Jameela interjects, using her sleeve to wipe noodle-soup steam off her glasses. 'We have no idea when the undertaker will come back, or when the Hunt will breach the spell. Shouldn't we try to find help?'

'Yes! And there's somewhere *I* could go for help, even if the rest of you can't.' I stab my fork into the pile of noodles on my plate, determinedly ignoring the singing ghost. 'The Other Ways.'

'I cannot have you going through those portals, alone, into strange worlds,' says Annie. 'You know that.'

'But where is he?' I demand. 'And what if someone else comes here, and takes his place? What if we didn't have a single say in it?'

'What do you mean, takes his place?' asks Isla.

What *do* I mean? Something is nagging at my mind. I know Shranken Putch is important. I know he should be here, where he belongs, and that it *matters*.

'Never mind any of that,' says Isla, fiercely. 'I say we get ready to fight back. We're witches, aren't we? They're afraid of us.'

Egg thumps the table. 'Yes! Let's give them cause to be afraid.'

Annie frowns. Before she can speak, the ancient twiggy broom propped by the back door falls over, with a loud *thwack* against the tiled floor.

'Broom fell,' says Mariam, pointlessly. Her cheeks are swollen with noodles.

'Old lore says that means company is coming,' says Annie.

I hope it's him. I hope and wish with all my heart it means the undertaker is returning home.

6
The Putch Pact

After dinner I rush down to the basement, carrying the Swiss roll on a baking tray. I shoulder the door open. 'Grael!' I call. 'Sorry it's late!'

I stand in the shadows, breathing hard. Then a shiver races across my skin. The weird mushroom has erupted further into the corner of the basement; shiny and reeking. It's now the width of a frying pan, and smooth as a worm.

We're going to have to do something about it soon. I put the baking tray down and make a quick note in my Book of Shadows. *Weird mushroom – cut it back? Talk to Annie.*

The ground quakes beneath my feet. Grael is swimming up through the well. When her head emerges, silvery beads of water roll down her scales.

I grab the tray with the Swiss roll on it, silently praying it hasn't already gone stale.

You realise you owe me two puddings now? This is last night's.

'Oh, you get a pudding every day, do you?' She chuckles as I climb on to the edge of the well and hold out the tray for her. The Swiss roll disappears in the time it takes me to blink.

I wish you would learn to make dragon-sized puddings instead of witch-sized ones, rumbles Grael, spraying me with crumbs.

'One step at a time,' I tell her, distracted. The water sparkles with little glowing lights from the portals far below. Would it be so bad if I just went to *look* at them? I nibble my lip.

The knucker dragon regards me for a moment. *You are plotting, wildish one.*

'Annie has said that we can't even go outside now, at all. I think it might drive me mad,' I whisper. What I really mean is, this is my birthright. I'm Shadow-Born. They kept me locked up for the first thirteen years of my life. I want safety, of course. But I also want freedom.

Grael bows her head. A thrill stings my belly as I scramble over the lip of the well and on to her smooth, leathery scales.

On the stone ledge at the bottom, I watch the portals. Each one is a different colour. Each one is doing something that tells me it's awake: stinking, sloughing off gunge, seeping fluid or sighing. The Shadow Way portal is in the centre of the five.

'Why have you all woken up *now?*' I say. 'I thought you were meant to be closed off forever.'

Who knows what has woken them, ripples Grael's thoughtful voice. *But it has something to do with you, shadow witch.*

'Why does everything have to have something to do with me, these days?' I grumble.

You shall have to get used to that, she retorts, a hot chuckle hissing out between her teeth.

I wrap my arms around my knees. 'Grael, do you know anything about the burial mound underneath the Ring?'

She turns her head to look at me. *It is old. Filled with bones, including those of my ancestors. It surrounds us now.* She lifts her tail to brush the wall, and I startle. Of course. The parlour is on top of the burial mound and the well is underneath the parlour. The well is part of it.

'We saw things emerging at the Ring,' I tell her. 'Trinkets. Tiny animal carvings and jewels.'

Humans and dragons both used to be buried with sacred treasures, she murmurs. *But they should not be on the move in such a way. Energy is stirring.*

'Is that anything to do with the portals opening? Or the Hunt?' I whisper, increasingly aware that the boundaries of this world have become less solid.

I do not know, she answers. A trace of sadness skims her voice like a thread of gold. *But dark forces gather, wild-eyed one. And you must take care-pains.*

Speaking of the Hunt makes me remember the last time I saw Tobias Barrow, the Witchfinder General – and Shranken Putch, who had been struggling to hold him off while I went after my sister into the Shadow Way. 'Grael, why hasn't Shranken Putch come home?'

He did not return here after you went through the portal, she says, walls rattling with the power of her emotion. *I suspect the Witchfinder took him away. I also suspect that he is the key to lighting much of this darkness.*

'The key? Why?'

The Hunt keep too tight a control on our Shranken Putch, she breathes, sending ripples across the water. *They are too interested. They are anxious about him.*

'I need to find out where he is,' I say, gripping the edge of the shelf of rock. 'Could you help me get a closer look at the portals?'

I climb back on to her head and she carries me from left to right, visiting them one by one.

The oval portal furthest to the left is covered in a thick layer of mud. *My grandmother once told me that this portal leads to the Way of Bones,* Grael says. Vines and twigs poke through. When I try scratching off a fingernail of mud, the oval flickers and seeps a sour smell, so I think I might have *hurt* it.

'Sorry,' I whisper.

Next comes the Way of Frost; a smooth, grey-blue oval. A sighing sound ebbs from it. When I put my ear close, I realise it's actually breathing tiny slivers of ice that bite my cheek.

After the Shadow Way portal in the middle of the five, there's one that feels warm to touch, like a sunned stone.

The Way of Flame, says Grael. *The forge of the worlds.*

The furthest to the right, half concealed beneath tumbled roots from the trees outside, is an oval veined with blue squashy protuberances, like blisters. A rushing sound comes from it, like a tide. *The Way of Fins*, according to Grael.

And all these doorways lead to worlds only I can step in to and explore. Without warning, a huge sigh escapes my lips. My fingertips itch, and the plasters Annie applied give a distinct *tug* against my skin. I lift my hands and watch as a tiny curl of shadow squeezes from underneath the plaster on my left index finger.

Show patience, child.

As though trying to undermine her advice, the scabbed Way of Flame portal begins to ooze gunge from its seal. The membrane is cloudy, but deep inside something is beating, like a half-dead heart.

I lay my hand gently on the membrane, and just behind my ear, the dragon snorts a hot breath that singes my ear. 'Ouch!'

But when I push the membrane, gently, I feel it bending under my touch. A coppery smell lifts off its surface, and red dust comes away on my fingertips. I put my ear to it, and inside there are faraway voices, and the clatterings of a world busily turning.

You'd better not let the witch Mistress find out what you're up to.

'There must be a way,' I mutter crossly, while Grael belches strawberry jam smells into the cramped space. 'A way that I can fulfil my duties here and search for Shranken Putch.' Above us, tree roots creak and shudder, dislodging mud that falls into the dragon's skin creases.

I pull the silver watch from my pocket and push the second hand until it begins to tick backwards. My stomach lurches as the well water begins to spin the Other way. The dragon makes a startled sound. She lifts gigantic, clawed feet out of the water and clings on to the wall. The whole well judders.

The scabs smooth out and the milkiness thins until the surface gleams purple. And then it unfolds like an ancient eyelid, peeling open before me, revealing the mouth of a dark tunnel. The air in front of it shimmers like heat. I crawl into the mouth of the portal.

But then I hear Annie and Egg calling for me.

Witch-ish one, coaxes Grael. *Come back, now.* She plucks at the back of my raincoat.

Frustration needles my stomach. I was born for this. The living world isn't even my real home. No one can understand that. Not even Grael.

My excitement dies and leaves a bitter taste in my mouth. I return to Grael and let her lift me back on to the stone ledge. I've been thinking lately about how valuable our magic must be, if the Hunt want it so badly. But instead of keeping my magic locked down, I want to learn it. I want to let it grow, watch it expand, even if that makes life more dangerous.

'Spel!' Egg screeches again, muffled from the world above the well.

The huge dragon watches me with calm, liquid-gold eyes. *Topside with you, now.*

I crawl back on to her head. Then a voice thumps against the opposite side of the Way of Bones' portal. It sounded very close. Too close.

What was that? Grael's own voice is edged with ice.

A hand pushes through the portal, small and cold-cracked. It crooks a finger and beckons to me.

I lean forward, staring. Grael begins to move me away. But she's not quick enough. The hand grabs my wrist. It advances further into the well, followed by a sleeve made of black feathers.

Another hand pushes through, holding a lantern, glass dome buzzing with fireflies. And a face begins to press against the membrane, eyes bulging through, questing for me.

I struggle against an iron grip. Grael pulls backwards. The hand slackens, and I almost lose my balance and fall into the water below.

'Aaagh!' I grab for the feathered arm.. A feather loosens. It comes away in my fingers, and the hands finally withdraw through the portal.

I sit upon the dragon's neck, clutching the feather in my hands. I graze it with a fingertip. An oily sheen wriggles along its edge. 'I think I'd better go back up now,' I whisper.

Grael wastes no time in obliging. *Perhaps it is right to stay away from the portals*, she says, when I've climbed off her and on to the lip of the well. *Whatever just happened is not a thing to risk again.*

When she bids me goodnight and tucks into a dive, disappearing in a coiled mass of scales and teeth, a huge sense of defeat crashes over me. What just happened? I grab a towel that I stashed in the corner, wrap it around my shoulders and sit down on the well to make notes in my Book of Shadows. First, I gently lay the feather inside the back cover to keep it flat. Next, I pull the stub of a pencil out from the rim of my beanie hat, open the book at the last page I wrote in and press the lead to the browned paper.

Just then, Egg barges into the basement. 'Spel! Annie's

looking for you. What've you been up to?' She squints at me. 'Why are you *wet*?'

My pencil snaps, cracking all the way from the lead to the stem. 'Hellish thickets!' I screech.

I wake in the night, in the cold, dark attic. Artemis is lying on my feet. The air feels thick as broth, and my limbs are strangely heavy. I lean over to turn on the bedside light, but when I click the button the room stays dark. Artemis stirs, climbs out of the covers and miaows at me. Her breath is full of silver dots. I reach out to touch one, but it bobs away from my finger.

'Am I still sleeping?' I bite my tongue, and it hurts.

We're awake, clarifies the little black cat.

I gape at her. 'So now you're *talking* to me?'

She ignores that, instead stepping her cold toe-beans on to my legs and using me as a springboard to leap on to the bedside table.

The pocket watch in the drawer has stopped at 04:00. When I move through the funeral parlour, the clock on the mantlepiece in the sitting room has stopped at the same time. No one else is here.

'Where is everyone?' I ask Artemis, who's pressed close to my ankles.

In another fold.

'What?'

She blinks calmly up at me.

When I step into the kitchen, the clock on the wall crunches to a stop, and the hands click backwards until it reads 04:00 again. It's just like that time when I woke up and Egg was sitting on the lip of the well. The parlour is freezing. All the fires have burned to blackened ashes. The floors and walls are tilting.

Artemis's tail brushes across the kitchen floor. *The Ring cannot be without a Putch. He is on his way.*

My skin prickles. 'Shranken Putch?' I picture him, then, tramping up hill and down ditch, fingers of wind and rain seeking the gaps in his threadbare clothing. Finding his way home, against the odds that the Hunt – as much as I don't want to let myself think it – have made that impossible for him.

She chatters her teeth at me. *No. The new Putch.*

'What do you mean?' I rub my arms against the chill. My skin crackles with ice.

The Putch Pact is a spell written on a scroll inside the burial mound that the Ring and the funeral parlour grow on. The treasure of ancient warrior kings and queens, barrowed under our feet. It created a recurring summons – the Putches. An ancient pact with the land, to protect and guide the poor, it means there will always be a protector of the dead, in this place. There are rings in the burial hoard, each inscribed with a spell. One per Putch. It is a great legacy.

I glance down. I feel swirled like the well water. 'Things are emerging from the burial chamber.'

She miaows, low in her throat. *That's where the cursed ring came from, the ring the Witchfinder used to throw your sister into the Shadow Way. Stolen grave jewels, stolen magic.*

Her tiny breath paints a cloud in the air. *Shranken Putch gave it to the Hunt as a bargain to protect this place and the dragon after they threatened to tear it all down. But he knew it was a mistake. They didn't leave this place alone. And loss of the ring uprooted him from the Ring, so now he has no tether to home.*

I shudder, feet frozen slabs on the floor. An image blazes in my mind. My forehead aches. The Wayfaring Tree, eye wide, roots snaking through the well and into other worlds. I think of the trinkets hatching out of the fruit. 'Could a new ring help bring him home?'

Artemis chirrups, tail draped across my feet. *When the Putch arrives, Shranken will not be able to return, regardless.*

'But Shranken has to return!' I say. 'This is his home! He is my teacher!'

She whines, low in her throat, eyes never leaving my face. *He cannot return, once the new Putch comes. The new Putch is almost here.*

I scoff at that. 'I'll find the *right* Putch, Shranken Putch. I'll bring him another ring.' I throw as much stubbornness behind my words as I can muster. The little cat merely blinks.

I remember the ring Isla found inside a fruit, hatched out of the burial hoard. When I find Shranken Putch, I'll give the ring to him.

I pass through the parlour like a ghoul. My mind grows vague. I lose track of Artemis. Then with a great ragged breath I wake up, in my bed. A dream pulls at the corners of my skull, but it's just a tangle of feelings and colours. I turn over in bed, frowning into the darkness. I need to remember something. But sleep drags me back down.

7
By the Pricking of My Thumbs,
Something Wicked This Way Comes

Next morning, the pallbearers help Annie transport the body to the funeral. She puts an enchantment on the hearse, making it appear the size of a shiny black beetle, so they can emerge from the Ring undetected.

It's a beautiful day for a ceremony, all washed gold and birds bursting across the sky, feathered bolts of black on blue. But an undercurrent of danger laces the air like a bitter taint.

I'm passing the sitting room when I notice a puddle of black material at the bottom of the mirror. 'Who left a mirror uncovered?' Is it that hard for the others to remember the funeral customs?

I grab the heavy black crepe. But a movement under the mirror's surface makes me pause. There – a hand pokes up from the bottom of the frame, fingers wiggling.

A face smears against the underside of the mirror glass. Smudged blue eyes. A mouth making shapes, though I can't hear the words. Dark blonde hair and – feathers, splaying against the glass. It's them, again. The kid in the cloak. I drop to my knees in front of the mirror. 'Who are you?' I hiss. 'Why are you haunting me?' Their face appears, closer to the glass, and I jerk backwards.

Mariam pops into the doorway. 'Everything all right, Elspeth?'

I rock back on my heels. 'Someone left a mirror uncovered. I could really have done without it.'

Mariam throws the cover over the glass. But covering it up doesn't change what's happening to me. I lift my sleeve to my mouth and nibble the edge of the chocolate-chip cookie that I stowed up there for emergencies. This whole situation is turning into one long emergency.

I head to the kitchen to shovel down some cold baked beans. But when I'm emptying the beans into a bowl, I remember my dream in a flash.

He cannot return, once the new Putch comes.

I abandon my beans. In the attic bedroom, I open our sock drawer and reach to the back, fingers closing over the ring that Isla found. The ring that, if I really wasn't dreaming, I'm going to need to give to Shranken Putch, to help him return. I put it in my pocket.

Then I race around the funeral parlour, searching for the suddenly elusive Artemis. 'Where are you, you wretched thing?' I mutter viciously.

Isla has obviously been in the kitchen, because most of the packets of food look like they've been ripped open by a bear.

Egg's voice booms from the top of the parlour because she can never just talk at a normal volume like a normal person. The Mistresses of Cluck (as we collectively refer to the hens) are scratching around in the cereal dust someone hasn't bothered to sweep up.

There's no sign of Artemis in any of her usual spots.

As I'm leaving the kitchen, Jameela rounds the corner too fast and crashes into me. Her eyes are bloodshot and puffy. 'Urgh!' she yells, as though I'm a centipede or something. 'I have to get out of this *shoebox* of a run-down, middle-of-nowhere, rat-infested hell-place.'

'Jameela!' I exclaim, awkwardly. 'How are you?' I sneak a look down at her ankle, but she's wearing black jeans and socks, so there's no way of seeing if there's a mark.

'*Fine.*' She narrows her eyes at me. 'Why are you being weird?'

Artemis trots across my slippered feet, and proceeds to rub her face and neck against the corner of the wall. Then she flumps abruptly on to her bottom, lifts a leg and starts scratching her neck with her claws.

'*There* you are!' I sigh. She's behaving exactly like a normal cat. I don't know how I expected to confront her about a strange dream I had.

Jameela smirks. 'You and that creature are practically inseparable.'

'So?'

Artemis gets her claws right underneath her collar, pauses – with the most intent expression – and then *pulls*.

'She's been trying to get her collar off all week,' murmurs Jam, kneeling beside the cat and scrubbing her between the ears. 'But that thing is not budging.'

When Annie returns to the parlour she looks drained, half wasted away, grey around the edges and bent over like an ancient. Despite all this, she says that it's time for a witch lesson. She asks us to gather the magical equipment for casting a circle. The parlour buzzes with a mixture of emotions. Mariam and Layla seem anxious, whereas Isla and Egg are ready to fight, talking about how we might be able to defend this place from the Hunt.

But Jameela storms up the stairs. 'Are you kidding me?' she shouts. 'After what happened yesterday? I am not going anywhere near *witchcraft* lessons.' In the distance, a door slams.

And what's the point in me attending lessons if Annie doesn't know how to teach me? I wonder, following the others into the sitting room. Everyone else is allowed to practise their magic. Most of the time I don't even feel part of this coven.

Annie sits in an armchair. Her breathing is ragged. 'Villagers are gathering with torches,' she tells us, gravely.

'There are more Hunters, too. They are determined to locate this place and break through the spell. The part of it that made people forget about the Ring has been broken, now. The spell is simply a veil. They know we're here.'

A chill dances through the room. The thought of our magic being drained from our blood and bones is a physical fear, making it harder and harder to breathe. My muscles feel coiled tight, ready to spring. My fingertips itch so badly that I'm forced to clench my hands into fists. Candle flames shiver on the mantlepiece, throwing shadows.

'Should we try and get Jam to come down?' asks Isla, resting her chin on her knees.

'We cannot force her to change her mind,' says Annie. An unmistakable tinge of sadness plucks at the corners of her mouth. 'Do you have the things I asked you to gather?'

We nod. There's a rough-looking old cauldron, a bag of white tea-light candles, a tub of earth and one of rainwater, and some herbs, gemstones and other little items hanging from Layla's wrist in a plastic bag. Egg brandishes the hilariously ancient-looking broom. Artemis sniffs its gnarled twigs, and sneezes twice.

'We're going to need to sew some nice big pockets into all the clothes you own,' Annie tells us. 'Pockets make everything easier, and also, they're a form of activism. Did you know that they stopped making pockets in women's clothing to discourage them from carrying magical ingredients, and to control them? It's easier to prove you're not a witch if you don't have pockets.'

'Here she goes,' whispers Isla, and I grin. Annie does love to give a lecture.

'That broom has *seen* things,' comments Layla. Mariam laughs so hard that she gets the hiccups.

'Focus, please,' says Annie, sternly, but then her face twitches with something close to a smile. 'First things first. We draw down the moon.'

She cranks open a window. I reach for a blanket as cold bites my exposed skin. Annie pronounces a rich, guttural power word in the back of her throat and produces a series of rapid craftwork movements with her forefingers and thumbs. Ribbons of moonlight connect with her arms, turning her veins silver. Then, little pearls of moonlight race down her forearms. Layla catches one as it rolls across the ground. 'It's so cold, and squishy!' she gasps.

'Put that down, Layla Dixon,' chides Annie. She snaps her fingers, and each little bead of light flies into the air, bathing us in gentle light. The bead in Layla's hand shoots up to join the others.

Annie sits cross-legged, looking round at us all. 'Merry meet!' she sings out.

'Merry hearth!' we reply.

We make an altar to the elements. A feather for air in the east, a stone for earth in the north, a small basin of rainwater in the west, a candle in the south, and a small silver star in the centre of the circle, its five points shining.

'The star signifies spirit,' says Annie, a twinkle of mischief agleam in her eye. 'The fifth element. Ether. The element you and your powers are aligned with, Elspeth. I would ask that you cast the circle for our ritual, and then be seated. The circle cannot be broken once cast – until we choose to dispel it – so I ask that you all make sure you are properly ready to begin.'

The weight of her words has made a grave moon out of everyone's faces. Annie laughs a little. 'Well, then. We begin.'

She moves her hand, and a long, slender stick appears between her fingers, and then, although she didn't move again, it's alight at one end. Incense.

'Isla,' says Annie, pulling something else out of her pocket. 'You walk behind Spel, scattering salt.'

With a small moan of irritation, Isla climbs to her feet, and Annie hands her a small bowl of salt crystals.

'Don't even think about stepping on my heels,' I tell her.

She flicks a chunk of salt into my face.

I take the stick of incense from Annie and start to walk in a clockwise direction – which is apparently called deosil – watching the delicate curl of smoke weave into the air. 'We cast this circle as a safe, sacred space between the worlds, where no positive or negative energies may enter to disturb our rite,' I mutter, as Annie has taught us.

A soft, thick silence descends over us like a blanket.

I start off imagining a silvery circle of light surrounding and protecting us, but soon it's as real as everything else in the room. In mine and Isla's wake is a silvery-blue band of light, that reflects on to the others' faces. Annie nods encouragement.

Next, Annie directs Egg to sweep the edge of the circle to get rid of any unwanted psychic debris. To my amazement we see it happen for real – as she sweeps, little fragments of shadow glide away under the direction of the sweeping. Egg gives a grim, satisfied chuckle.

'A quick reminder, girls. This is the only space where you are permitted to practise magic, under my direct supervision.'

In turn, they manifest their abilities. I sit hunched over my knees, fingertips itching. Mariam opens her palms skywards, smiling as vines lengthen from the bracelets at her wrists into flowers that bloom at her fingertips. The beads of moonlight pick out her thick plait in pools of silver on black.

Egg flips her hair, as though to dismiss the other girl's efforts. With the barest lift of her chin she sends the cauldron spinning in a circle before rising up into the air. As it goes, the ends of all our clothing rise like weeds in a gathering wind. She doesn't break a sweat.

Isla utters a little roar. All the candle flames shoot upwards, veiling us behind a wall of flame. Artemis screeches until the flames settle down. An ashen smell tinges the air. When we look back at Isla, a flame is balanced on each of her fingertips.

She grins, all sharp little teeth.

My heart plummets. Even if I knew how to control my magic it wouldn't show as a pretty elemental display. I'm still on the outside, even now.

Layla gives us a wink. The rainwater in the basin in front of her begins to shiver. Then rain beats the branches outside the window as though trying to snap them.

But then Layla snatches a breath. Her eyes have peeled to the whites, and the lids flicker. 'Someone else is here,' she croaks.

I gaze into the silver surface of the star in the centre. Then I feel my shoulders tighten. In the slim spokes of the silver is a reflection that isn't mine.

'That can't be right,' says Annie. 'The circle was properly cast.'

I look at the basin of rainwater, and the same face is there as well. Blue eyes, dark blonde hair. A stubborn mouth that's shaping words I can't understand. They're here again. I last saw them in the mirror, and now they're watching somehow from our altar. Overhead, the moon beads shiver.

'What's happening?' asks Mariam. The plants on her wrists sharpen into defensive spines.

Annie stands. 'We need to open the circle. *Now.*'

'Don't,' I plead. 'Just wait a minute.'

'We're under attack.' Egg's eyes shine with a thing like delight. She moves into a squat, fists bunching.

I move closer to the rainwater, which shows the best image of the tiny face.

'Elspeth,' warns Annie.

I stare down into the water. 'Who are you?' I whisper.

Behind them, a scrap of black glides through the sky. A rook.

The face disappears from the basin, the ripples of the water the only evidence they were ever here at all.

Artemis hisses from the pool of darkness at my elbow. She steps on to my leg and settles on my thigh, balancing in a perfect loaf shape. I bury my fingers in her soft fur. Her purring throbs into my bones.

Annie clicks her fingers, and something changes in the air. The smokiness dissipates and the magic leaks away. Moon beads pour through the window like a flock of silvered birds, flying home. The heavy drape of silence splits apart, leaving the sound of our breathing and the rain hitting the leaves of the trees beyond the window.

'No more magic,' whispers Annie, features pinched with anger and fear. 'Just the cloaking spell, to keep us safe. Nothing more. I don't know what I was thinking.'

'But –' gabbles Egg.

'We focus instead on the task of remembering,' says Annie, cutting her off. 'Part of our task is to remember the witch community. It will be the most important and difficult thing we will ever do. We are scattered, we are hiding, we are dead, or we are terrified. But they did *not* burn us all.'

The sitting-room window is already laced with frost, and beyond it, the sun is tumbling towards the horizon. A shiver dances through my bones.

The circle broken, the clews totter towards us with a tray of drinks. Annie ignores them and heads straight upstairs to bed. I lean over and take a mug of spiced hot chocolate, wrapping my hands gratefully around the warmth.

Something about what happened has the others restless. Or maybe it's not being allowed out, or to practise magic. They dance around the sitting room, hot chocolate slopping over the sides of their mugs. The clews get upset by that, scurrying to clean up the mess.

Even Mariam lets her hair down – literally, flinging her head around to the loud music Egg plays on the radio. Egg gets a sugar rush, and when she does a cartwheel in the sitting room she collapses, laughing, on to the sofa.

Artemis catches the fun-spark for a while, prancing around the room, fur puffed up with excitement. But inevitably she starts to disapprove and retreats to a bookshelf, where she hunches stonily and rasps at us.

I sit with my back to an armchair, my hot chocolate slowly going cold. I feel sick. All I want is to stop feeling like the world is spinning out of control. Why am I being chased by someone from another world?

8
Trouble with a Capital T

When everyone's gone to bed, I lock myself in the bathroom and climb into the empty bath with a blanket and a candle, which I light and place on the sink. Then I pull out my Book of Shadows and a fresh pencil. When I open the book, the feather slips into my lap. The sheen is still there, clinging to the black curve like essence from a dream.

I pick it up and turn it in the candlelight. Then I flip through the pages of the book to find my current writing page – but a black smudge transfers from my fingers on to the paper. I check my hands, but they're clean. *'What?'*

The black smudge begins to pull apart into smaller blots. Watching it makes my heart squirm. A drop of black falls on to the page, then, like a tear.

It fell from the tip of the feather. Another drop rolls off it while I watch. The oily sheen rolls along the feather's edge, now liquid.

There's a sliver of a cut down the centre of the white tip that once grew from a wing. It makes the feather look like a pen.

I try pressing the tip to the black drops on the paper, ignoring the warning clang of my blood. And it writes. Finally getting a chance to write feels like the biggest relief. I imagine that I'm writing to my mother, Amara, because I really need a friend to talk to right now. It's easy to feel like I'm writing to her. This book was hers, after all.

The secret life of Spel Wrythe: finding Shranken Putch

1. *I don't know much about the mystery of what's happened to Putch, but I have some clues.*
2. *I have the note he left for me, which means he knew he was going.*
3. *I have a ring that hatched out of a fruit, and I think it might have come from the burial mound beneath us.*
4. *Maybe if I can find the undertaker and give him that ring, he'll have a way of coming home.*
5. *Because in a sort of dream, sort of not, Artemis told me about the Putch Pact, and how he needs a tether to this place. I know it matters, because Grael told me that she thinks Putch is the key to lighting the darkness, whatever that means. Either way, the Hunt wanted him gone. But I'm not going to let them do it without a fight.*

Writing with the feather ink is odd because it stretches instead of flows, the words growing from the original splodge.

I lift the nib off the page while I think about how to order my next list. But then something changes in the air, and my words begin to slip about on the page.

My stomach plunges, and the breath tightens in my chest.

Putch flutters to the edge of the book and then slides off, landing in a spot of silver grey on the side of the bath. It looks like ash. I stay very still for a moment. Then I throw the quill away from me, insides itching with a rapidly swelling fright.

The tension in the air breaks, and the other words stop moving. Instead they settle deeper into the paper, fading as though the ink has soaked in.

When I check my pocket watch, it's almost midnight. I have to get to bed. The death phone could ring at any time, and I'm the closest thing this place has to an undertaker, after all.

I return the pencil to my hat and the book to my pocket, then clamber out of the bath. The feather waits on the floor. A shine ripples along its edge, like a wink.

Next morning, Egg and I are sitting at the kitchen table, surrounded by buckets that have been positioned to catch the rainwater that's now leaking through the ceiling in multiple places. We're both using mugs of hot chocolate to warm our hands, since using the heaters is too expensive and there's no fireplace in here. The hens have migrated to other, warmer rooms.

There are so many things I want to tell my sister about. But it's hard to know where to start, and these days she feels so distant from me, even when we're physically together.

'I can't believe we're still expected just to wait here under the cloaking spell,' I whisper, frustration scraping the underside of my skin. 'Maybe if Annie trusted me, I could find a way to help.'

Egg rolls her eyes. 'Yeah, fine. Except what have we done so far to make her think any of us can help? See it from her side, Spel. We've made things worse.'

Irritation prickles. 'We?'

'Oh, that's nice. Thanks so much.' She kicks out at the table leg a little too hard, and liquid spills over the brims of our mugs. 'You think you're invincible now, huh? After the Shadow Way?'

Her jaw tightens around the name of the realm where I was born, against nature's laws. I know she's far from over the trauma of her experiences there.

'Hardly.' I kick out at the table legs, too, meet Egg's glare, look away. Hellish thickets. I literally *never* said I was invincible. 'But I do think there are possibilities for me to help us, given that I'm the only one that can get out of here.' I tug my beanie lower over my head. 'Into the portals, I mean.'

'Have you ever thought that maybe you should just go,

then?' Egg slams her hands down on the table and pushes herself to her feet, before storming away.

Her words from after we went to the village echo into my brain, still stinging. *Missus Special-Face.* But that's not what I'm saying I am at all! Why does it feel like she doesn't understand me any more?

When tears come, I blink them away furiously, which gives me a headache. The others are in the sitting room, so I climb the stairs up to the attic and grab the Book of Shadows from where I've wedged it between my bed and the wall. Sitting cross-legged on my bed, I press the nib of the feather to the paper. Black gloopy ink pools on the page, and then the ink stretches into words by itself.

Elspeth Wrythe. Shadow-Born witch.

My heart skips like a hare. Another message appears, borrowing the thread of ink from the previous one. *The undertaker's cat wears the moon charm.*

A frown drawstrings my brows together. An electric feeling passes from the Book of Shadows into my wrist. More words bleed on to the page.

Never take the moon off.

'Huh,' I whisper, cold fright sliding through me. Artemis has been scratching at her collar more and more lately, and everyone is now convinced she has fleas. Annie said she was going to see if the food bank had any pet medicine. Artemis had positively *bristled* when Annie said the word pet.

I take a deep breath. As long as I've had this book, I've felt comforted by it, because it was my mother's. Confiding in the book feels safe, so maybe it's just the weirdness that's scary. Maybe it's okay to trust it. I press words into the page. *Why can't the moon come off?* I think for a moment, before writing again. *And who are you?*

I don't dare let myself think it. It couldn't be her. Surely it couldn't be.

Footsteps creak up the attic stairs. I know the sound of Egg's walk well enough to know it's her. I slam the book shut as she sticks her head round the door.

'Can I not just get five minutes' peace?' I blurt.

She pauses, staring at me sullenly. 'I was coming to apologise,' she snaps, before turning on her heel and marching off again.

'Egg!' I call. She doesn't come back. Jagged thorn patch that she is.

I open the book again but Artemis chooses that moment to leap on to my lap, startling half the life out of me. She must have come in when Egg opened the door. I snap the book shut again, lifting it out of her way. A small cloud of grey ash puffs out of the edge of the book, like the ash that dropped into the bath.

Artemis kneads my leg, gazing at me with glowing eyes. The silver moon around her neck catches the light. A gleam shudders along the moon's back.

'Why shouldn't your moon be taken off?' I ask her, leaning down to scratch the exact spot between her ears that she always butts my hand with.

She utters an annoyed whine.

I lean over to put the book and the feather on the bedside table. Then a dizzy feeling swishes round my brain. A flurry of hearth ashes and rook feathers blow out of the tiny attic fireplace, as though a gust of wind has swept down the chimney. The ashes settle on the floor between the beds, and begin to form words. I clutch handfuls of bedding, itching with horror.

Do you want to speak to the undertaker?

'*What?*' I whisper, my own voice hardly audible over the blood rushing in my ears. After the writing has appeared, the magical feeling subsides slightly. 'Yes, I do! Come back!' I huddle on my bed, chewing the inside of my mouth.

Then the ashes start moving again, and I jump into a squat with my arms wrapped around my knees as I stare down at the floor. Artemis growls.

'Who is writing this?' My voice is barely a breath.

A tree branch scritch-scratches against the window.

I stifle a scream as the hearth ashes scurry around, forming more letters.

Come to the portal.

9
Undertaking 101

I'm on my way to tell the others what happened when Annie's voice drifts up from the kitchen. 'It cannot be overstated, girls. Elspeth could fade out of existence entirely, at *any* moment. We have to be careful with her.'

'That's what I'm worried about,' says Egg.

'I'm glad you understand,' Annie replies. 'Spel is fragile. We have to remember that.'

'Don't you think there's also a risk that she might – you know,' says Mariam, quickly.

'What?' demands Egg.

'*Ruin everything?*'

A hissing squabble breaks out, and I rock back on the stairs, hugging my knees. *Fragile?* Their words leave me breathless. I'm not made of glass. It's like they're saying that I can't be trusted, because I might break at any moment. And as for ruining everything? It hadn't really occurred to me that they might think I'm that much of a liability.

'Oh, come on.' Layla laughs. 'What is there to ruin?'

'That's not exactly what I mean!' wails Mariam. 'I mean – I don't know – bring something worse to our door?'

'Don't be daft,' snaps Egg, and a tiny glow of sisterly pride – only the ghost of what I used to feel – burns in my chest. It fizzles out quickly. Egg sounded doubtful.

'It's like the only person she really wants to spend time with is the cat,' murmurs Jameela.

'Spel processes things more deeply than you lot,' says Annie. 'You're all much too loud for her. Perhaps Artemis is a better companion.'

I flinch. Because isn't it a great feeling when adults single you out as different?

Curled on the stairs, a flame of defiance ignites in my bones. Any intention to do as I'm told evaporates completely.

I tiptoe downstairs, avoiding all the creakiest steps. If there's any chance of talking to Shranken Putch, I have to take it – even though I don't know who wrote that message. Could it be something to do with the hand that grabbed my wrist?

I pause on the first-floor landing, gripping the banister. *And what if it's a trap?* whispers a tiny voice inside my head. I shake the voice away. This time I'll be prepared. I'm not letting anyone grab me again.

When the coast is clear in the hallway below, I rush down the last flight and nip down the stairs to the basement.

In the basement, the weird mushroom in the corner has

started faintly groaning. Hellish thickets! I swallow a yelp of frustration that I forgot to mention it to Annie. Since it's not my priority right now, I decide to try to ignore it. But that's far from easily done – as I climb on to the lip of the well and call for Grael, the mushroom seeps a wet, gurgling whine into the darkness. Urgh.

The floor vibrates under my feet as the dragon makes her way topside.

Witch-ish one, says Grael, pupils expanding and contracting as she looks at me. *I had not thought I would see you again so soon. Your Mistress has forbidden travel, and I do not like what happened last time we met.*

'I know,' I reply, leaning forward to climb on to the damp, scaly folds of flesh at the back of her neck. 'But I think I might have found a way to speak to Shranken Putch!'

Grael makes a rippling sound, as though surprised, and despite her wariness she carries me to the bottom of the well.

A chill traces my spine as a hand pushes through the same portal as last time. But when the firefly lantern appears again, glass dome crowded with trapped creatures, I feel a stab of determination.

It *is* them. I'm not waiting around in here to be grabbed again. I want to know who this person is, why they keep haunting me, and what's happened to Shranken Putch. This time, I'm taking charge, rules or no rules. I swat the hands away. They retreat, the lantern's metal shrieking.

I lean towards the portal, stretching out my arms. Then I take a breath and push myself inside, wriggling head first through the cloying copper mud of the snoozing portal.

A distant music scatters overhead like metal stars. Memories flit past, scudding clouds across my senses. Annie Turner pointing into the night sky to show us a planet. Mariam, sweeping the kitchen floor, asking what our plans should be for the moon meet. Egg's mouth forming words that I can't hear. Her face growing blurred.

I use my elbows to drag myself further into the realm of the unseen – roots, small, scurrying creatures, dead leaves, even tiny skeletons, cold and jagged under my touch.

On the other side is a tunnel entrance, half filled with a puddle. I splash through on my hands and knees, pull myself free and stand in the glow of a late-winter sunrise. Balls of mist rise like ghouls from graves.

A silhouetted figure stands waiting a little way ahead of me, but there's too much sun in my eyes to be able to see. The air feels different here. It's thicker, more sluggish. It crawls across my skin, tickling. Clouds of black moths, delicate as charred scraps of paper, dance on a lazy breeze. The noise is different. There's a constant low droning sound, like a bell being struck over and over until the sound runs into itself.

It smells different here, too. Of stagnant air and water, a trace of salt, of dusty books, maybe, and wood smoke. I blunder forwards, squinting in the sun.

Spiralling away from me is a chalky-white path that slopes down to a squat building with steam rising from its chimney. Pine trees scatter the space between here and there. In the distance are a series of domed hills.

In the fresh blue sky above the pines, a delicate arc of pale moons bloom, awaiting darkness. I count. There are *thirteen* of them.

Thirteen moons?

The figure moves towards me, emerging as the sun clears from my eyes. It's the kid who appeared down the plughole, and underneath the floor, in a silver star, and a dish of rainwater, and a mirror. The kid who grabbed my wrist through the portal, whose cloak the feather came from. They look about my age, with dark blonde hair pulled into a topknot tight enough to stretch the skin taut. Their blue eyes are rimmed with grey circles.

The cloak they always seem to wear is made of a thick, glossy cascade of rook feathers. A gust of wind makes the black lantern squeal in their fingers, throwing the fireflies against the glass. Their fingers are covered in dark purple stains, and their nails are bitten bloody, to the quick. They're watching me with a sort of carved-open curiosity. Like they can't believe I'm here.

'Well?' I gasp, failing to stop the shake in my voice. 'What do you know about the undertaker?'

They cock their head.

'It was you that sent that message, wasn't it? *Come to the portal*. And here you are.'

Nothing. Fear nibbles my edges. How did they do it? And why won't they answer me? Maybe we don't speak the same language.

Then impatience flares, sweeping away my fear. 'Look, I'm in a rush! My home is in danger. I need to find him.'

'Nice to meet you, too.' There's a note of challenge in their voice. And, unless I'm imagining it, a slightly wounded look in their now steely eyes.

'Okay, sorry.' I clench my jaw. 'I'm Spel. What's your name?'

'Flux.' They rock on their heels, grinning. 'I'm a student undertaker.'

Student undertaker? We'll come back to that. 'Why do you keep appearing all the time, in my house?'

Flux smirks. 'Don't you like it?'

'The other day I was minding my own business and you popped up at the bottom of the plughole!'

'Ha!' yells Flux, excitedly. 'That must be when you pushed your whole stupid great head through my bedroom ceiling and had a good goggle around at everything. It was creepy enough, I can tell you that much.'

So I've been doing the same thing to them? Appearing where I shouldn't?

I scan the sky above us again. *Thirteen moons. There are*

thirteen moons in this world. The Otherness of it makes me feel like an alien, vulnerable and exposed as a wound.

When I look at Flux again, the front of their feather cloak has begun to bulge and wriggle. A very small, fleshy creature pops its head out of an invisible pocket and peers at me through lidless eyes. As it pushes out further and grasps the edge of the pocket, three hairy prongs are revealed on each side of its neck, and there are four pointed fingers on each tiny pink hand.

'What's that?' I stammer.

Flux glances down, then back at me. 'Grenwald.'

Maybe I wasn't clear. 'But *what* is it?'

'He's my axolotl.' They stroke its head. 'And the most beautiful axolotl ever to sprout gills, aren't you, Grenny?'

That's debatable. Also, what the jagged thorn patch is an axolotl, anyway?

A slippery pink tongue sneaks out of the creature's – Grenwald's – mouth, testing the air in my direction. My legs itch with wanting to escape. But I can't run away now.

Flux's eyes widen as they stare past my shoulder.

'What?' I twist to look. 'Oh, hellish thickets.'

A couple of ditchlings have followed me through the portal. Dismay drags at my skin. I stamp my foot, and they startle like cats. 'What do you think you're doing?' I hiss.

A grating sound meets my ears. Flux is laughing, their raspy voice translating into a coarse chuckle. 'So much for being undertaker in residence,' they gasp, through tears of mirth. 'Even first years would be thrown out for allowing ghouls to glue themselves on like that.'

I blink. 'You – you know how to stop this from happening?'

'A haunting?' they ask casually, studying their bitten fingernails. 'I should say so. That's Undertaking 101. It's for babies.' The cackling starts again.

I haven't got time for this. 'Did you send that message to me? How? Do you know where the undertaker is?'

My questions tumble like a stream, and they don't answer. The excitement has faded from their face.

Another question rises through me, chilling my blood and bones. 'How did you know I'm undertaker in residence?'

10
Lych and Screech

The moons darken, until they're a curve of ink-black orbs dominating the sky, which is, in turn, growing lighter.

The itchiness that I keep getting in my fingertips grows more intense. A tiny puff of black smoke twines out of my left index finger. I try to swat it away, but Flux's eyes hook on to the smoke like a fish to a line.

'Shadow-Born, you are.' It's not a question.

I snatch for breath.

'I am, too.'

'You're –' My tongue feels too big for my mouth. 'You're *Shadow-Born?*'

As if in answer, coils of smoke puff out of the end of their own fingers. 'I came through into your world to fetch you, didn't I?'

'You did,' I reply, slowly, realising with a sharp pang that I didn't use my pocket watch to open the portal. Flux had already opened it.

'Come on,' says Flux, bounding down the chalky slope.

'What? Wait! You haven't answered any of my questions!'

'You want to talk to him, don't you?' they call back.

Muttering curses, I set off after Flux, boots scrunching over a fine white gravel, smooth as glass. My hands are clenched into fists inside my pockets. It never occurred to me that any other witch could be Shadow-Born. And what were the chances that I'd actually *meet* another one?

I catch up to Flux as we skirt past the squat building I noticed before, which turns out to be a train station. A tall figure stands just inside the door. It looks like a man with impossibly long, bendy legs. He's wearing a hat with a wide brim, and even from a distance I can hear the tap of his polished shoes on the wooden station floor. The figure turns slowly to watch us pass. Except they have no face, only a smooth oval sitting on top of their shoulders.

Flux takes my elbow and steers us quickly away from the station. 'Don't look back,' they whisper.

'What was that?' I breathe.

Flux shakes their head. 'Not now.'

We pass a wooden sign declaring *The Snags*, in peeling painted letters. A series of hills rise and fall against the darkness. I squint in the lamplight. No – not hills. Snails. Giant snails.

As I approach the nearest of the shells, so huge that they rise into the sky like tower blocks, I crane my neck to stare at the little lights within. People are living inside the spiral shells.

With lamps lit, the shells are almost see-through. Some of them have holes bashed in their sides; others have people crammed into makeshift dwellings tethered to the very tops of the shells.

I pause outside a shell that's different from all the others. It's pulsing with coloured lights that move around inside – purple, pink, yellow, and blue – and throbbing with noise.

'Oh, this place is great,' enthuses Flux. 'It's –'

There's a flurry of movement behind us. Flux yells in surprise as the faceless man we saw waiting at the train station scuttles towards us, holding on to his hat, a briefcase banging against his leg.

Somehow, I have time to think a few morbid thoughts. Annie was right to tell me not to do this. I'm such an idiot. What if I die – I mean, *completely* – out here?

'Quick! Get in!' shouts Flux, pushing me towards a thin door in the giant shell. I slip through, into a world of noise and colour, flashing lights and pounding music. Flux barges in behind me. People glide past on roller skates. Some race each other, others skate backwards, or do jumps and spins.

I weave through the crowd, ignoring their shouts for me to get out of the way. Flux stays close behind me, but when I twist to look, the faceless man is following. I fly across the room, shoving past people lounging on skates and sipping a frothy green brew that looks like a cup of neon frogspawn.

'Hey!' someone shouts.

'There's an agent here!' calls another voice, and panic erupts.

Everyone scatters. Abruptly, the music stops.

An agent? Could they mean the faceless man?

I shove through a door on the other side of the shell. The snail shells are divided from the gloomy field beyond by a fence. 'Keep going!' yells Flux, and we leap the fence, haring towards a town huddled under a blanket of fog.

The grasses are long and purple. A sound shivers out of the undergrowth, like a cross between glass shattering and a high-pitched scream. 'Watch out for skeleton toads!' puffs Flux.

I wince, glancing nervously at the damp grasses as they brush my trousers.

By the time we reach the other side of the field, there's no sign of the faceless man. We walk down a dirt track leading between two huge gateposts in the shape of rooks, stone eyes lit with torches. The shadow of the thirteen moons is dappled across the stonework.

Flux points at each rook in turn. 'That's Lych, and that's Screech.'

'What is this place?' I pant, heart slowing as I catch my breath.

'Rookery Hollows,' Flux replies, wearing an expression that's hard to read.

We walk between Lych and Screech, into a jumbled town full of old buildings, bridges and spires, all stained a pinky-peach colour. Here and there, dragons adorn the rooftops, scales winking. The sky buzzes with activity – a network of angular white shapes zipping like lanes of traffic. 'What are those?' I point.

'Bone gliders,' says Flux.

An electric thrill rushes around my body. I've done it. I've stepped into another world. Only I can do it, and I've done it because no one else has a clue how to stop the Hunt. So it's going to be down to me.

The streets are covered in the fine white gravel I noticed when I first entered this world. I wrinkle my nose at the way it squeaks under my feet. Then I realise what it is. I stoop and cup a handful of the gravel, letting it filter through my fingers. 'This is bone,' I say, glancing up at Flux. 'Tiny little chips of bone.'

'Bits of bone fall off the gliders,' they tell me, opening their palms. They're soon coated in a thin layer of white dust.

'Great.' I press the sleeve of my sweatshirt over my mouth and nose, and try to separate out all the different smells and sounds of Rookery Hollows but it's so difficult. There are wafts of seaweed, fish, freshly baked bread, sewage, frying onions, and the bitter vapour from brewing coffee.

'Where is he?' I ask, staying in step with Flux.

Grenwald rides on the back of Flux's hand as we walk. 'Not far. I'm taking you to him now.'

Rookery Hollows is a labyrinth of crooked, misty lanes, flooded paths or skinny twittens – which Flux says is a Rookery word for alleyway – that loop around and spit you out where you started. The whole place is like a maze. As we step into the mouth of a particularly dark, misty twitten, I can't shake the creeping dread that we're being followed.

'A word of advice about surviving in Rookery,' Flux whispers. 'The Underside and the Other sides of things – they rule. Never read what's written on the Underside of your dinner plate. Never walk on the Other side of a lamp post to your companion – you will split into different worlds. Okay?'

'Um, okay?' I whisper back. 'I guess.' *Just get to Shranken Putch*, I tell myself. *Just find him and speak to him, and you don't have to worry about anything else right now.* 'Good,' they reply, snatching a papery black moth out of the air and feeding it to Grenwald. The creature softly chatters his teeth, before unleashing a startlingly loud belch.

Why should I trust you? The words tumble through my brain, and when I imagine telling any of my coven about this, I feel sick. They would think I'm so beyond stupid.

The end of this twitten is still nowhere in sight. 'I have some *questions*, about all this,' I say, partly to distract myself.

'You can ask three,' they chime, in a slightly mocking tone that scrapes my nerves.

'That's pretty rude.' I point. 'How can there be thirteen moons?'

'One for every month?' they reply, as though I'm forgetting the colour of grass.

'But there are only twelve months.'

They give me a look. 'If we're not careful there's only going to be twelve *moons*.'

Sure enough, if I look closely I can see how the last moon on the right side of the arc has a rough edge rather than a smooth curve. As I watch, a piece of it crumbles into black ash that smears down the sky like distant rain.

'It's being eaten away,' says Flux, and the words make all the hairs stand up on my arms.

'By who?'

Flux hesitates, giving me a sidelong glance. Grenwald scampers up their arm, disappearing into the hidden pocket in Flux's cloak. 'The Hangman,' they answer, finally. Then they stride on ahead of me.

I hurry to keep up, boots scrunching against the chalky-white bone gravel.

The twitten finally spits us into another tangle of ancient streets, peppered with alley mouths and heavily bolted doorways. The streets are deserted. A shadow falls across me, and I look up to find that the sky has been blotted out by a hill crowned by a series of white towers, shining under the black moon shadow.

'That's the College of Macabre Arts,' Flux tells me. 'Every day, at tide-turn, it's severed from the rest of Rookery Hollows by the sea.'

I stare up at the towers. 'And – there are people in there, when it's sea-severed?'

'Oh yes,' says Flux. They turn to me, eyes shining. 'Do you want to play hide-and-seek?'

'No,' I say, firmly. 'I told you. I came here to speak to someone who you said you could take me to. I don't have time for games, Flux.'

They nod, the light fading from their eyes. Then they dart away to the left, leading me down a narrow alleyway and into a hedge maze sculpted from ancient yews.

It feels like we'll never find a way through. But then the hedges part and we stumble out in front of a sprawling building with a giant bird's nest bursting out of the windows and along and across the top floor.

'This is the Rookery itself,' says Flux. Their eyes harden. 'This is where I live.'

We walk up a flight of stone steps and Flux pushes open a heavy wooden door, gesturing for me to enter. 'He's here?' I ask, searching Flux's face.

'You can speak to him,' they reply, slipping through in front of me. When I follow, the wooden door falls shut behind us with a boom that echoes into the distance. Inside, the light is mostly gulped by shadow. Our footsteps ring on the stone floors. Flux's home smells like gravestones and midnight.

We move through a warren of narrow passageways, until the space opens out into a cavernous hall. Like the moons, the lamps in the hall throw shadow instead of light. At the back of the hall is a black throne. I squint at it, trying to make sense of the fact that, very slowly, it is *squirming*.

'The rook throne,' Flux whispers. 'The most important part of the Rookery.'

A long wooden table is strewn with the remains of a feast. Pot-bellied goblets stand in red circles of blood-coloured liquid. There are dishes of rotting fruit, oozing sour froth. The walls are covered in huge, old tapestries. My palms begin to sweat. Egg was locked in a haunted tapestry in the Shadow

Way, and though this one looks lifeless, the sight still makes my heart hammer with dread.

'Putch?' I call, faintly, the stained air snatching my voice and drinking it into the walls.

Flux presses both palms against my spine. 'Come,' they whisper. 'It's through here, in the courtyard.'

'What is?'

'The Wayfaring Tree.'

I feel my eyes widen. 'How can there be another one?' I whisper.

Flux gives a shrewd smile. 'Everything always has its Other.'

We cross to a door in the opposite wall. The stones are slippery from what must be centuries of footfall. Then Flux shows me into an eerily silent courtyard. Silver raindrops fall even though the sky is absent, and they fall as though in slow motion. As the drops land, they illuminate the shapes filling the space all around – and I realise with a start that this is a graveyard, filled with an array of crooked grey headstones like a mouthful of rotten teeth.

'Why have you brought me here?' I ask, turning angrily to Flux. 'He's not dead, is he? What have you done to him?'

'Know peace, witch,' says Flux, flicking little shadows off their fingertips. 'I've done nothing but bring you to speak to him.'

I step between the gravestones. In the centre is a tree that is an exact double of the Wayfaring Tree back at the Ring.

The pain in my forehead instantly returns, and I press the heel of my hand against it, fighting a wave of dizziness.

I scuff around over the moss and roots and dips in the earth. 'Shranken Putch!' I call. A raindrop ripens on a branch very near my face. It grows rounder and hangs long off the tip of the branch, and then Shranken Putch's face appears inside it. His scrutinous, mutinous eyes bulge and his brows seethe as he turns his face this way and that. Then his gaze locks on to me.

'Wrythe girl? Shadow witch! Measly thing. Hellish thickets!'

11
Lost

I stare into the raindrop that's swollen with the image of the undertaker. 'Shranken Putch?' I whisper.

'They called me that, once,' he harrumphs. 'How are you performing this trickery?' Behind him is a glimpse of a dark space.

I stamp down my annoyance. 'Where *are* you?'

'I don't know.' He screws up his face. 'A prison, of some sort, I believe.'

'Oh, good.'

'*Good?*'

'Well, you're alive, aren't you? The last time I saw you, you were being threatened by the Witchfinder. I was worried you might be dead!'

He snorts. 'If I was *dead*, answer me how I would be talking to you?'

'Seriously, you should see my life. Dead people are *mostly* who I talk to.'

He winces, wearing an expression that suggests he knows

what I mean only too well. 'How is my parlour?'

I shrug. 'Okay? I'm managing to help the souls through. There are too many of them, though. I'm exhausted. The hens are running the place. I usually find one in my bed.'

Shranken Putch practically evaporates under the stress this seems to cause him. 'Hens, indoors?'

I shuffle. 'The girls thought . . . the hens might get cold outside.'

Putch stares at me incredulously. 'They're all *living* indoors?'

'Yes?'

He looks very disturbed about the hens even though there are blatantly other more important things going on right now. Adults are so weird.

'Hens live outside, it's what they do!' he squawks, looking very much as though he himself is laying a very difficult egg. 'They have their own house!'

'Never mind, never mind,' I say quickly, hoping to smooth over his fretting. 'So, when can you come home?'

This is, of course, when I notice the ice picked out across his beard and hanging from his eyebrows. The gaunt lines of his face. The bruises lining his eye sockets.

'I can't, small Wrythe.' He lowers his voice. 'Listen. The parlour will pass to you, now. And that jagged old cat.' He curls his lip. 'And the new Putch.'

'No,' I whisper, my voice snagging in my throat. 'You can't mean that. Where are you? We'll come and find you!'

'There must be a Putch at the Ring. It doesn't have to be me.'

'But Grael said you're the key in all this. The key to stopping the –'

Shranken Putch shushes me, violently. He speaks more quietly, and quickly. 'What have you noticed about that aircraft?'

'The one that passes overhead all the time? You know about that?'

'Less asking, more answering,' he demands. The raindrop has stretched so much that his mouth is now speaking from knee-height, and his eyes are level with my chin.

'I don't know.' I squat down and think for a moment, arms wrapped around myself. 'It makes a lot of horrible noise. It's trying to break through the cloaking spell Annie put on the parlour.'

He nods. 'It is spying. Don't trust anyone you don't know – do you hear me?'

I swallow, uncomfortably aware that I have been doing exactly that. But I had no choice. Urgency crashes through me, then. There's too much to do and I need him to understand. 'Putch, I know about the pact! I can bring you back; I found a ring for you. Where are you?'

Panic flashes across his face. He opens his mouth. Begins to speak. But the raindrop lengthens dramatically on the branch. It falls. I spring to catch it. His stretched face slips through my fingers. He's gone.

'No! No, come back!' I watch more raindrops sliding off the branches, but however hard I will it to happen, none of them show his face. Instead, infinite other faces shine in the drops, mouths and eyes stretched wide, words chattering and mixing with each other to make a swelling sound of panic.

I turn away from the tree, covering my ears, but all the light in the Rookery has snuffed out. I don't know if it's real or not, but I'm alone in a night as thick and deep as treacle.

'Flux?' I call, fear rising like bile. There's no answer. Somehow, I knew there wouldn't be.

I find the door to the hall by walking very slowly with my hands outstretched, bumping painfully into gravestones. I keep calling for Flux, and the fear turns to anger when no answer comes.

The door has no handle. Panic ripples through my veins. I scrabble at its edges, but I can't find a way to get it open. Then I thump at it with both fists, again and again and again, and finally it thunks open. I crash through and on to the floor, hitting my face hard enough to make a *cracking* sound. After a dull pause, pain splinters through me, and blood rushes out of my nose, over my mouth. I gasp for breath, letting blood on to my tongue.

Fighting tears, I climb to my feet. The hall flickers with those lamps that seem to drain the life from the air. The throne continues to squirm in a way that makes my skin itch. I lick the blood off my teeth and cross the space as quickly as I can, with my head down. I duck through the entrance and turn right, which I'm almost certain is the way we came. Then I start walking in as straight a line as I can manage. I whisper nonsense to myself, trying to hold off the terror. In the dark rafters, above me and to both sides, there's a rustling of feathers and a glinting of eyes.

After a while, a knowing begins to gnaw at my gut. I slow to a stop. Flux has abandoned me. I've been walking for too long. I should have reached the way out by now. I feel like a rat, trapped in the wall.

But I shouldn't have stopped, because now I think I might have slightly changed direction. I stand, blinking for a moment, trying to slow the frantic hammering of my heart.

Thoughts of the Hunt begin to swarm the back of my brain, along with the memory of the rats I saw with the tree's eye. A shiver traces along my spine, delicate as though made by a fingertip. But it chills me with the force of a blizzard.

I probably shouldn't, but I start to run.

The world simmers down to passageways and slipping and rooks brushing me with their wingtips and the harsh, ragged sound of my own breath. Sometimes I think I can hear a man's voice, or the scraping of bones. Then I'm stumbling on to a hard surface, and my boots are as loud as hammers. I stop, pressing my hands over my mouth. And suddenly I'm bathed in light.

I'm outside in the street, and the moons are on the floor. I take a step away, legs shaking, whispering prayers to a god I thought I'd forgotten. Then hysterical laughter descends upon me, and I rock on my heels, hugging myself against the painful hilarity that can't be stopped.

When I'm able to see through my tears, I look down again. The moons are still below, but understanding trickles through me. I must have crossed water. They're reflections. I kneel down, and knock wood with frozen hands. I have stumbled on to a bridge.

I am very lost. Did I come out through a different door? I feel like the Rookery spun me around and turned me upside down and spat me out into another world all over again.

Unseen creatures slide out from the reeds and into the water. I can hear their bodies plunking in. But I can't see a hand in front of my face.

I turn on the spot, just able to make out the shape of the Rookery hulking against the sky. Then I pick a direction – any, as long as it's away from there – and set off at a jittery walking pace.

A lot of trudging follows. Should I stay in this world and search for Putch? Or should I get home before I'm in too much trouble? It might be too late to avoid that, though.

Even though I'm freezing, a heat begins to build in my head and chest and the back of my throat. My eyes are burning. I follow a scattering of lights until I'm back in the antique streets of Rookery Hollows, where a fog has snuck in from the sea. I try to ask for directions to those giant snail shells, or just the Lych and Screech gates, but the rare times when I see anyone, they don't want to talk to me.

A man wearing a long, flapping coat and carrying a briefcase is walking alone past a row of houses. I step towards him, clearing my throat. But when he jerks his head suddenly in my direction, I stop in my tracks. His face is a smooth, blank oval. It's the faceless man again. I dive into a deep doorway and crouch down, watching while he peers into pools of shadow or down alleyways. I freeze, hardly permitting myself to breathe.

The door opens behind me. 'What are *you* doing here?'

I turn around. Flux steps through the darkness carrying that firefly lantern again, pushing the shadows back. They look startled to see me.

'Don't say a word,' I whisper, as I shove my way inside and shut the door. We wait until the faceless man has passed by and out of sight. Then I round on Flux.

'Where were you?' I demand.

Flux arranges their face into an expression of supposed innocence. 'My master summoned me. Imagine my shock when I went back and you'd disappeared! I didn't mean to –'

'Save it,' I say, more harshly than I'd expected. 'Where is the undertaker?'

'Didn't he tell you?'

'No!' I stare at Flux, slowly understanding that my expectation is misplaced. Flux either doesn't know as much as I assumed, or else is deliberately keeping the truth from me. 'How did you know I'd be able to speak to him, if you don't know where he is?'

A stubborn look crosses their face. 'Why is this turning out to be more trouble than I bargained for?' they mutter.

'What do you mean?' I hiss.

'I did you a favour,' Flux tells me, eyes hard. 'I'm not supposed to take anyone to that tree. He doesn't know I helped you.'

'He? Who?'

Flux looks around, before whispering very, very quietly. 'The Hangman.'

I watch Flux's face. They're terrified. But I'm still angry that they took me to that place and left me there. I definitely can't trust them.

'I'm going home.' I keep my anger fully stoked, because if I give way to fear it's going to be a lot more unbearable. If I'm angry, I'm hoping Flux won't dare any tricks.

I push the door open and Flux gives a furious huff. 'Be careful! Agents are abroad.'

'There's more than one of the faceless men?'

'Oh yes. Troops of them.'

We creep into the street and hurry in the direction of two points of flame in the distance – even I know that they're the twin beacons of Lych and Screech.

We head down a twitten that intersects with the main street through the town. 'I don't need you to go with me,' I tell Flux, keeping my eyes fixed ahead.

'Yes, you do,' they reply, coolly. 'This twitten is sensible, but lots of others are silly. They'll twist around and throw you out somewhere else entirely.'

'Fine,' I mutter, teeth gritted so hard it makes my jaw ache.

Rain begins to tip out of the sky; long, icy daggers that slip down the neck of my sweatshirt. The night is wet enough that scores of skeleton toads are summoned. This time I can see them, sitting in the gutters, wearing their skeletons on the outside like white armour. They scream under the shadow of the moons.

'You'll have to promise to come back,' says Flux. 'If you want to speak to him again.'

'I'm promising nothing,' I reply, despite my fear that I'll be abandoned for the second time, or worse.

When we reach the end of the twitten, a cluster of faceless men are walking past, all clutching briefcases and wearing the same beige hats and coats. We flatten ourselves against the wall, waiting.

'What are they?' I whisper once they're gone, my voice only a husk.

Flux smiles grimly. 'They'll quest forever for their stolen faces. They are the Hangman's agents. Even though he's the one that did the thieving.'

Exhaustion rolls over me. I can't try to process anything else right now. I have to get home. When we step out of the twitten and turn right, we're standing again between the two huge rook gates, eyes blazing with firelight. We move between the gates, tramp through the field towards the skyline of giant snails beyond, and then I'm running.

Flux yells after me, pelting through the grasses in my wake.

When the tunnel to the portal thumps into view, desperation makes me clumsy, trainers slipping on the rain-swollen grass.

'Bye, then!' calls Flux. Then other sounds are called out, but the shape of the words is blurred by a sudden swirling wind.

I whip round to face them. 'Would *he* know where Shranken Putch is?'

Fright pinches Flux's features. 'No.' They shake their head. But I don't believe them.

'How did you send me that message, to come to the portal?'

They step closer. 'The Book,' they whisper, fever-bright eyes wet in the gloom. 'The shadow witch's Book of Shadow.'

Understanding swoops over me, cold and certain. 'When the Book replied to me . . .'

Flux smiles, bitterly. 'I had one, once. My own book.' On their cloak is a wound where the feather I wrote with came from. 'Your words have been scored into my bones,' they whisper.

'What?'

But they turn and race away, up hill and down ditch, lantern screaming into the wind.

Even in the rain, the strange, sluggish air of the Way of Bones crawls across my cheeks like a fat-bellied worm.

Then thoughts of the Hangman's faceless agents sneak up on me, turning my mouth dry. I fish my watch out of my pocket and touch the second hand. The slim needle shudders, before clicking backwards. Then I throw myself to my knees, crawl down the tunnel and tumble head first into the portal.

Grael is waiting.

She's so upset that she actually refuses to speak to me. I'm quite touched, because I assumed dragons would be far above the level of human drama. I love that she cares. When I get upstairs, I creep around to the foot of the main staircase. But Isla flies out of the sitting room, sees me, and screams in my face. 'She's back!'

12
Disgrace-on-Toast

Everyone is yelling at me. It's a great squabbling cacophony, like the funeral parlour is filled with geese instead of humans. I can barely get a word in to explain what happened.

The sight of all their concern and outrage is exhausting. I'm too tired to even flinch when Annie hauls me upstairs by the elbow.

The secret life of Spel Wrythe: all I know for certain
1. *I know how I must look*
2. *Bloody, bruised*
3. *Sodden, shivering*
4. *And I know I stink*
5. *Fear always makes me stink, but only from my right armpit, for some reason*

Annie dries me with an incredibly rough old towel that practically flays off my skin.

It takes a bath, a fire and a hot chocolate to bring

functioning words to my cold-numbed lips. 'He's in trouble.'

'Who?' demands Egg, furiously. We're all crowded into the attic. I can sense my sister is going to take ages to forgive me. Even though all I've done is something similar to the type of thing she used to do – and I wasn't even running away. Maybe she's jealous.

'Who do you think?' I demand, sounding even in my own ears like the crotchety old undertaker himself. 'Shranken Putch!'

Isla's brow puckers. *'Who?'*

I fold my arms. 'The person who owns this parlour that is keeping you safe.' *The one who is the answer to defeating the Hunt, though I'm not exactly sure how, yet.* 'The last person in this entire world who cares about us!'

Isla peels back her top lip. 'All right, drama llama.'

Annie is purple in the face and already administering a lecture, but the others are all talking at the same time. Here and there I catch snippets about *risking everything* and *searching everywhere* and *can't just disappear like that, without telling anyone.*

'Why won't anyone listen?' I yelp. 'I spoke to him! I spoke to Shranken Putch!' I break off into a fit of coughing.

No one hears what I'm trying to tell them. My sister stares at me like I'm an alien thing she's never encountered before. 'How could you willingly go into another world, and not tell anyone?' she asks, in disgust. 'How could you make yourself that vulnerable?'

Her words spark off a fresh bout of exclamations and hand-wringings.

'I didn't make myself vulnerable!' I rasp, wincing inwardly. She's got a point, given what happened in the Way of Bones. But what am I supposed to do? Wait around here indefinitely when we have no idea how to stop the Hunt and nowhere else to go, ever?

'We're surrounded, Elspeth,' says Annie, miserably. 'There's an angry mob out there, galvanised by the Hunt. I don't want to have to worry about what you're up to as well.'

The relief I felt about getting back here is fading very rapidly.

'Listen! He said the aircraft is spying on us! He said he doesn't know where he is, but – ' I trail off, too exhausted to try to shout above them all. Too annoyed, as well. What I have to say is important, and they can't even be quiet to listen.

'The fight is here, Elspeth,' says Isla, lofty as you like. 'But you'd know that if you cared to stick around and help us.'

The audacity of it makes me gasp. I tell her to do something very rude. At the same time, I feel the itch at my fingertips and look down in horror as a big curl of shadow pops free and sails over our heads, coiling like an eel around the lampshade.

'Right!' Annie exclaims, weariness plucking at her edges. 'That's enough, Spel. When I said no more magic, and no straying outside the parlour, did you somehow imagine yourself exempt?'

Isla nods at me, smugly.

'This place is more like Mouldheels' School with every passing day,' I grumble.

Egg chuckles wryly at that.

Annie's face is puckered into one giant ball of anguish and fury. 'There will be no more going down that well.'

Later, Jameela steps into the attic with a stack of toast that she puts on the bedside table. Egg, Layla, Mariam and Isla follow her. I crack open an eye, then slip a hand outside the blankets to snaffle up a buttery slice.

'Mmmm,' sing-songs Isla. 'Delicious disgrace-on-toast.' Everyone tells her to shut up. Isla's eyes have gained new-found respect for me since I fetched my cursed sister back from the underworld. But the respect has only been layered over ancient disgust, like cheap paint. It's already started to peel.

'We also brought you emergency cookies,' says Layla.

'Thanks.' Unexpected warmth glows inside me. It's really sweet of them to have noticed that I keep emergency cookies for troubling times. 'Where's Annie?' I venture.

'Too cross, still,' says Layla, with a sympathetic squeeze of my shoulder. 'But she'll cool down, Spel.'

'I did speak to him, you know. Shranken Putch.'

'How?' asks Egg.

'Inside a raindrop? It fell from the Other Wayfaring Tree.' I pull my duvet tighter around me. I'm shivering violently.

'She's given herself a fever,' says Mariam, as though I'm not here. 'Until we treat it, she probably won't make much sense.'

'I *am* making sense. It's just that no one's listening to me!'

Egg's hands are actually on her hips. 'Why did you give yourself a fever, Spel?'

'It's not my fault!'

'Well, it is, isn't it? Running off into other worlds.'

'We'll need a very strong pot of tea,' Mariam declares, playing with a vine that has wrapped itself around her wrist.

'I detest that brown ditchwater you call a drink,' I mumble. Then I pull the blankets over my head.

'Where is he, then, this Mister Putch?' asks Layla, perched on the side of my bed.

'No mister!' Egg guffaws, as though the old man's favourite saying is our own private joke. I get a horribly good view of the mushed-up toast in her mouth.

'Charming,' says Mariam, queasily.

I stick my head out of my covers and meet each of their eyes in turn, though my own are throbbing inside my skull and hurt like fire. 'He said he's in a prison.'

'Would you Adam and Eve it?' whispers Isla.

Egg's face is thunder-slapped. 'Prison?' she declares, as though I've reported that he's taken to laying eggs out of his nose.

'What's he doing there, when we were so worried about him?'

'I don't know,' I say. 'It's not like he chose to be arrested. Also, none of you have been worried about him at all!'

Egg throws herself face down on to her bed, groaning. Artemis leaps on to my lap and climbs me until she's able to drape herself around my shoulders like a scarf, purring so loudly in my ear that – despite the sick anticipation in my stomach – a giggle escapes my mouth. 'He thinks the plane – or whatever it is – is spying on us,' I tell them, chewing my cold toast.

'How did you know where to look for him?' asks Isla, suddenly alert.

I wince. 'I already *said*. Through a raindrop.'

'But how did you know where to go, to do that?'

I look at Egg, wishing we could be alone. I feel like I could get through to her, without all these other opinions and interruptions. But she's sitting cross-legged on her bed, aggressively flipping the pages of a magazine.

I swallow, suddenly nervous. 'A message appeared in the ashes from the fire, asking if I wanted to speak to him.' I twist my mouth, feeling defiant. 'So I went to speak to him.'

A collective look of horror swoops around the room.

'Why would you do that without telling us?' gasps Mariam.

'Did you not stop to wonder what untoward forces might be writing you messages made out of ashes?' demands Isla, all high and mighty as usual.

Then something worse happens. Jameela stands up, waving her hands dismissively. 'Don't worry so much,' she tells the others. 'Spel hasn't even got any sort of grip on her powers yet. And look – she's sick. How do we know she didn't imagine it?'

One by one, doubt crosses their faces. Doubt mixed with relief.

'But I didn't imagine it!'

'I think we should let her get some sleep,' Mariam tells the others, ushering them out of the room.

I open my mouth to tell Egg that she doesn't have to leave, but her leggings brush straight past my blankets as she steps out of the room.

Anger and frustration swirl through my blood. But worse than that is my fear for Shranken Putch, and for us. A low grumbling throbs in the beams of the house. The aircraft is scouting again, trying to prise apart our spell with its search beams. I put my face in my pillow, and scream as loud as I can.

Why won't anyone listen to me? Why won't anyone believe me? Why are Jameela's words worth more than mine?

I think of Flux, living in that gruesome Rookery. There was a sadness running like a river under their skin. I felt it. They said they're a student undertaker, and that they know how to deal with a haunting.

I'd like to see what a school for undertakers is like. I definitely need to help Shranken Putch. Maybe if I went back to the Way of Bones, I could try to find out where he is.

When I lift my head from my pillow, Artemis is fervently washing her chest. Then she looks up at me with her tongue still out.

'You've left your tongue out again.'

The pink sliver disappears, and the cat's eyes squeeze narrow. She pushes her claws up through the band of her collar, as though trying to prise it off. I lean towards her, taking the silver moon charm between my fingers. The message in the book warned me not to take this collar off. But why shouldn't I? And if that really was Flux, can I trust them? Artemis yowls, but I let the moon drop.

The candlelight eats a hole out of the darkness. 'How could they all just dismiss me like that?' I ask her, scrubbing the fur between her ears with a fingertip. 'I feel like no one trusts my judgement.'

Artemis butts my hand with her forehead, demanding more strokes. So helpful. She pulls at the collar again.

Flux's face floats into my head again. It's so strange to think that they're living a whole other life, right now, in the Way of Bones.

I pull the soft, worn Book of Shadows out of my pocket, and flick through the pages, admiring my mother's handwriting – a wide, looping, generous style. I run my fingers over her words. She touched these pages, many more times than she ever touched me. The sadness that wells up in me turns quickly to anger, and I flip the pages more roughly.

I take the quill from the little elastic loop I made to hold it to the book, and press the nib to the page. *Flux? Can you see this? I really need someone to talk to.*

Artemis sits facing me, tail coiled around her paws. She utters a small whine.

The night breathes through the window.

Then there's a terrible crash that makes me cover my ears, and sends Artemis scattering across the room. There are screams from downstairs. I freeze on my bed for a few seconds, then slam my book shut, spring up and race on to the landing, taking the stairs down to the first floor two at a time.

'Careful!' warns Annie, from the hallway below, where everyone else is already huddled.

'There's a lot of glass around,' adds Mariam.

The hallway mirror has shattered into hundreds of glinting shards of jagged glass. So has the mirror in the sitting room. Upstairs, the mirrors in the bathroom and the bedrooms have all smashed, too.

'Every mirror in the parlour has broken,' says Layla, stating the bloodcurdlingly obvious.

'How did that happen?' mutters Isla, grimacing.

But that's not my main question. 'What came out of them?' is all I want to know.

13
Sunken Putch

The rumbling noise of the aircraft passing overhead grows louder, until it's almost unbearable. Blindingly bright light stabs through the windows. I drop into a crouch on the floor, covering my ears. How have the light beams breached the cloaking spell? Could it be weakening?

'I'm going to close all the curtains!' bellows Annie. 'Stay together!'

A screaming engine punches our ears. Mariam braces herself against the sitting-room doorway, then turns to us, face aghast, pointing.

We pile into the doorway, staring through the windows into the night's open mouth. The aircraft is there, hovering directly opposite the parlour, purring, grumbling, belching out great gusts of steam. The steam seeps inside, smelling of blood mixed with water. It's round and white, with wings like those of an insect, whirring so fast they're a cobwebby blur against the night sky. It's held behind the shimmery veil of the cloaking spell, but only just. Whoever is flying that thing

is clearly determined to break through.

'Get down!' I yell, snatching the curtains closed.

We drop to the floor and crawl into the hallway. Annie races back down the stairs. 'Into the basement!'

But when we get there, we're greeted by a hideous gargling sound and a stink like rotten vegetables and feet.

The strange fungus in the basement floor has lengthened even more. At the base are two bushy protuberances that I understand, with a painful thump in the chest, to be eyebrows. This isn't a weird mushroom at all. As I stare at the floor, the growth begins to push further upwards. The eyebrows rise, followed by two tarnished silver eyes and a long, crooked nose just like Putch's.

'Putch?' I squawk, dashing across the floor and kneeling next to the emerging face.

'Elspeth, wait!' shrieks Annie.

The mouth pulls free. 'Yes,' it says, but my heart crashes because the way he spoke wasn't like Shranken Putch. It's not him.

That Other fold Artemis told me about is coming to pass – this is the new Putch. He's taking root here, and there's nothing I can do about it.

When the Putch has advanced up to the elbows, he calmly hoists himself up and out on to the stone floor. He peers around the dimly-lit basement with an expression of disgruntled disdain. Grael has appeared at the top of the well and watches him expectantly.

'Don't even think about asking for pudding right now,' I mutter.

'You're back,' declares Egg, half-heartedly. 'Um, congratulations.'

'It's not him,' I whisper, but my throat is too dry and the words are dead leaves in my mouth. All three Mistress Clucks saunter past, as though an actual person hasn't grown out of the floor. God, their hen lives must be easy.

The Putch swivels his head to goggle down at me. 'Sunken Putch,' he garbles, words sharper than Shranken's, as though he's filling the air with needles. 'Name. No –'

'No mister. We know.' I plant my hands on my hips and summon my strongest voice. 'You're not needed here, Sunken Putch. There is another Putch and this is his home. And anyway, I'm the undertaker in residence until he returns.'

Sunken Putch watches me with barely disguised contempt. 'Evidently, there is no other Putch in this rat hole. Or I would not have been summoned by the ancient pact. Or curse, as I would prefer to call it.'

'Elspeth Wrythe,' whispers Annie. 'Would you care to explain what's going on?'

The Putch dusts himself down, leans back into the hole he grew out of, to retrieve a brown leather case. He steps away from me with an air of relief, as though I am a very unpleasant thing indeed. Then he screws up his face.

'What, pray tell, is that dreadful cacophony?'

'We're not sure,' I answer falteringly. 'It's some kind of aircraft, searching – well, for us. It seems.'

He nods, once, face hardening. 'Witchcraft, is it? Oh, that fool. Harbouring the wretched Wicked should never have been Putch business. My first job shall be to unravel whatever threads he has tangled himself in.'

'Oh, will it, now?' says Annie indignantly, crossing her arms.

'Yes, *madam*. It will.' But when he takes a step away from the hole he grew out of, an invisible tether wrenches him backwards.

'Where is it?' he burbles, eyebrows quirking furiously.

'Where is what?' asks Annie, trying to keep us all shielded behind her.

'The ring,' he confirms, jaw flickering.

My blood jolts. *One ring per Putch.* The ring from the burial mound. I know exactly where it is. It's in my pocket.

'Oh, I found a –' starts Isla, but I jab her hard under the ribs. 'Ouch!'

The Putch goggles around at us, through two furious silver eyes, half squashed by the weight of wild eyebrows.

The aircraft passes overhead again, search beams piercing the windows. Shouts begin to filter in as well, from the hillside. They're coming closer.

Sunken Putch clicks open his leather bag and riffles

through the contents, becoming more and more disgruntled. 'Ridiculous pact,' he grumbles. 'It must be malfunctioning.'

He can't properly become the Putch here without a ring, I realise, heart leaping. I've got to make sure he doesn't find out I've got it. I've got to take it to Shranken Putch. But how am I going to find him?

Annie calls us into a huddle in the opposite corner of the basement, while Sunken Putch tries and tries to free himself. 'There's a potion on the stove,' she whispers, eyes frantic. 'We need to strengthen the spell again. If they get in –'

'We'll be ready for them,' promises Egg, and Isla gives a snaggle-toothed grin.

Annie rakes a great tattered breath. 'Just – please, whatever happens, be careful. Don't burn the house down.'

We wait while Annie ventures back upstairs, listening to the sounds of her hauling the cauldron outside to feed the contents to her cloaking spell.

'If anyone here is attempting to thwart me,' says Sunken Putch, voice creaking and puttering, 'they will be sorry.'

When Annie calls us, we rush out of the basement and up the stairs, no one wanting to be the last one left down there with Sunken Putch. Annie locks him in, even though he can't leave anyway. Then she gives me a pointed look.

'Like I've already said – you're not to go near that well.'

'You said *down*, not near,' I reply, tartly.

'Sassy!' says Isla, with something like approval.

In the attic, Egg clambers over me and sits with her back against the wall and her legs across me. I offer her the packet of cookies and she takes one, pulling it to pieces and eating them one by one. 'What's going on, Spel?' she says. 'I feel like you don't tell me anything these days.'

I take a deep breath, powered by sugar. How do I begin to tell her that being Shadow-Born feels so much more like freedom than anything I have ever experienced here, or could probably ever hope to? How do I explain how horrible it is that when I try to tell her and the others about talking to Shranken Putch they say I'm imagining things? I'm still angry that she didn't stand up to Jameela about that.

I open my mouth to try to begin, when Layla comes back from the bathroom. She looks really tired and anxious – maybe that's how I look.

Egg takes my hesitation as an answer.

'See?' Her mouth is hard and her eyes are glossy black stones. 'You don't even want to talk to me.'

'No.' My voice is small. Lonely. 'It's not that.' But she and Layla are already thick as thieves, whispering their private secrets, and I can't get their attention.

I grab my Book of Shadows, flipping to the page where I wrote earlier. But there's been no answer. I swallow back my disappointment. There are so many thoughts tumbling in my head that I start scribbling them down, using the scrap of light from the dying fire in the grate.

Sisters are weird. We've always been a package, like buy-one-get-one-free, except that everyone's always seen me as a side serving of something that tastes bad, accompanying the main event. Egg assumed she would be the most powerful witch. But why? It really bothers me.

Now maybe she's having a taste of what it's like to be the one that's not that special. It's up to her if she wants to react in a spiteful way. And considering that, why shouldn't I do my own things and spend time with other people, and not tell her everything about it? Why shouldn't I have my own secrets?

I dream that Egg and I are adrift at sea, holding hands, heads slipping under the rough swells. The water grows wilder, hungrier. We're pulled apart, fingers unlocking, and when I open my mouth to scream her name, seawater rushes in. Her name is drowned before it leaves my mouth. We're carried away, on two separate paths.

14
Gone

By morning, my fever has passed. I wake up before Egg and Layla. Artemis is sleeping on my pillow, face tucked inside my curled hand. I lay still for a moment, not wanting to disturb her, but then a growl of hunger forces me to move. The cat lifts her head and her left cheek is all smooshed. Her tooth has made a dent in my palm.

Then the parlour is splintered by the unmistakable sound of Isla screaming. The sound clangs around, curdling the blood. I shoot out of bed, closely followed by Egg and Layla.

When we reach the sitting room, where Isla and Jameela sleep, Isla sits alone in a nest of blankets and cushions, weeping. 'She's gone!'

'What? Who? What do you mean?' babbles Annie, hair all sticking out and pillowcase creases on her cheek. In her nightgown she's shockingly thin and grey-tinged. Frail.

'Jameela!' shrieks Isla, and Layla sits next to her, putting an arm round her shaking shoulders.

There's a weird emptiness where Jameela should be.

'She hated it here so much,' babbles Isla desperately to each of us. 'She was panicking about everything.' She bursts into tears. 'That rat bit her! It wouldn't heal. But I didn't think she'd really try and run away!'

'What rat?' Annie asks, sharply.

'The rat in the tea shop! She made me swear not to tell. But now I'm wondering if I should have.' Isla looks so distraught that I feel an unfamiliar pang of sympathy for her.

'A rat bit her?' Annie presses her fingers over her mouth.

'I'll just check she's not in the bathroom,' whispers Mariam, and Annie nods. But Mariam soon returns, dark eyes brimming with tears. She shakes her head.

Isla dithers on the spot and then flings herself out of her blankets and into the hallway. We follow, calling her. She hurls herself at the door, but Annie grabs her round the waist.

'Isla Thomas, that's enough of that now,' she says, holding her until she stops struggling and collapses into sobs. She deposits Isla with Mariam and grabs her coat from the hallway, before striding into the kitchen.

We straggle after her.

'All of you stay put – in *this* world, Elspeth – until I return.'

'What?' I croak. 'You're going, too?'

'But you're not well!' protests Mariam. 'The spell has drained you too much!'

'How would Jameela have got past the people hunting for us?' asks Layla, eyes wide. 'How will you?'

A gurgling wail echoes from somewhere underneath our feet. 'And what do we do about *him?*' demands Egg.

Annie doesn't pause. 'Nothing! Just feed the cloaking spell like I showed you. Don't let it grow hungry.' Then she peels open the back door and disappears into the sodden morning.

There's a terrible silence in her wake. Isla flicks filthy looks at me. As though this is all my fault.

We grip the backs of the kitchen chairs and stare at each other, wide-eyed. 'Didn't Annie say that the Hunt use vessel creatures for stolen magic?' whispers Mariam.

That sets Isla off again. Mariam drops the subject.

The parlour feels quiet with two people missing. They've been gone less than five minutes when a rat falls through a crack in the wall. Artemis chases it. We use wads of paper or cotton to plug up any holes or cracks we can find in the walls, in the backs of cupboards, in the floors. Then we tape the repairs to reinforce them, though I'm pretty sure a rat could chew through almost anything if it wanted to.

All the rest of the day we listen to the creatures scratching in the walls. The cloaking spell presses against the windows. 'How often do we have to make the potion, to strengthen it?' asks Layla.

Egg squints dubiously into the cauldron. 'Let's just make sure it never runs too low?'

'Good idea,' says Mariam.

'You realise it's all over, don't you?' crows Isla, from the corner where she's arranged herself a blanket fort.

'No, it's not,' says Layla, briskly. 'I'll make you a hot chocolate, and then you can pull yourself together and help us.'

But while Isla hurls curses, I start wondering. Isn't she right? If I don't find Shranken Putch, maybe it really will all be over.

Artemis leaps up at my leg, startling me. I can read the determination in her expression; her imploring green eyes. She releases the most outrageous screech.

Layla glances over. 'I think it's cruel to keep that collar on any longer,' she says. 'It's really bothering her.'

'I think you're right,' I reply. The skin around the band looks really sore from all the pulling and scratching she's been doing. Honestly, what's the worst that could happen if I take her collar off?

'Hey,' I whisper, leaning down and taking the slender silver moon between my fingers. 'Is this feeling too tight?'

Artemis's eyes somehow become even more intense, if such a thing is possible. I wriggle the clasp open. There's a brief, brilliant flash, like someone has lifted a veil between night and day, and a spark nips my fingers like the electric shock Artemis sometimes gives me from her nose. Then there's a sense of space opening up. I'm pushed backwards on to the floor by Artemis, who for some reason has shot upwards towards the ceiling, and outwards towards the back wall.

Someone screams. I think it must be me.

Artemis has vanished. A woman has appeared, with large green eyes blinking behind a pair of owlish glasses, a mass of curly dark hair, and two fists clenched at her sides.

A scar in the shape of a crescent moon sits in the hollow of her throat, thick and shiny as a worm.

15
A Muddlewood Demon

'Finally,' she says, voice thick with sarcasm. She dusts down her ripped wide-legged slacks and adjusts the bow on the front of her crumpled silk blouse.

I scramble upright. 'It can't – *Art* – what –?'

'Who're *you*?' demands Egg.

Layla and Mariam are gaping at the woman, but Isla, in her unravelled state, is blunter than ever. 'She's that wretched fleabag, you fools.'

The woman gives her a quizzical glance. 'Diana, in fact,' she replies, as though it's the most obvious thing in the world. 'Once a dryad of the Muddlewood, displaced when it was felled, demonised. Bound by the moon – a barrow jewel – in cat form, in order that a wake cat would always be present at the Ring – which is the heart of the wood, if you don't know by now.' She clears her throat. 'Now listen, dears. It appears service is lacking around here. Ought you to fetch me some tea?'

'But,' I stammer. 'We don't really have time for tea. Everything's going wrong.'

'Cats don't even drink tea,' chimes Isla, sullenly.

'Oh, pish.' The person that was until recently a little black cat with anger issues flaps a slender hand. 'They certainly do, it is simply that no one offers it to them.' She pulls out a kitchen chair and sits, looking at us expectantly. 'There is always time for tea. I know where the good teapot is, too. Heaven knows why that old thorn never took out the good china.'

The clews stream out from under the skirting board. But before they can even assemble their tower, Diana snarls at them and they scurry away again.

'Oh, for god's sake, I'll do it,' says Layla, breathlessly. When she takes out the china and puts the kettle on the stove, her hands are shaking.

'Good,' says Diana, approvingly. 'Now. Elspeth. You were right about Shranken Putch, and everyone else was being completely daft not listening to you.'

'Really?' I yelp, dashing across the kitchen to her and pulling out a chair.

'Yes, really,' she says, looking vaguely annoyed. 'Now don't get silly, there's no time to lose. I remember telling you, when I was bound, that the Ring was *in want of an undertaker*, and that there were to be . . .'

'No adventures in the Other Ways until Shranken Putch returns?' I breathe.

'Exactly. But that's all gone out the window now that this

new Putch has arrived, and the Hunt are beating down the door. You have to find Shranken Putch and bring him home. You have a plan, don't you? I think you whispered it into my silky little ears while I dozed, at some point.'

Egg snorts.

'Yes, I've got the ring that hatched out from the burial hoard.' I pull it out of my pocket and rest it on my palm. The spell etched around the inside winks in a similar way to the moon charm.

'Hey!' snuffles Isla. 'You stole that from me!'

'It's not for you,' I fire back, impatiently.

'What do you mean, she was right about Shranken Putch?' asks Egg, leaning against the kitchen counter.

'If the Hunt unravel the Putch Pact, and drain the magic from the heart of the Muddlewood, untold power will be bestowed on them. By prising Shranken Putch away from his post, they've corrupted the spell.'

The kettle begins to shriek. 'So how will that ring help?' asks Layla, pouring the water into a teapot. Her hands are still shaking.

'A ring from the burial hoard passes into the possession of the Putch when they first home here. Bringing this one to Shranken Putch might – and I stress *might* – just work to bring him home and protect the pact from Hunt manipulation.'

'That's what I'm hoping,' I tell her, eagerly.

'What is a Putch, anyway?' asks Mariam, while Layla brings the tea to the table.

'They're sort of brothers,' says Diana, searchingly, as though unable to decide where to begin. 'Brothers through time, and place. Whenever one disappeared – or more commonly, worked until death – another would worm up through the soil like a sprouting bean. In olden times, people worshipped and feared them. They were something like a wizard, in your stories. But darker, and more powerful. Closer to a god.'

I blink at her. 'Are they always undertakers?'

'They are what their pact demands.' She sips her tea. 'The Putches *here* are always undertakers.'

I slump back in my chair, a grim triumph settling over me. I was *right* about Shranken Putch being so important. I knew it! 'Where is he?' I babble, excitement rushing through my veins. 'I'll go and find him. I need to go right now.'

'Oh, I don't know where he *is*,' says Diana, casual as you like.

My excitement evaporates. 'Um, sorry, what? You're a magical cat-not-cat person and you don't know any more than I do?'

She replaces her cup into its saucer with a sharp clack. 'Excuse you, Ms Wrythe, but have I or have I not indeed been stuck here as the undertaker's cat with all of you for the past however long? How should I know any better than you?'

Mariam clears her throat. 'Um, because ... magic?'

'*Magic*,' splutters Diana bitterly. 'Magic is not some kind of explain-all, mystical swizzle stick, you know.'

'What's a swizzle stick?' whispers Egg.

'I don't know,' mouths Layla.

I dig my nails into the edge of the table. 'So, all you're saying is essentially what I already knew? But worse – that the stakes are higher than just the Hunt finding us in here. That they want to drain the last, most ancient magic in this world, and if they do they'll become all-powerful and be able to cross into all the worlds?'

'It goes a little something like that,' she says, obnoxiously. If she were still a cat, she'd be getting slash-happy by now. 'He's being entombed, but I don't know where.'

'Why? What does that mean?'

'It's the only way for the Hunt to fully break the Putch Pact. First, take the ring that binds. Then, another Putch will be birthed from the barrow – but manipulation is not the way the spell works. Next, if the Putch is entombed elsewhere, the pact will be shattered and that means no more protection of this place. They will take the heart of the Muddlewood, and the last knucker dragon, and all the treasures of the burial hoard. The portals will be exploited, and souls will have no way to find peace.'

'Then they would be able to drain every world of magic,' I whisper.

She makes me hold out my hand, and tips the moon collar

into my palm. It's an innocent-looking pool of silver and silk against my skin, except I know better. A silvery wink shines along the edge of the moon.

'Wear it,' she tells me. 'Never take it off – if you do, I will be summoned. But I will not take kindly to it, and remember: the summons will only work *once*.'

'It won't – turn me into a cat, will it?' I venture.

She fixes me with a stern look. 'Are you an immortal of the Muddlewood, old as time, bound by bone and spellwork to this place, and untethered to fixed form?'

'Um, no?' I fasten the moon around my neck.

Then the aircraft is back, hovering directly outside the window, held back by the spell. Voices are shouting, near the back door. But they can't get through the cloaking. Mariam scrambles over to the stove, stirring the potion. Layla ransacks the cupboards, pulling out the ingredients. 'Cinquefoil's running low,' she tells us, shoulders sagging.

'Elspeth,' says Diana, reaching for my hand. 'You must go and search for Shranken Putch. Now, or all is lost. I'll help them as best I can.'

'But if the Hunt find you –' I stammer, blinking away tears. I don't need to say any more. We all know how much the Hunt would glory in discovering an ancient of the Muddlewood, immortal veins thrumming with powerful magic. And I look round at the others, all woefully underprepared for whatever they're facing. Partially trained, with erratic magic, food and magical supplies running low, and no way of knowing when a break in the spell will expose them. It might only need to be a hairline break.

'Elspeth.' Diana gazes at me, pupils still the long black diamonds worn by cats. The moon scar in the hollow of her throat appears to glow. 'Do not imagine me defenceless,' she purrs. 'I'll look after them.'

'Hang on,' says Egg. 'Who's going to look after *her*?'

Diana smiles. 'Child, you still think she needs looking after? Elspeth Wrythe is the most powerful witch of a generation.'

Don't say that, I think, wishing I could shrink. But my sister's face softens, and she grins at me. 'I know. I just worry about her, it's what sisters do.'

'But she's not in control of her magic,' quavers Isla. 'And Annie said – '

'We're going to have to let go of what Annie said,' I tell her. As for my magic, I'm not sure what to say.

'You're right, Spel,' says Mariam. 'You can do this. You'll get to grips with your magic as you go.'

'Oh, wow, thank you Ma –'

'No time, no time!' Diana grins, a pearlescent fang gripping her lower lip. 'Now. Go. Quickly!'

I stumble out of the kitchen, flinching against the noise of the aircraft. There's only one person I know that can help me. I have no reason to think I can trust them. But hope soars when I open my Book of Shadows and read the words that have bloomed on the page, answering mine.

I'm here. I really need someone to talk to, too.

I scribble the words quickly, using the rook feather. *Meet me at the portal!*

Then I curse, remembering that Annie locked the basement. I race up to her bedroom on the first floor, riffling through drawers and clothes, until the key falls out of a pair of folded trousers.

Then I slip-slide back down the stairs, patting my pockets to check I have what I need – book, feather, pocket watch, barrow ring. *Check.* When I put the key into the lock and turn it, a scroll unravels from the metal like a yellowed tongue, and makes an announcement in a maddeningly loud voice.

Witch, witch, attention, spell-casting witch! You who put a spell on me have had your trust betrayed, times three!

It's like a siren going off.

'She's not here!' I growl. 'Stupid spell.'

But Sunken Putch is waiting for me, right behind the door. I dart away from him, squeezing through, but he grabs the back of my sweatshirt. My feet slip on the shattered floor where he grew. 'Oh no, you don't!' he roars. 'You've got the grave trinket, haven't you? You've got *my* ring!'

'It's not for you,' declares a voice, and Egg steps into the basement, knocking the Putch away from me. 'Run, Spel!'

I give her a nod and then I'm tearing away from the

struggle, screaming for Grael. When the dragon emerges in a bulk of black and gold, I'm already vaulting on to her back.

Then it's down the gullet of the pitch-dark well and back to the portals, where I push the watch's second hand until it ticks backwards and the water in the well swirls the Other way.

When I open the portal to the Way of Bones and slip through, head spinning with the sound of scattering metal stars and a tangle of disjointed memories, Flux is already leaning on a tree a few feet from the tunnel entrance.

The shadows of the thirteen moons cast a chill across the landscape and along my spine. 'I have to find Shranken Putch,' I gasp. 'All the worlds depend on it.'

PART TWO:

ROOKERY HOLLOWS

16
Sea-Severed

Flux pushes away from the tree they're leaning on. 'We'd better get going, then.'

I nod, gratefully, and hurry down the crunchy white path that snakes between the pines, towards the train station on the right, and the giant snail shells – the Snags – on the left. I'm out of breath and every part of me is still ringing with what's just happened.

I mean, I knew Artemis wasn't exactly your usual cat, but the truth is way wilder than I'd ever have imagined. The way she believed in me – and had been silently trying to encourage me, all along – has made a fresh burst of energy sing through my bones.

But the thought of what they might all be facing back at the parlour is such a terrifying one that I feel overwhelmed and –

'You all right?' asks Flux, looking askance at me. They've lagged behind.

'Um, no. Not really. We need to hurry up!'

'You really need to speak to him, don't you?'

'*Yes.*' Without slowing down, I turn to look at Flux. 'You don't understand, do you? Where I'm from, all the magic has been drained. Almost all the witches are gone. We're not free, they won't even let us live peacefully. And I've been picking up clues, here and there, about why the undertaker who gave us a home matters, more than just as a person, and a teacher –' I stop, gulping back tears. 'What happens to him matters for the fate of every magical creature. For one of my best friends, who happens to be a dragon. For the only place I've ever called home.'

Flux is staring at me, mouth slack, wisps of dark blonde hair blowing loose in front of their eyes.

'I have to bring him back, Flux. He said he's in a prison, but he doesn't know where. My cat – I mean, Diana – I mean, oh, never mind! She said he's being *entombed*. I have to speak to him again and try to get more information.'

Flux stays silent, scanning the way ahead with great damp eyes.

We're approaching the Snags, but this time they're unlit and quiet. If I didn't know about the skating and the people living in them, I'd have thought them abandoned. 'What happened to the snails?' I ask, suddenly.

'Extinct,' Flux replies, shrugging. 'People used to eat them.'

'That's sad. Also, a bit gross.' As my breath slows and

my heart steadies, I'm struck again by the weird way the air moves across your skin, in this world. A scent of decay dances with sea salt and brine. It's colder here than it was last time, too. The grass sparkles with frost, and the mud underneath has a crust of ice that snaps under our boots. I pull my beanie lower over my head and tug my sleeves over my fingers.

As we pass beneath the flame-eyes of the gates in the shape of giant rooks, Lych and Screech, the town of Rookery Hollows is slowly stirring. Smoke coils from a few chimneys, and the smell of baking bread makes my mouth water.

In the middle of the town, where twittens intersect with a crumbling fountain in an old square, the formidable-looking College of Macabre Arts rises on its hill that becomes an island when the tide comes in. Its sea-nibbled foundations support four shining bone towers and a fifth that's ruined. Each tower swarms with rooks.

When Flux steps on to the causeway that leads to the college, I call out to them.

'I need to go straight to the Rookery, to speak to the Hangman!'

Flux turns to me, bruised eyes straining against the sockets. 'Why?'

'The tree is in his courtyard,' I say, biting back my impatience. 'That's the only place I know to start. And maybe he'll know something.'

'You want to speak to *him*?' they whisper, and at the same

time, all the rooks on the ruined tower overhead burst away from it, as though a gun's been fired.

'Yes,' I insist, over the noise of flapping wings and cawing throats.

'But we have to go to the college, first – that's where I'm doing my training.'

'I don't have time!'

Flux walks back to me, pushing the hair out of their eyes. 'Don't worry, it'll just be for a few minutes. I've forgotten my key, and we won't be able to get into the Rookery without it.'

I honestly could scream. But what's the point? I was hardly going to stroll into the Way of Bones and find Putch immediately. But any delay feels agonising. My stomach is turning somersaults and my hands are sweating. 'Okay, but please – can we be really quick?'

'Yes, of course.'

We set off along the path that separates the College, and all its towers of bone, from the rest of Rookery Hollows. The path is scattered with starfish, seaweed and pearls that rime the edges like salt on lips. When we reach the other side, there's a long, steep climb up steps cut into the side of the hill. At the top, I'm able to see past the college towards the open sea – Rookery Hollows is shielded from a sheer cliff face by this building alone.

We pass through a huge, gated entrance into a courtyard. 'My school is in the fifth tower. Come.' Flux leads me towards a door in the corner of the yard, which has a skull symbol at the top. I crane my neck to stare up at the rickety fifth tower. It has chunks of stone missing, and it's leaning, like at any moment it could topple backwards into the sea.

I hesitate, wondering if I should just wait outside. But it feels eerie out here, with no one else around and sea spray blowing through the cracks in the stone. Thoughts of those faceless agents have me hurrying to keep up with Flux.

We cross the courtyard and go through the skull door, and then head down a cool, musty corridor. There are empty classrooms, piles of dusty books, and even a walk-in cupboard full of coffins. 'For training purposes,' clarifies Flux.

Setting foot in a school again makes my palms sweat even worse, and my chest ache. I find myself tensed in case a Mistress emerges from the gloom.

'Where is everyone?' I whisper.

Flux's voice echoes too loud against the walls. 'Term hasn't started again yet.'

At the end of the corridor we push through another door and climb a circular set of stone stairs. The tower is ancient, draughty and full of gaps.

We wind all the way to the top. Each gust of wind shakes the bone structure of the tower. Grenwald pokes his head out of Flux's pocket and sniffs, fronded hands testing the air.

'Gren! You can't be hungry again *already*?' says Flux, stroking the axolotl's head. They shove their shoulder against a thick wooden door, which swings open to reveal a round room full of squashy armchairs, beanbags and tables crowded with books. There's a wide fireplace and several cats sleeping on chairs, or shelves. Long windows provide dramatic sea views. 'This is the skull-tower common room,' Flux announces.

A squawk makes me startle and look upwards. A dull brown, whiskery elfin creature is asleep in the rafters with its head lolled forward, startling itself awake every few seconds with a muted cry that sounds as though it has a sore throat. Its claws are wrapped tightly around the beam. It's a tiny owl.

'That's our mascot – a long-whiskered owlet,' whispers Flux.

'I like its eyebrows,' I say, and Flux smothers a laugh in their sleeve.

Flux tumbles into an armchair and reaches into the grate, feeding hearth ashes to Grenwald, who laps up the tiny, charred flakes.

'So where's this key?' I ask. 'We need to go.' My limbs feel jittery. Maybe I should've gone to the Rookery alone, and tried to find a way inside.

'Oh, we can't leave now,' says Flux, blue eyes wide. 'The tide's come in.'

'*What*? No!' I rush across the room and press my face to the window. Sure enough, miles below, the causeway path has been flooded by seawater. Deep, grey, churning seawater.

We've been disconnected from the land. 'How long until the
tide goes out again?' I mumble, through lips that feel numb.

Flux lolls on the armchair, playing with Grenwald. 'Oh,
about seven hours, maybe?'

'Seven *hours*?' For a moment I just stare at Flux, while the sea crashes against the cliffs, and the rising wind howls through the gaps in the stone. Then doom rattles through my bones, and I realise what it's cost me that we're stuck here. I also become suddenly aware of how cold, hungry and exhausted I am. 'I'm gonna *kill* you!' I scream.

Flux laughs. 'You're not.'

I rush at them, but they roll off the armchair and scuttle away across the common room. Grenwald clambers on to their head and watches me while belching ashen smoke. I can't believe this is happening. 'You knew we'd be cut off, didn't you?'

Flux glowers at me, pale brows furrowed and chin jutting stubbornly. A small scar puckers the skin under one eye. 'And if I did?' Their fingertips are permanently stained purple, as though they've been picking berries. 'Why are you assuming that I am the villain?'

'Why are *you* trying to ruin everything? Why did you meet

me if you're not going to help?' I feel like I'm losing my mind. 'I've told you what will happen if I fail!' I put my arms around myself, afraid that if I'm not careful I'll give way, I'll crumble to the floor, I'll never be able to get up again.

'But you *will* fail,' they tell me, expression troubled. 'There's no way you can win.'

'Why would you say that? There is, if I can at least try!'

'You may not choose to believe it,' says Flux. 'But I'm trying to protect you.'

'Why would you do that?' I demand. 'And why would I trust you?'

'Because, dear Spel, we are the same.' Flux holds a finger aloft and brews a little purplish shadow, which swells until it becomes a bulb that flies off and dances around us. It wasn't a berry stain. It's a stain of magic. 'I meant it when I said I needed someone to talk to.'

'So you trapped me in a tower?' I shriek.

The tiny owl in the rafters hoots and shuffles its feet, eyeing the bulb of magic as it drifts underneath where it's perched.

'No – yes – *no*, that's not why!' Flux screws up their eyes, streamers of shadow rolling from their fingers and cloaking the floor in a thick cloud of dark fog. 'No one should enter that place.'

'The Rookery? You do,' I snap. 'And you let me in before.'

'I live there. And that time was different. I was sorry, afterwards. You were lucky to get out again.'

'Can't you run away, if you hate it so much?'

A small smile, like a thread of thin light through a grubby window. 'No. I cannot.'

'But you're Shadow-Born. You can travel anywhere!'

'You know better than anyone that being Shadow-Born does not relieve you of your duties at home. Yes, I can travel – on the Hangman's bidding. I cannot *leave*. Not even for a night. Every night, I am summoned home.'

The Hangman's bidding. A shudder rolls through me, top to toe. 'Is he your father?'

Flux gapes at me. 'I have no family remaining.'

I think about the things I wrote in my Book of Shadows, that somehow Flux must have seen. Things about the ring from the burial hoard, and about thinking Egg was jealous of me, and all sorts of other thoughts and plans and worries.

It occurs to me that Flux has all the power. I know next to nothing about them.

I pull my Book of Shadows out of my pocket. 'You said you had one of these, once. What happened to it?'

More shadows stream out of Flux's fingers, and they pinch and shape them, until little shadow bats and birds flit around the circular room. 'I had to give it up.'

'Why?'

Flux gives a small, brittle laugh. 'To cheat true death.'

I start. 'You aren't dead.' A tingle steps across my skin. I *know* death. Flux is half alive, like me.

'Exactly. But I should be. I am an ancient, like roots and rocks, though I appear as a child.'

The weirdness of their words scatters goosebumps along my arms. 'How did giving up your Book of Shadows cheat death?'

Grenwald pops his head out of Flux's pocket, then darts up their cloak and on to their shoulder. Flux strokes his head, gently. 'Sometimes I wonder if it truly did,' they murmur.

Outside, a storm grumbles into life. Rain hisses against the tower, slicing through the cracks. Puddles form on the tables and the floor. Lightning blinks, and thunder shakes the sky.

'Can you smell that burnt smell?' Flux asks. 'That's the smell of the storm. It's so much fun to watch storms from here.'

'Nothing about this is fun,' I spit, shaking with fresh anger. 'You might have killed my friends by doing this. You might have caused the future draining of every magical creature. How does that feel, murderer?' The violence of my own words shocks me, but I don't take them back.

Flux flickers, lightning blinking the common room in and out of existence.

I grit my teeth, frustration swelling in my chest. I touch the moon charm around my neck. Home feels a million miles away, and I can't stand wondering whether they're holding back the Hunt. Whether the spell has been breached. Whether Grael and Diana, the witches and the Ring, are being drained of their magic while I'm stuck in this tower. I can't let myself get too drawn in to Flux's story.

'I'm still going to the Rookery,' I vow, staring Flux down. 'With or without your help.'

Flux looks out of the window, then back at me. Their blue eyes have darkened as though clouds have passed over them. I notice the rows of glinting silver studs tracking the shells of their ears. 'Who am I to stop you?' they say, finally. 'You have had your warning.'

I begin to pace the common room. Normally I'd be desperate to get my hands on the undertaking textbooks stacked on the tables, but now I can't settle. It doesn't matter that I know I'm stuck here; all my muscles want to do is run.

'Since we're going to be here for a while, shall we get food from the canteen?' asks Flux, with optimistic cheer.

I'm about to tell them to take a running jump out of the window when my stomach grumbles loudly enough to rival the thunder.

'I'll take that as a yes.'

The canteen is a hopeful way of describing a loft above the main room, accessed by a wobbly ladder. It contains a rusty urn of coffee on a stove, and a counter lined with old, congealed puddings. Flux lets Grenwald clamber around all over a livid green jelly, which is soon covered in his tiny handprints.

There's a metal cupboard in the wall, which Flux says is called a dumb waiter, for having food sent up if you can't be bothered to go anywhere.

At which point I remind them that in this case, I've been *forced* not to go anywhere. And they at least have the grace to look a bit sorry.

'I'll have something sent up,' they tell me, pulling on a thick rope that hangs from the middle of the loft.

'How? There's no one else here!'

'Yes, I know,' says Flux, wrinkling their nose. 'That doesn't matter.'

Flux heads back down to the main room and starts building a fire in the grate, bustling about with kindling and logs, striking a spark against the stone mouth of the hearth.

Rain slants in, and I wipe it from my face. 'When you grabbed my wrist through the portal – why were you looking for me?'

'I was not particularly looking for you,' Flux replies. 'But you had been appearing to me, in the strangest of places. I went checking the portals. I wanted to know if you'd be able to cross them, like I can. I have never known another Shadow-Born. Not in all my thousands of years.'

'Never?'

'Not ever.' The fire gains strength, and Flux drags two

beanbags and a pile of blankets towards it. 'So, imagine my surprise when you trotted along.'

I try to emulate one of Egg's best milk-souring looks. 'I do not trot.'

Flux grins.

'I never thought there could be another person who's Shadow-Born,' I mutter. 'I thought I was a –' A *what?* I wonder. A *freak, a fluke?*

'We are proof of eternal love,' says Flux, with a warmth that surprises me. 'Our birth-parents, even in their death, found a way to send us back to the living world. No one should be birthed in the underworld. But we were.'

We gaze at each other. I feel guilty for thinking about myself as an accident, when Amara – my mother – shifted the laws of life and death to ensure my survival.

Then thunder cracks directly overhead, and I twitch with fright. 'Oh, come and look!' chatters Flux, excitedly. At the window, I see how a series of lines have been etched in the dark clouds. 'Thunderstones are coming,' says Flux.

They point to the other side of the causeway, where the tiny shapes of people are creeping towards the edge of the tangled sea, too close to the centre of the storm. Lightning arrows down, biting the earth around the people.

'What are they doing?' I ask, unable to tear my eyes away from what I'm seeing. 'That's insanely dangerous.'

Everywhere the lightning hits, people scurry across the

ground, swarming to the spot. They're too far away for me to be able to see what they're doing.

'Getting money.'

I squint at the tiny figures in the distance. Every time lightning strikes again in another place, the swarm breaks apart and they all rush across the scarred ground. 'What are they looking for?'

'Thunderstones,' says Flux, with a touch of exasperation. 'The highest value money. They're spat out when a storm writes in the clouds. See – those lines?'

'To get money you have to risk being struck by lightning?'

Flux shrugs. 'Some people do, yes. The poorest.'

'That's disgusting.'

Flux looks surprised at my venom. 'It is the Hangman's way.'

The miniature owl in the rafters starts hooting and flapping its feathers.

Flux glances up. 'Supper is here.'

'Is that owl just here to announce food?'

The dumb waiter makes a clanking, creaking, scraping racket that sets my teeth on edge. Flux scampers across and up to the loft, opens the hatch, and lifts out two greasy paper packages. 'Help, please!'

'Hellish thickets,' I mutter.

A pot of tea comes up in the dumb waiter, too, as well as mugs, milk and a jar of brown sugar lumps. I help Flux carry everything down the ladder, and then we throw ourselves on to the beanbags, in front of the fire. I pull a blanket over me and unwrap one of the paper parcels. Inside is a large fillet of battered fish and heaps of warm, salty chips.

Before Flux has even opened theirs, I'm desperately ripping off pieces of fish and eating them, barely chewing. Apart from snacking on a piece of toast here and there, I can't remember when I last had a full meal. I hadn't realised I was so ravenous.

Flux kneels to pour two mugs for us. 'Tea goes so well with chips and a storm,' they say.

'I hate tea,' I retort, even while reaching for a pair of silver sugar tongs. If I'm forced to drink tea, I'm putting in a lot of sugar.

Flux gasps, then grabs my sleeve. 'Don't touch the tongs.'

My muscles stiffen. The tongs shimmer slightly, like the heat coming off the pavement on a very hot day.

Flux risks a quick glance at me. 'Can you see it, too?'

'Yes.' The tongs are – and I see it with sharp, painful clarity – simply *seeming* to be tongs.

Flux offers me a brief, reassured smile. 'I'm glad it's not just me.'

I grasp to find the right words. But I keep my voice low. 'They're like – creepily calm.'

'Yes, that's it!' hisses Flux.

I bite my lip. 'So, there are things – objects – that are kind of like, impostors?'

'Don't let them hear you!' whispers Flux. 'They're – aware.'

'Sorry,' I whisper back.

I snatch a sugar lump from the bowl, throwing it at the tongs. There's a sensation of time and place bending in that one small spot, folding like a blink. The sugar lump vanishes with a crisp *pop*, leaving a smell of burning.

'The sugar lump – disappeared.'

Flux flinches. 'There are Other folds. Things can get lost in them. We have to watch out because whole people have been known to . . .' They snap their fingers for effect, and I jump. *Other folds* – just like Artemis said, in my not-dream.

The storm swells to sound like a mountain giant throwing metal rubbish bins around overhead.

Flux uses their foot to push the tray with the tea things away from us. Then they settle back on their beanbag. 'This is probably my most recommended experience at Rookery Hollows,' they yell, over the din of the storm.

'You've come up here in a storm before, on purpose?'

'Yes. We're getting more and more storms with the thirteenth moon being eaten,' they tell me, abruptly sombre. 'It has disrupted the natural balance of things.'

'You're totally mad!' I scream. 'I'm going back down!'

Flux leans across to me and grabs my arm, eyes wild, mouth smeared with grease and salt. 'No, you can't! The tower's too unstable in a storm. You might get sucked out through a gap, plus the courtyard floods at high tide, too.'

I really am totally isolated up here, with *them*.

We finish our food and Flux pours more tea, carefully avoiding the sugar tongs. I take a mug just to warm my hands on. Flux settles back on their beanbag to watch the storm. I clutch the edges of mine like a life raft, as the tower quakes and icy arrows of rain are fired in. The light fades until the room is lit only by fire and lightning.

Shadows sneak from underneath the plasters on my fingers. With a snarl, I put my mug down and rip the plasters off. The shadows lend me pools of darkness with which to weave shapes.

Flux coaches me.

'Put more feeling into it, and feel the ache in your bones, and sense the spaces where light and darkness meet,' they tell me, eagerly. 'Think of when you open a portal and step through – that strange tilting of the earth, everything flowing the Other way. Harness that sensation.'

At first, I'm convinced they're talking nonsense, and it confuses me and adds to my overall frustration. But then I stop resisting and take a deep breath. I'm so relieved that I'm not holding back any more, and I'm not afraid of my magic any more, that the inky, smoky shadows flow like I've turned on a tap.

Making shadow creatures feels a bit like braiding my sister's hair. I pull a mass of shadow towards me, gathering heavy strands between my fingers, then start to weave. I pinch, stretch, pull, weave, tighten, knot. The shadows crowd closer to watch. When I think of an animal, the weaving takes its shape.

'Very good,' says Flux, with what seems like genuine approval.

Hours pass in a way that's like nothing I've ever experienced before. Flux wolfs their food, laughing wildly every time a wave slaps the stone and the tower wobbles. Every time the wind thrashes and the sea churns, the tower is engulfed in spray that showers everything in the room with freezing seawater. Meanwhile, the creatures we crafted from shadow flicker around the walls, like a strange theatre production.

Much later, the storm finally calms. 'This place is abandoned, isn't it?' I ask, more gently than I expected to.

'Yes.' Flux scrubs the end of their nose with their sleeve. 'The school was closed down. Too unsafe. Everyone scared of the Hangman. Everyone leaving Rookery Hollows.'

'I'm sorry.' I say it because I really am.

I'm half asleep when Flux speaks again.

'Have you ever felt so lonely that a crowded room felt like an empty space?' they ask, almost too quietly to hear.

I look up, startled. The fire is mostly ashes. Our eyes meet. 'Yeah,' I whisper. 'I have.'

I must have dozed off on the beanbag, because the next thing I know, Flux is shaking me awake. The room smells of cold and smoke.

'What?' I moan, pulling my blanket over my face.

'Tide's out!' says Flux.

I fling myself off the beanbag and scramble to my feet.

18
Dislocation

'Don't run so fast!' yells Flux. 'It's dangerous!'

'I don't care! Come on!' I shout back, as I dash down the winding staircase of Skull Tower, splashing through puddles of sea and rainwater.

We stumble into the afternoon light of a day scrubbed clean by the storm. Then it's across the courtyard, through the main doors and down the stairs that lead to the causeway.

The sea has strewn an assortment of storm-gifts on to the path; mussels and oysters, seaweed and egg cases, fish and pieces of driftwood.

We reach the mainland and I stare back over my shoulder at the towers of the college, sticking like bone-pins into the sky. Skull Tower sways slightly in the gathering breeze, and Flux must notice the queasy look on my face.

'You get used to it,' they tell me, with a smirk.

'The isolation, or the fact that the whole thing's likely to topple at any moment?'

'Both.'

We enter the town's labyrinth of old streets. I'm sure I spot a faceless agent watching from a doorway, but someone walks between us, and when I look again he's gone.

Then we're in the yew-hedge maze, and finally the Rookery looms over us, twigs and feathers and vines tangled into a nest that sprawls out of the upper windows and across the front of the building. Something moves amidst the mess; a figure, shrouded in shadows and feathers, concealed by a dense thicket of matter. Surrounded by raucous, warring birds.

Flux freezes, staring upwards. They flex their shoulder blades, wincing in pain.

'What's wrong?' I ask, but before they can answer a bell begins to toll, and then a hideous grating sound overtakes it, like broken bones scraping against each other. The Rookery starts to shift, whole walls sliding apart in the middle and being replaced with other sections, windows finding new positions, the giant nest splitting apart and being fitted back together in new and even more untidy ways.

Rook eggs fall and smash at our feet, spattering our ankles in goo. 'What just happened?' I breathe.

'The dislocation,' replies Flux, seemingly recovered. But when they look at me, that river of sadness under their skin is tumbling near the surface, threatening to flood. 'Are you certain you must enter here?'

'Yes.' I nod. 'Yes, I must.'

They usher me through the huge wooden door, which

is carved with distorted images of rooks, skulls, snakes and toads. It must have been too dark to notice those, last time.

We stand in the dank entrance hall, slabs of mossy stone radiating a bone-numbing chill. 'That doesn't really answer my question,' I whisper, trying not to take proper lungfuls of the stagnant air.

Flux presses a finger to their lips, and we move across the entrance hall, our footsteps too loud against the stone. I peer into doorways, black pits like toothless maws, wondering where he is. '*Putch?*' I hiss, afraid that I might walk straight past a hidden place where he's being entombed. No answer comes, except the sound of other things moving against the stone flagstones or scraping the walls – but when I whip round to look, nothing's there.

When Flux grabs my arm, their fingers grip hard enough to bruise. 'Be quiet,' they whisper, close to my ear. 'Someone might hear.'

'The Hangman? But I want to talk to him.'

Flux shakes their head. 'Not just him.' They refuse to say more, leading us deeper into the Rookery, up a flight of stairs that twists round and round, and finally to a room tucked up under the eaves.

A bed with an ornately carved wooden headboard stands against one wall, and a huge dark wardrobe hulks in the corner. A sketchbook is open on the bed, full of smudgy charcoal drawings of an assortment of creatures. They look like the shadow-beings we made, except grotesquely anguished – terrified eyes, wailing mouths, crouched poses, as though hiding from something. A long mirror spotted with age is hung on the far wall, and next to it is a fireplace, the grate choked with rook feathers. Grenwald slips out of Flux's sleeve and scuttles on to the bed, where he curls up and begins to snooze.

Flux closes the door behind us. 'You do not understand what sort of a place you find yourself in, witch.'

'Yeah, I do. I remember what it was like when you abandoned me in that courtyard, *witch*.' I cross my arms. 'Was that the Hangman I saw outside, in the nest? I have to get back to the Wayfaring Tree to speak to Putch, and if I can't find out where he is, I need to speak to the Hangman.'

'All that must wait until morning. Then I'll take you back to the tree. The Rookery will be more dormant, then.'

'I'm *not* waiting.'

'You must. The Hangman is entertaining this evening. It won't just be him, and his Rook King, and his faceless agents. It will be guests for the Dreadful Banquet, also.'

Their words send shivers across my skin. But there's no chance I'm hanging around in here until morning. If Flux won't help me, I'll have to do it alone.

Flux moves across to the fireplace and starts cleaning the feathers out of the grate, and that's when I notice the tapestry. It's behind the door, which strikes me as odd because it's not displayed in a place to be noticed easily. It's small, faded and gloomy.

The scene shows a funeral procession on a hillside, moving down from a ring of trees at the top to a church at the bottom. The uniform worn by the undertakers is the same as we wear now, but they lead a horse-drawn hearse before the mourners. As I stare up at the tapestry, a prickle stirs on the back of my neck. The leading undertaker is surrounded by a glowing haze of silver thread, and is apart from the others, as though not really part of the living world. And that ring of trees looks so familiar. But surely there are lots of hilltop trees, planted in circles. Aren't there?

Flux steps to the wardrobe and pulls out a pair of thick flannel pyjamas and some warm socks. 'In case you get cold,' they tell me.

I pull my gaze away from the tapestry. 'Thanks,' I mutter. I really hope that tapestry is dead. At Mistress Mouldheels' School for Wicked Girls, witches' souls were drained through a tapestry that was enchanted.

'I'm going to get us some bone broth,' Flux announces. They slip out the door, and Grenwald opens one eye, studying me.

I try to slow my galloping heart, and push the uneasy feeling away. Tapestries must be everywhere, in loads of places. I can't let it bother me – otherwise, it'll have power whether it's bewitched or not.

I pull the door open, but Flux is already coming back up the stairs, carrying two steaming mugs. 'How did you do that?'

They press one into my hands, and I pull a face – the mug is carved from bone, and the rich-smelling broth has droplets of oil floating in it.

'We need our broth to keep us warm,' Flux tells me, a smidge defensively.

'I can believe it,' I reply, not at all interested in trying a drink with the word *bone* in its name.

Flux closes the door again, and sits on their bed, settling to drawing more creatures in their sketchbook. 'I'm to serve at the banquet this evening.'

'That could be helpful,' I muse. 'If there's any chance of them seeing me, you can create a distraction.'

'No, I told you –' they start, before folding forward on the bed and whimpering in pain.

'Are you sick?'

'Not sick. Summoned. Remember – this place isn't safe, and you must not go wandering around alone. The dislocation happens hourly, and even if you knew where you were before it happened, you would not have a clue afterwards.'

Before I can argue, they've ducked out the door. I listen to their footsteps fade away. As I mull over what they said about this place, an idea strikes me. What if I drew myself a map of the way to and from this room, and the main entrance? When the dislocation happens again, maybe a sketch would help me match up the landmarks I need to recognise.

The light beyond the window begins to fade. I put the bone mug on a table and reach into my pocket, feeling the cold metal of my pocket watch. Then I check the other side, fingers closing around the ring I brought for Putch. My breath is a cloud in the freezing room, despite the fire. And despite the cold, my hands begin to sweat with nerves. I check my pockets again, then cast around me, eyes frantically searching. But it's happened.

My Book of Shadows is gone.

19
Moon Meat

Lanterns flicker on the landing outside Flux's room, casting thin, sickly light across the stone floors and walls. I can't believe the book is gone. All my mother's notes, all my own, all the spells, the lists, the observations, the details I hadn't even had a chance to read yet. Gone. Tears snake from my eyes to my chin, and I brush them away, anger snapping at my nerves and heating up my belly.

I wait for a moment, making sure no one's coming, and then plunge down the stairs and follow them round until I reach the floor below. I'm in a huge dark corridor, which feels horribly exposed. It smells like a graveyard and it's just as silent. I want to run screaming for Flux, demand my book back, but I force myself to wait, clinging to the wall and the shadows.

It must have happened when I dozed off on the beanbag in the tower. I can't think of any other time it would have been possible. After everything we talked about, and the magic we made together, they were still capable of stealing from me?

I snort, fury scraping my insides. So much for *loneliness*. I can't believe I started to feel sorry for them.

A bell rings, somewhere in the guts of the Rookery. It makes a sound like a choking drain. I follow the noise, along the corridor and down another sweep of stairs, and I'm a few steps from the bottom when another bell tolls. Then a clicking, crunching noise begins, as the joints of the Rookery prepare to dislocate once more.

'No,' I whisper. I fling myself the rest of the way down, but I'm too late. Before I hit the ground at the bottom, the whole staircase begins to rumble and quiver. It splits in two, the upper half swinging away to the right. The lower half – that I'm clinging to – grinds and grumbles, before sliding through a seam that's opened in the opposite wall. I slam against the banister, grabbing on with both hands as the stairs sail away through the bowels of the Rookery. I crouch, shaking, until finally the movement stops. Flux was right about the dislocation – how am I ever going to keep track of where I am?

I'm faced with an open corridor, wide and dark as the throat of a beast. Footsteps are approaching from the left. One by one, firefly lanterns pop into life along the corridor, spitting pools of measly light on to the flagstones. Unless I move, whoever is coming will see me huddled here.

I jump up and dash into the hollow under the stairs, palms sweating and heart drumming.

Faceless men swarm down the corridor, followed by a troop of lumpen figures, gargling and snarling. One shivers along the floor like a stack of jelly, and their voice sounds like a toilet flushing. I still feel like they could see me here. I need the shadows to be thicker.

As I think it, my fingers begin to itch. Shadows curl out of my skin and cloud my face. I blow them outwards, using my hands to smooth them into a blanket. It's thin enough for me to see through, but feels like a screen to help keep me out of sight. I hope it works.

Before they reach the stairs I'm hiding under, the strange procession turn left, filing through a doorway. I wait, holding my breath, until I'm sure no one else is coming. Then I creep across the floor into the corridor and sneak up to the threshold, peering around the edge of the door into a long, draughty hall.

Flickering firefly lanterns illuminate a long banquet table, groaning under the weight of cauldrons of steaming bone broth, dishes of boiled rook eggs, bowls of grey gloop and tankards of thick liquid; some purple, others deep green. The guests take their seats, and from a darkened doorway in the far corner, a squealing trolley rolls out and is pulled by two faceless agents until it reaches the table. A cover is thrown back to reveal a massive chunk of cratered flesh.

The faceless agents begin to saw slices off it and soon platters of dark blue meat have been distributed along the length of the table. *Blue?*

A voice quavers into the air, dripping with pleasure. 'Venerable guests, welcome, welcome!'

I stifle a gasp, finally noticing the throne in the gloom, just beyond the head of the table. This is the hall I passed through the first time I was at the Rookery.

This time, the squirming throne is occupied. *So this must be the Hangman.* He's a small, balding man swathed in a feather cloak and hunched over a silver platter. A massive statue of a rook sits to his right on a wooden stand, gleaming an obsidian black. The rook has one eye, the other socket wrinkled and empty. The very centre of my forehead begins to ache, in exactly the place that hurt when I saw through the tree's eye.

The Hangman speaks again, knuckles flexing against feather and bone. 'Revel in my moon flesh, all gathered here! Remember I, who mined this most illicit and hard-sought resource for you. Feel the power it bestows! Feast!'

A gargled cheer rings around the walls. The guests dip their faces, ripping, rending, feasting.

The Hangman tears a piece of meat, and the flesh is chalky, blue-black, and raw. Full of crater marks. As he bites into it, there's a meaty squeak as his teeth sever the sinews. Bluish juices run down his sparsely bearded chin, chiming on to the platter in front of him.

The throne is comprised of many bodies – the bodies of countless rooks, arranged into one squirming structure.

The sight of it makes my mouth turn dry.

Behind the throne is a tapestry.

It hangs on the back wall, and green blooms of mould cling to the thread. It shows a hunting party, all gathered in front of a castle, dressed in old-fashioned finery. There are horses and hounds and falcons. And in the distance, between the trees, are witches wearing headscarves. Green headscarves, like we wore at Mouldheels' School.

This is a hunting tapestry, telling the story of a witch hunt.

Every inch of my skin tells me to run far, far away. To run back to the portal, to my own world, to help fight the Hunt as best we can, and if it's too late, to at least be captured in a world I know.

A world drained of magic, with no place left for magical creatures.

No. It's all wrong. Fresh determination stirs in my chest, and anger. So much anger. Shranken Putch is the only one who can help me stop the Hunt for good. The only one who can ensure a safe place for the magical ones. I came here to find him, and I'm not giving up now.

All around, the trapped fireflies fling themselves hopelessly against the walls of their glass prisons. And here and there, through cracks in the stone, the Other Wayfaring Tree has pushed inside, roots beginning to reclaim the space.

Flux stands in the shadows behind the guests. Every time one grunts or clicks their fingers or slams the table, they dart forward, topping up tankards or clearing plates, or dashing for more moon flesh.

I grind my jaw, wondering if they've got my Book of Shadows in their pocket right now.

I also remember them telling me that the gradual destruction of the thirteenth moon has been disrupting the natural world in this Way, and causing more and more wild weather. The Dreadful Banquet is endangering lives, all for a taste of illegal meat.

Flux told me when we first met that the thirteenth moon was being eaten away. That must be why I saw it crumbling in the sky. What will happen to this world when it's disappeared?

All around us, within the stone walls, comes the sound of claws scratching and scurrying. The smell of rook droppings and moon meat builds to a fogging stench that gives me a headache.

It's now, or never. I brew another cloud of shadows that fan around me like a cloak. Then I tiptoe through the door, sticking to the far wall. I follow a tree root that's broken through, and I keep my shadows close. When I glance back, Flux is goggling at me, eyes shining.

They drop a platter, with a jarring crash that makes rooks cry and guests groan and the Hangman roar from his living throne. 'Shadow child!'

Flux created a distraction for me, just as I suggested. I run in a half crouch until I reach the door to the courtyard.

As I'm easing it open just enough to squeeze through, the giant bird next to the Hangman moves, shaking out its feathers in one shivering movement. Then it lifts off its pedestal and flies at Flux, cawing.

It's a real bird. That must be the Rook King. Flux covers their face, cowering.

A bell rings. The floor rumbles. No. No. *Not again.*

'Agents!' bellows the Hangman, across the hall. Faceless men stream out of the walls like rats, chaining the table down as the dislocation starts again, and all I can do is grip as hard as I can to the partly open door. The stone slabs and wooden supports scream with effort as the bones of the Rookery dislocate, and the ceiling switches places with the floor.

The world swings around, my legs fall into the air, bile rushes up my throat.

When the Rookery settles back into temporary stillness, the door is underneath me.

I brace myself, gulp a breath, then relax my grip on the door. I'm falling, down and through the floor, away, into the middle of a thicket of branches silvered with orbs.

There's the briefest moment to realise I've fallen into the Other Wayfaring Tree before I'm crashing down through the branches. I land at the base of the trunk, in a mess of gnarled branches and surrounded by gravestones. Pain blossoms in the centre of my forehead. When I stand up, clothes torn and skin bleeding, my breath catches. The tree has sickened. Stooped and shrivelling, it sags towards the ground.

From every branch hangs a raindrop. Inside every raindrop is a face.

20
Witchful Thinking

Raindrops ripen on the branches, stretch, fall. They bud again, with the same face inside. The faces stare blankly, the distorted mouths weep, or growl. Some chatter, endless loops of one-sided conversation. They look straight through me.

Freezing smog coils around the gravestones, poking through the rips in my sweatshirt. I stare up at the raindrops as they bud, ripen, swell, stretch, fall. My forehead throbs, that same pain I first noticed at the Wayfaring Tree in my own world. 'Shranken Putch!' I call, voice fracturing. Then I find a splinter of fierceness waiting in my heart, and call him again, shadows erupting from my fingertips. 'Shranken *Putch*!'

I search the faces, desperately wishing I'd thought to ask Flux how they found him the last time. The open door, high above the tree, bangs in a stagnant breeze. I flinch, squatting between two crowded gravestones. 'Putch, please,' I whisper. 'I need you. I think you might need me.'

The ring from the burial hoard is a cool circle in my pocket. I lift it out, clenching it tight in my fist as I whisper his name, over and over, rhythmic as a spell.

A raindrop lengthens from the tip of a branch, and my heart gives a painful swoop. The face that appears inside the drop is the face I most wanted to see in all the worlds. But it's slack and bloodless, all grey skin and bone.

'Putch!' I whisper, glancing overhead again.

There's a tarnished greyness tightening about him, as though he's turning – into stone. Lumpy stone, full of cracks where his life is still fighting not to be sealed away, as though into a tomb. *Entombed.*

'Why are they doing this to you?' I rock on the balls of my feet, unable to stop the tears from rolling. 'Why do they want to destroy everything?'

The raindrop bulges, stretches, lengthens on the tip of the branch.

'Putch!'

His lips move, very slightly. A sigh whistles through his teeth. 'Small Wrythe,' he murmurs, face twisting as though in pain. 'No – run! Run away!'

'Putch,' I yelp, getting closer to the raindrop and staring up into it. 'Wake up, please! Don't let them win!' I think of the wasted hours Flux cost me, stuck in that tower, and bite down on my tongue to keep from screaming.

His eyeballs flick from side to side, and his eyelids crack open a sliver. 'Shadow witch,' he murmurs, lips split and lined with dust.

The raindrop drops violently lower, stretching on a silvery cord. I flinch. 'Yes, it's me! I need to know where you are, Putch. Tell me anything you can about how to find you!'

'New Putch,' he mutters, muscles twitching. 'Same as I, many moons past. No fighting.'

He's too sick and trapped for this conversation, but I have to keep going. I need a piece of information, just one gem that's enough to tell me what to do next.

'No,' I tell him, blinking through a sudden blur of tears. 'You thought another Putch would be fine to take your place, but I've learned that's not true. They're trying to break the Putch Pact. They're trying to destroy the Ring's protection, and steal the heart of the ancient Muddlewood. We have to stop them – or the dragon will die, the portals will be breached, the Ring will be cut down, and the witches will be drained.'

He gasps, the sound like air being sucked through a crack in a gravestone.

'I've taken the barrow ring meant for the new Putch,' I whisper, putting emphasis on each word, praying he's able to follow what I've said. 'I'm going to bring it to you. So you can come home.' I search the image in the raindrop, trying to spot anything – a single clue – as to where he might be. But all I can see is his pained face, and the stone crawling up his neck and on to his cheeks.

'Small Wrythe,' he mutters urgently, as the raindrop lengthens, threatening to fall.

'What?' I whisper.

'Witchfinder's seat . . . castle,' he wheezes. A tear pearls in the corner of his eye, rolls a track through the dust and grime. 'I am *sorry*.'

'Oh, Putch!' There's a painful lump in my throat and my head pounds with waiting tears. 'None of this is your fault!'

He turns his face half away, crumpling in pain, and that's when I see it. A glimpse of a tapestry, high on a wall in the distance, beyond the growing tomb. My forehead burns enough to make me whimper with pain. 'Use the pain to see,' mumbles Putch. 'Wield wisdom.'

'What?' I look again. But I can't see anything else that might help.

Then Putch turns his face back to me. '*Spel*,' he says, eyes snapping wide open. He stares at me through their tarnished silver.

My neck prickles. 'What?'

'Take care-pains,' he whispers, barely audible. 'Another set of ears is listening.'

I frown, glancing around, and then a voice pierces the quiet, making every nerve in my body jangle.

Trespasser.

It's the Rook King. He's sitting in the tree, eye glittering down at me.

'No, no, shhhh –'

The bird dives, rasping, wingspan blotting out the thin

light trickling from the Rookery's windows. His beak ripens as he barrels for me.

'Get away from me!' I dart into the tree's lower branches, trying to shelter, and the giant rook switches direction without missing a beat.

Shranken Putch's raindrop is barely clinging to the tree branch. I crawl forward to stare into it again. He drops his voice until it's a scratch in the air, like the creak of a tree when the wind is sleepy. 'His *eye* lurks in the well water, beneath the tree. Seeing – all things. All worlds.' Pain finds my forehead, sharp, disorientating.

The raindrop falls on to my shoe. For half a moment the undertaker's face stares up at me. Then the water breaks apart, and he's erased.

Seeing all worlds? What does that mean?

The Rook King dives at me again, throat opening to utter murderous incantations. His wings beat my ears, leaving my head bruised and my arms bloody with scratches. I run, arms shielding my head. I need to find my Book of Shadows and write down my clues about Shranken Putch, because my head is hurting and I can't make sense of it all.

The great ragged bird circles back to the Other tree, where he alights on a branch which creaks under his bulk.

A bell rings, inside the Rookery. Around and above the courtyard, the Rookery dislocates and reforms, walls scraping across each other while the courtyard stays still.

It's all working around this one central point, I realise.

I find a skinny tendril of root veining the wall just above eye height. I follow it, hardly daring to breathe, until I find a door that leads back inside the Rookery. I creep through a narrow, unlit passageway, flagstones worn slippery and frozen to a glitter.

My first thought is to find Flux's bedroom again and confront them about my Book of Shadows – or wait for the banquet to finish, if that's still going on. I need somewhere to think, too. But trying to find my way back there feels impossible.

Every corridor looks the same, and every staircase I follow leads to somewhere else. I'm tiptoeing back down another flight of steps when suddenly, somehow, I find myself back outside the Hall of Bones.

I freeze, ducking down in the hollow of the stairwell. From inside the hall, the Hangman's voice carries across the stones. But the longer he talks, the more confused I am. There's only one voice – his – speaking.

I creep out of the hollow and poke my head around the edge of the door.

His throne has swivelled around to face the back wall. And the Hangman is speaking to the hunting tapestry.

21
The Grimoire

The tapestry twitches with life, all the little figures of the witch hunt animated in a scene that should be hundreds of years dead. A stitched figure stands at the front of the scene, the castle at his back. I drop into a crouch, gasping for breath.

It's the Witchfinder General – Tobias Barrow. Head of the modern-day Hunt. The last time I saw him, he was attacking Shranken Putch and me, and wishing my sister a cursed eternity in the Shadow Way. Why is he talking to the Hangman?

'Remember my tethered shadow child, Witchfinder,' croaks the Hangman. 'Capturing any other Shadow-Born witches means they too can be used to perform tasks across the Ways, at our whim.'

My spine prickles. Shadow child is what he calls Flux. What does he mean by *tethered*?

'Yes,' drawls Tobias, teeth shining. 'We shall truly have a network across the worlds, trading in witch powers and draining magical creatures. Distilling them into energy.'

'What of the rest of the plot?' the Hangman rumbles.

'Arundel is primed. The entombment is in progress, and the ancient Hunting texts say that will mean the pact will be broken. Then we can move in – not only to seize the last witches of this Way, but to claim the magic of that last patch of wildness. The text tells of a dragon – if that is true, the wealth shall be boundless. Dragon blood will power our movement and bring untold riches, by the drop. We will bleed the beast until a river runs.'

Crouched in the threshold, my own blood simmers with rage. Then his words untangle themselves in my head. Arundel . . . there's a castle in the tapestry, and Shranken Putch mentioned one, too, and the Witchfinder's seat – Arundel Castle *must* be where the undertaker is being entombed.

I've been tricked. I know it as surely as the sun rises. *Do you want to speak to the undertaker?* That's the message that appeared in the ashes, which Flux was able to write after I started using the feather to write with. *Come to the portal.*

Shranken Putch was in my own world after all. True, I only found that out by coming here, and I have no idea how I would have searched for him in my world with the Hunt outside our door, but still – he's not even in the Way of Bones. The Hangman can see into other worlds, which must be what Putch was saying. That's how I saw him in a raindrop at the Hangman's Wayfaring Tree.

For a moment I let my head drop on to my knees, exhaustion and fury and fear crashing over my head like a wave.

'And when you have distilled the power of the place, and enter the portals, my hospitality shall await you,' gruffs the Hangman.

Tobias Barrow sweeps a bow. 'For that, my lineage and the whole Unwicked world thanks you.' Then he walks away, his stitched likeness becoming smaller until it fades from view. The Hangman brushes a hand in front of the tapestry and the life falls from it – the threads lose their oily sheen, and the tension in the air slackens.

A slow, insidious understanding trickles from my scalp to my toes. The Hunt and the Hangman can communicate with each other through tapestries. The Hunt can't step between the worlds – but that doesn't mean their influence can't reach into every space, spreading rot. It must be stolen magic that lets them do it. And now they want to grow their power – they've hunted almost every living witch in my world, so they want to start taking from other worlds. The greed makes my head swim.

I'm turning away when the Hangman's voice echoes again. 'Shadow child. Come.'

The breath rushes out of my lungs. He must have seen me. But –

'Yes, sire.'

The words didn't come from my mouth. I look up.

Flux is there, by his side. I remember when they said they'd been summoned, before.

'What is the meaning of this?' asks the Hangman, producing a small leather book out of the depths of his cloak. My Book of Shadows. I feel my mouth turn dry.

Flux gapes at it. 'It's the grimoire, as you asked, sire. The most important spellbook we've ever hunted for.'

'This is nothing but a mess of scrap paper!' he roars. 'Petty country spells, personal diary entries, pressed flowers!' Spittle flies from his lips.

'But, sire! I saw the grimoire when I peered into the Drained Place,' Flux gabbles, desperation inching into their voice. 'It is the very same one.'

'It is worthless,' says the Hangman, throwing my Book of Shadows at Flux. Then a note of cunning enters his voice. 'But, truth is spoken – your excursion did reveal the grimoire. What else was in that room, with the child?'

'I only saw them, and the book,' Flux stutters, clutching my book to their chest.

Flux was looking for me. Of course they were. They lied when they said they hadn't been looking for me on purpose – we didn't start appearing to each other just because.

I'd begun to let myself believe it might have been because of some kind of Shadow-Born bond. I couldn't have been more stupid. They were hunting me with the Hangman, and they led me into this world. The only thing I did right was to bring the ring with me, so that Sunken Putch couldn't take root and the pact couldn't be broken.

'Need I remind you of what is at stake? All I need to do is snip –' the Hangman mimes sawing with an imaginary knife. 'And everything that tethers you to consciousness will be lost. You will be dust.'

From the shadows, I flinch. Flux raises their hands to their face, visibly trembling.

'That Huntsman thinks he rules the business of magic-theft,' grumbles the Hangman. 'But when I get my hands on that grimoire – the one coded with more power than the heart of the Muddlewood itself – it is *I* who will be controlling their access to magic. The Barrows are one of the most ancient, elite Hunting families. But how they shall bow and scrape to me.'

'Yes, sire.'

'Where is she?' demands the Hangman. 'Keep that book safe, and bring her to me! Even if that's not the grimoire, I'll still use it to tether her to my bidding.' The Hangman half chokes on a piece of moon flesh, filmy eyes bulging. He hacks and splutters, tears coursing down his whiskery cheeks. I flinch when he bashes the table with a fist, spraying the hall with flecks of blue-black moon meat.

Trespasser, neck-breaker. The Rook King is in the rafters, eye glittering down at me.

'No!' I hiss. 'Shut up!'

'Who is there, my beauty?' rasps the Hangman.

Instead of replying, the Rook King descends upon me, stirring my clothes into a gale with the strength of his wing beats. Heavy weights drop on to my shoulders. I twist and yell, covering my face with my hands, but then I'm lifted up into the air, and carried the length of the hall.

The Rook King drops me on the floor at the foot of the throne.

22
Cover the Mirrors

Trespasser, neck-breaker, croaks the Rook King again, swivelling its eye to my face.

'Ah,' rasps the Hangman, reaching out to stroke the giant bird. 'Not a trespasser, Rook King. Surely a welcome guest.' He spreads his hands in a supposed gesture of generosity, but his eyes stay cold and flat. Dead.

This close, I can see the throne writhing and shifting beneath the Hangman's weight. The rooks closest to him are being crushed, and towards the bottom others are hatching. The whole structure is edged in broken, jagged bones, smashed shells and jutting quills.

As I stand in front of the Hangman and Flux, the tapestry behind the throne animates. The oily sheen returns, and new stitches pick themselves out across the weaving. In the distance, across from the castle, there's a hill and a ring of trees. As I watch, the trees thicken, grow, spread. Shadowy creatures move between them, nest in their canopies. The ring is now a forest. The Muddlewood.

Why is the tapestry showing it?

The Hangman's glance swivels between the tapestry and my face, and back again. 'Fool child!' he bellows at Flux, before turning to me. 'You,' he murmurs, almost reverently. 'It's not that –' He gestures roughly to the book in Flux's arms. 'It's *you* that I have searched for.' His mouth widens into a raw grimace, his teeth stained bruise-blue by moon flesh. 'This is what I do not tell Tobias and his cronies. This is how I shall overcome them in strength and power. You whose blood and bones are etched with the richest magic imaginable. How long I have awaited your birth.'

'What?' I blurt. 'That's mad!'

'The spells are written on your bones,' he rasps. 'The incantations dance within your blood; codes to unravel the fabric of life, blink a flower out of being, or breathe sparks into weather.'

I scowl up at him. 'I don't want to unravel the fabric of life!' I shout. 'I don't want to blink anything out of being! That's not how I'm going to use my powers.'

His stare pierces me. 'What arrogance. There is nothing to say *you* would ever be able to do that. But were someone to borrow from your blood –' He smiles, the flesh of his lips sliding back from his teeth. 'Oh, who knows what they might achieve.'

While we're speaking, a tendril of thread sneaks out of the tapestry behind him. 'Would you like a way to cheat death?' he wheezes.

'Is that what you did to Flux?' I snap.

He grabs a handful of moon flesh from a platter and cracks open his mouth. 'That child should be five thousand years cold, but I have provided an alternative.' His teeth sink into the chunk of moon.

Flux's gaze meets mine. Theirs is terrified. The shining bones around the edge of the rook throne gleam. The tendril hangs from the tapestry. And it lengthens another inch.

His long, tapered fingernails stroke the feathers on the arms of his throne. My Book of Shadows grows spines, and Flux yelps, loosening their hold. It flies through the air towards me. I hold it to my chest, brewing ribbons of shadow at my fingertips at the same time. 'Why are all of you so power mad?' I whisper.

'What?' he demands, feet slipping as he thrashes on his throne. 'Speak up, shadow child!'

I won't speak up. I'm going to make people listen to me, but not by shouting over their noise.

'I won't let you win,' I say, and he squints at me. His laugh is a coarse sound like a saw being scraped across metal.

The Hangman stands, but before he can take a step towards me I throw armloads of shadow into his face, making him stagger backwards. I weave little beasts with sharp claws and teeth that tear at his face, making him shriek.

Then I run. The Rook King swoops behind me, and I feel his talons snick at my sweatshirt. But Flux bellows like a warrior, and beckons shadows out of the walls that surround the giant bird, making it screech in fury and pull away from me.

I race out of the hall and into the corridor, rushing in the direction I think might lead to the front doors. As the walls close in around me, it's like being swallowed whole. I trip and fall, smacking my cheek against the stone. Pain spreads across my face and I have to bite my fist to keep the shriek in.

I'm bruised, and covered in scabs and scratches, and my limbs are heavy with weariness.

I get up and keep running, and up ahead I see the door. I'm almost free. But then a chiming rings out through the air. The bell is striking the hour. Stone rumbles as the Rookery begins to dislocate. I feel a pulling, twisting inside my skull, a knot of sickness deep in my stomach. As the chiming stops, I stagger, and gulp a huge breath as the room stops spinning.

The door is gone. I'm in another passageway, with a staircase spiralling away to my left. Footsteps shush the stone in the gloom to my right, in the darkness. I fling myself up the stairs, weeping, and wind up and up until I can't go any further. I've ended up back at Flux's room under the eaves.

I throw the door open and duck inside. No one else is here. But within seconds, footsteps ring on the landing outside.

'Flux!' I pant, as they burst into the room. In the corner of my eye, movement catches my attention. The large, age-spotted mirror on the wall is swirling with activity.

Faces and shapes are brushing about underneath the glass. Trapped spirits. The faces in the mirror look terrified to the point of losing human shape. Stretched eyes, anguished mouths, muscles corded in jaws and necks.

'The mirror,' I breathe. 'What's wrong with it?'

Flux blinks, the tiniest flicker of movement. But otherwise they remain motionless, watching me without a trace of emotion.

I turn back towards them. 'Flux – how did you come here?'

'I've always been here,' they reply, sullenly.

As they turn away again, I see it – poking out from between their shoulder blades is a thread. A thread that's the same colour as the one that crept towards me out of the hunting tapestry. It's like a shimmering cord, translucent like a membrane. I remember when Flux said they'd been summoned, when they doubled over in pain. When they said they could travel, but never stay away from this place overnight.

A tether, that keeps them bound to a tapestry. I don't know which one – maybe they're one of the witches from the hunting tapestry in the Hall of Bones, or maybe they're an undertaker from the tapestry behind their bedroom door, and the only way . . .

I feel like icy water has been tipped down the back of my neck. 'Flux. Is the only way to free yourself from your tapestry to help the Hangman? Is that why you do it?'

Flux's dark blonde hair has fallen in clumps around their face. Their dusky blue eyes flick restlessly around the room. 'Not quite,' they mutter, giving a short, harsh laugh. 'He made me a deal – but it turned into more of a trick. Long time ago. The tether is what keeps me alive.'

Grenwald scurries out of their top pocket and on to the top of their head.

'We could help each other escape him,' I find myself saying. 'His power – it's linked to being able to see into all the worlds. And those faces in the raindrops are proof of it.' My mind races as I remember what Putch told me. 'The Rook King's missing eye – it's how he does it. If we could find it, could it be destroyed?'

A look of mocking passes across Flux's face. 'You are so thick in the head,' they spit. 'It's obvious now how I was able – so easily – to separate you from the people who should be closest to you in all the worlds. It's just pathetic.'

I stumble backwards, until my back is pressed against the mirror. 'What?'

Their voice has turned high-pitched, derisive. 'If you're that stupid, you don't even deserve friends and family.'

Their voice chokes slightly. Shadow creatures begin to squirm against the walls, peeling out of the cold stone and stumbling around the room on crumpled wings, or cramped legs. Flux's creations. The beings that started in their sketchbook and haunted Flux so much that they scrawled the same creatures across the walls.

Creatures from five thousand years ago, when Flux lived,

without a tapestry tether in their back and a contract on their soul.

'You don't have any friends – or family,' I whisper. 'Maybe we could have been friends. But you lied to me. You tricked me. You've been hunting for me all along.' I push myself away from the mirror and take a step forward, but Flux blocks me, their expression cold. A shadow creature flits past my face, scraping my skin open with agitated claws. Another creature plays games in the walls, taking the shape of a coffin-maker and hissing at me.

I need to defend myself.

I rub the fingers of my left hand across the palm of my right, flicking little coils of shadow out into the air. I layer them up until a fat gloomy cloud hangs in front of my face. I begin to sculpt the cloud, using the fingertips of my left hand – which I have learned has the most power – to add shadow here, to snip it away there. Soon a shadow dragon hovers just overhead, mouth brimming with angry sparks. I open my mouth to snarl, and the shadow dragon copies me.

Flux laughs, a harsh barking sound. They flick a thumbnail against a forefinger, and an army of shadow creatures slink out of the walls of the firelit chamber. They surround my dragon, devouring the smoky coils of its shape, sparing nothing. My fingertips ache.

'Your people will forget you.' Flux darts forward. I flinch. 'Because when someone was never even alive, it's hard to

miss them. You're dead, aren't you? As good as.' They step towards me, until my back is pressed hard against the glass.

'So are you,' I manage, throat dry. 'We're both Shadow-Born. And you're long buried.'

Flux watches my face for a moment. Then they click their fingers. The spirits stuck behind the mirror whoosh free.

The glass behind my back turns soft and damp. I'm sinking into it.

'Help, pull me up!' I cry, losing my balance. My hands flail, fingertips brushing Flux. But they're just out of reach.

Flux smiles, sadly. Their eyes have darkened. 'I'm sorry,' they whisper. Then they plant the heels of their hands on my shoulders and give me a firm, decided *shove*.

I'm slipping. I'm falling backwards. Into nothing. My heart lurches. I try to grab out at the sides of the mirror frame, the wall, scrabbling desperately, ripping my nails.

Flux shakes their head. 'Always cover the mirrors,' they say.

Then there's a wall between us. I press against the glass, begging, sobbing. I get my shoulder against it and press, certain I can just slip back out again and into the room. But nothing happens. Flux turns away, crosses the room, and leaves. I open my mouth, and let out a scream.

23
The Underside

The space inside the mirror is small and square, and not big enough to lie down in. Sounds from the outside world land thickly, muffled as though wrapped in cotton. I've worked out that I can see more of Flux's room when I squeeze to the sides. But Flux isn't there. They left, right after pushing me.

I haven't quite let myself think certain things, yet. But thoughts are crowding in anyway.

How will I ever find Shranken Putch now?

If I can't rescue him, how will we ever stop the endless destruction of the Hunt?

What if no one ever finds *me*?

What if I never get out?

Grenwald, Flux's axolotl, scampers about across the mirror, smudging it with greasy little handprints. I thump against the Underside, yelling at him, but he doesn't even cower – I'm as deeply entombed as though I'm inside a burial chamber.

Entombed. Like Shranken Putch. Perhaps we'll never see each other again, now. Perhaps I'll never see anyone again.

And it's this piteous thought that unravels me, sends me sliding down to the cold, empty floor. I huddle there, on the hard stone, arms around myself, weeping so hard that I feel like my throat is going to bleed.

Later, I wake up. My bones are sore and aching. I must have fallen asleep. I stand up, peering out of my prison. Flux's bedroom is dark. They haven't returned yet.

As shockwaves continue to roll through me, I think back to how they were able to know my deepest thoughts just by reading what I wrote with the quill.

I could actually kill the past me. But I could kill *Flux* more. How can a person be so cruel?

How can another person be so stupid?

I feel a pang of missing my coven. And the funeral parlour, too. I miss the squeaky floorboards, and the faded floral armchairs, and the layer of sticky dust coating the kitchen. I miss all the chocolate-stained milk pans, and the leaky attic roof, and the creaking of the trees' limbs when a storm rushes upon the Ring. I scream again, thumping the glass, bruising myself, but no one comes.

Time passes. Maybe a whole day. I stare out of the cold, empty hole, too numb to see. My breath makes a vapour that beads on the glass.

But then the door flies open, and Flux darts into the room. They cross to the mirror. When they see me, their face is a shock-slap. 'Spel, I'm so sorry,' they tell me, features distorted by bitter sorrow. 'I'm going to try to get you out, I promise.'

I thump the glass with both hands. 'Do it now! Get me out!' I screech.

There's movement behind Flux. A cloaked figure, gliding through the shadows. A sharp grimace, blue teeth. The Hangman.

He rasps, approaching the mirror. 'You belong to my Rookery now,' he gasps, eyes bulging. 'Like a rat stuck in the pipes. Do not struggle, dear one.'

I back away from the glass. But he plunges his hand inside, fishing around for me. His yellowed nails scrape my skin. I yell, kicking him away.

Then a noise clamours through the floor, and the Hangman sighs. 'The banquet descends again,' he mutters. 'They are moon-guzzlers indeed. Too bad. I shall return.' At the door, he turns to Flux. 'Try to relax the witch,' he murmurs. 'Too much fear taints the blood.'

After he's gone, Flux returns to the mirror, begging me to listen. But I turn away, ignoring them. 'Just shut up, and get me out!'

But as hard as they try, nothing softens the glass enough for me to get back through.

I reach for the curve of silver at my throat. The moon.

The silver moon, strung on a black cord, linking me to a Muddlewood demon and my own troubled world.

If I am even able to summon Diana, will she just be stuck here, too? Will she kill me with her own bare hands, given that she's finally got her freedom?

The decision arrives like thunder. I'm not willing to wait for the Hangman to come back. I fumble with the knotted cord behind my neck and slip the moon charm off, letting the silver pool in my palm, reflecting nothing but the grey murk of the Underside.

Diana is there, standing in front of me. I know that she wasn't there before, even though there was no pause between before and after her appearance. Her hair is matted and wild, her eyes are shining, and a cut on her lip is pouring black blood over her chin. When her diamond pupils focus on me, she groans.

'Where are we?' demands Diana, touching her chin and inspecting the blood on her fingers.

I wince. 'Um. Inside a mirror?'

She gapes at me. It's disconcerting, given that I wouldn't have expected to be able to surprise an ancient forest being. 'You – you allowed yourself to be trapped inside a mirror? And then – let me get this right – you summoned me into it?'

I glance around, at the sticky grey walls and the void above and behind us.

'You realise where we are now, don't you?' she says,

rounding on me, fabulous silk blouse billowing in the damp air.

'No, obviously not!' I retort, my own temper rising. 'I thought I was trapped forever behind a mirror and you were the only one who could help!'

She swoops a malicious bow, chin almost scraping the tops of her leather boots. 'We're in the Underside, you great, jagged dolt. And that is one of the worst places you can be – and one of the only places in all the Ways I have never glimpsed, in all my centuries. So I suppose I should at least thank you for a novel experience.'

'I'm sorry! I didn't know what else to do! And I've had enough of being responsible for everything, all by myself!'

Nostrils flaring, something in her eyes softens. 'Right. Well, let's go.'

'Where?' I kick out at the back of the mirror.

'There!' yelps Diana, shattering any brief illusion that she might forgive me. She gestures, with a wide sweep of a silk-covered arm, into the foggy space behind us. And to my amazement, a little clear patch in the fog appears. The grey space I've been weeping in gives on to a narrow grey tunnel. There is a path.

We follow it. Flux yells at my back, through the glass, but I ignore them. We walk stooped, our spines hugging the salt-sticky roof. How many tears have been cried into this mirror, how many secrets have been whispered into it? My fingertips are grazed by running them along the walls, seeking blindly for a way out. Diana grows a bulb on top of her head, an orb of light that hangs like a snowdrop, casting thin yellow light over the uneven ground.

We finally stagger out of the mouth of the tunnel, on to a dark road. Lamp posts spill an orange glow into piles of dirty old snow. The lantern on Diana's head shrinks back underneath her scalp, and before I can ask her about it, she presses a finger to her lips. With one looping arc of a wrist, she brushes a soft black cloak around my shoulders, which ties itself at my throat with a smooth satin ribbon. It is wonderfully warm.

Then she steps off down the road, boots scrunching slush, and I scurry to keep up. 'I spoke to him again, Diana! I know where he is. If I – I mean, we – can get out of here, and I can get back to our world, I know where to look for him.'

'Good work, Elspeth,' she says, with genuine approval that makes me glow inside. 'Unfortunately, you summoned me at the very moment I was patching a breach in the cloaking spell. The breach was made by that aircraft. Rats started pouring in. Villagers and Hunters were crowded outside it, too.'

The glow dies, very swiftly, leaving me numb again. When I tell Diana about what the Hangman said, about the power in my blood, she doesn't look at all surprised. 'Your father was an immortal creature. A demon of the Muddlewood,' she tells me. 'Half immortal, half witch, and Shadow-Born – that's why you're so valuable to the Hunt.' She pauses, while my brain reels. 'It's useful to learn about this Hangman, and his involvement with the Hunt, and the wider implications of their plan. In essence, it is worse than any of us thought.'

She passes a lamp post and I hurry to stay apace with her, and make to pass the post on its other side. 'What kind of an immortal creature was he?'

But Diana seizes my arm roughly, pulling me over to the same side as her. 'Never pass a lamp post on its Other side!' she rasps, in exactly the kind of voice I would expect of someone who spent years as a cat.

'Why not?' Dimly, I remember Flux warning me of something similar. Ironically.

'Each side is a different realm,' she breathes, slowly unpeeling her fingers from my arm. 'To stay in the same one as each other, we must not pass into any Other sides.'

'Could have mentioned that before,' I mutter, grinding my jaw as she strides away again, clothes swirling in the ice dust, lit golden by the lamps.

We walk. My body aches, but the cold is bearable inside the cloak. I can't see a thing beyond the blurred edges of the road, the piles of old snow, and Diana, stalking forward with her hood up and her hands folded into her pockets.

'Wait.' Her dry mouth clacks against her teeth. She licks them clean.

The moment hangs like a drop of water.

'I don't know how much longer we can stay here,' murmurs Diana. 'If we walk too long, we will forget we're trying to escape. We will join an endless loop.'

I nod. My head feels clumsy. Pain still throbs in my forehead. The place of the tree's eye.

Ahead, a door appears, a cavernous tear in the night. It's half hanging off invisible hinges, a wound in the dark. When we pass through, it's into a hush, like the inside of a tomb.

'Where are –'

My voice is severed by the sound of someone weeping.

To our left is a staircase. To our right, a grandfather clock, tucked into the shadows, face filmed with dust. The sound of weeping is louder now, but it also sounds submerged. My ears feel full of fog.

We pass empty rooms, laundry rooms, a huge kitchen hanging with glinting silver.

The crying starts again.

Shadows gather towards me. I feel the shadow creatures waiting in my left fingertips begin to stir. I point at the larger mass of shadows, adding to them with my own, sculpting a monster of my own making.

Because that's the thing. Monsters are only to be feared if you're not the one controlling them. In the darkness, I feel my lips pull into a grin.

'Ooh,' says Diana, licking the dried blood off her chin. 'You *have* been busy.'

I step out of the hollow with a towering creature at my back, purring softly. It's a bit like the dragon I made in Flux's room, except this time it's more like a panther, prowling on heavy velvet paws, keenly scenting the air.

I was never fragile, and my intuition and judgement are strong. I might be quieter and smaller than the rest of my coven, and I might take longer sometimes to think things through, but now I know those things are strengths. They're valuable.

When I stop, the shadow creature stops. When I lift my chin and sniff the air, it does the same thing.

We pass a room where a group of faceless agents are assembling intricate mechanisms from shining pins and plates of bone. They're miniature aircraft, like the one that's been hovering outside the cloaking spell at the parlour, but smaller. 'So this is where it came from,' murmurs Diana, jaw hardening.

'It must have been sent through when the portals woke up,' I reply. Maybe because of Flux's ability to open them.

We walk through a set of double doors. My shadow creature growls. I find my own throat forming the same sound.

At the front of the room is the back of an enormous tapestry. It spans the entire width of the room, and almost the length of the floor to ceiling. It's the hunting tapestry

I saw behind the Hangman's throne, except now I'm on the Underside. It casts a sour smell and the threads glitter with a sense of threat, like visible black poison is coating every fibre. The scene it depicts is a battle. The scenes are so horrible I know that they'll invade my dreams for a while to come.

This side is the reality, not the false, outward-facing version. Spears and swords and blood and horses and anguish and mud, all throwing their startling realness into the hall. Witches, dead, littering the ground. Worse, the Underside of the tapestry is screaming.

My shadow creature breathes quietly at my back. I'm comforted by its bulk and calm strength.

Then I see them. The kid in a feather cloak, a thick tether snaking out between their shoulder blades and tying them to the tapestry. Flux.

They dart left and right, vanishing in and out of folds in time and place. Returning skin-soaked, or ice-bitten, or fighting off attacks by strange, winged beasts. The work never ends. Centuries of servitude, and I wish I could cut that cord that connects them to the tapestry.

Flux said the deal they made was to cheat death. But I wish I could make them understand that, although no one is ever ready for their death, when it comes it must be accepted. There is no other way – the situation they're in with the Hangman proves it.

A bell begins to toll the hour, a beat that vibrates inside

my chest, displacing the dominion of my own heart. Dizziness folds me over, but before the world falls away, a hand takes my elbow and holds me until my head clears. I find myself looking up into Diana's green eyes.

She straightens my beanie and draws my cloak closer about my shoulders. Her dark silken brows are knitted in urgency. 'Do you know of any other mirrors in this place? We must find one and dig a path out through its Underskin.'

24
A Croak in the Dark

'Why another mirror? Why not the one I was pushed through?'

'The spell was set in motion there,' she answers, with a pinch of impatience. 'We must close the circle by linking to another mirror. They are connected. Like waterways, often teeming with spirits.'

'I haven't seen any other mirrors.' My heart sinks. 'What if –'

'Positive thoughts only, Elspeth!' Diana forges ahead. 'We shall simply have to find one.'

We worm our way through the depths of the Underside of the Rookery. We're like leaves choking a drain, mud sticking to shoes, blood oozing from gums, mildew clinging to walls. Diana's eyes are bright in the grey hush. She slinks forth, tongue tasting the alien air. But at some point, her form begins to shift. Some moments she's a twisting vapour, other times a solid creature – but nothing close to a human shape – fur matted and battle-worn, betraying the hardships of exile from her woodland home.

Time stumbles forward and she's a wild rabbit, I scoop her up and feel her heart flickering against my fingers. I press my nose against her head, inhaling the scent of bloodied fur. Then she bleeds back into her human shape again, starting from the tips of the ears, and she stands next to me wearing a disapproving look as though nothing ever happened.

Eventually, we find another tunnel that Diana scrutinizes at length before she declares it worth investigating. It's even lower than the last tunnel, so we're forced to crawl through, elbows dragging us like scale-bellied serpents. It makes me think of Grael, and the disgusting things Tobias Barrow said about using and selling her blood.

I wonder what will happen if the Rookery dislocates again while we're in a mirror tunnel and if that would tear us out of the proper order of things for good. I dig my toes in and crawl faster, thoughts of Grael and Putch and the Ring fuelling me.

We find the Underside of a mirror that's covered in a dust sheet, in an attic full of the tumbled shapes of long-discarded things.

'I'm staying here,' says Diana. 'When you get through, put my collar on again. That should send me back. The summoning won't work again, after that is done.'

'But how will I get through?' I push against the Underside of the mirror, the blind surface rough and cold against my skin.

The light is eerily vivid. Diana steps towards me and opens

her mouth. She croaks a miaow directly into my face. It's a croak in the dark, a scratch against time, a carving out of a heart, a power word, garbled to cut away a chunk of reality and mould it into something different.

I shudder. I know – with a certainty that makes me feel a thousand years old – that she worked a spell. A complicated, ancient, forbidden spell.

The spidery code of the spell she breathed threads through my vision like the premonition of a faint. I sink to my knees.

The texture of the Underskin changes shortly after the spell flies.

And then it's a membrane, thick and blubbery, giving under my touch. I twist back to stare at Diana, and her hands are on her hips but her smile is wild and wicked and her brown silks and orange velvets and damp green eyes conjure images of battles fought between trees.

When I call her name, the Underside eats it whole, stealing it straight from my lips.

I stumble into the attic and freeze there, in the middle of the room. My breath is a telltale fog. The Rookery's rafters offer scarce shelter against the open sky. My shadow creature has evaporated into the barest dark mist, which scatters the harder I stare at it.

Old possessions clutter the space. I pick my way around them, anxious that if I put a foot wrong, I'll plunge straight through the floor. The Rookery's dislocations are regular, but

I have no idea how to predict them. Praying that one isn't about to happen, I make it to the door and open it, the hinges whining in a way that makes my teeth ache.

Diana's cloak has evaporated. But when I unfold my palm, the moon is there – Artemis's collar. I tie the collar around my neck again. I feel her presence sigh away, the barest perception of a loosening in the air. *Get home safe, please. And stay safe once you're there.*

Strange noises leach up through the Rookery – bellows, disjointed music, clattering, the creaking of huge jaws. The Dreadful Banquet. What if they devour the entire thirteenth moon?

I retrace my steps, back into the attic, and curl in a ball on the floor with several dust sheets piled on top of me like shrouds. I can't risk stumbling upon the banquet, and my body is much too weary to move any further. I'll rest, but only for a little while.

My dream takes me to a mountain.

'Spel,' crackles the voice, so ancient it feels like it throbbed from my marrow. 'It's time to wake up, now.' There's more than a hint of impatience in that voice. I know it. I open my eyes to see an ancient-looking, wildly joyful crone, with a scar in her throat in the shape of a crescent moon.

'Artemis?' I blink. 'I mean, Diana? What are you doing dancing around on top of a mountain?' I push myself upright, suddenly furious about how little I understand of the worlds. 'For that matter, what were you doing in the shape of a cat?'

She chuckles, low and rasping. 'As you can see, I do what I want. Old hags can have a lot of fun if they want to.'

'The monsters are angry at being kept in the dark. They drink the light,' she says, suddenly nervous.

'Aren't the monsters entitled to their share?' I counter.

The old woman smiles crookedly.

'Their home is a wasteland, now,' she says, a challenge gleaming in her eyes. 'Why would you fight for that world? Why bother?'

I gasp awake. The darkness has ripened around me like meat on bones. My dream beats the walls of my skull. *Why bother?*

I think of all the creatures still living in the world – my world – which they call the Drained Place, and the people there, even the Unwicked who never granted me an ounce of compassion. But even so, it's still my job to stand up for what's right.

I stand up and shake my limbs awake. When I think of my sister's sparkling black eyes, the life drumming through her veins and blooming on her quick tongue and in her strong feelings, the idea of a world drained of life is so wrong I want to scream.

Why bother?

'Because it matters,' I whisper, to the watching walls, the Rookery's bated breath..

25
Cunning Darlings

The Rookery is silent in the pre-dawn. I creep out of the attic and find that the building has dislocated again. The staircase has vanished, replaced by another on the ceiling, and the windows have moved to the side of the opposite wall. A ladder leans against the wall to my right, so that the staircase can be reached.

'How thoughtful,' I whisper sarcastically, to the surrounding air.

The ladder is made of bone, and my trainers ring against the hollow rungs as I scuttle upwards, stomach equally hollow. I put my head through the floor above and climb out, grabbing the banisters overhead and hauling until I'm flipped the right way up, the world tilting into place again. I'm about to take a step forward when warning bells clang inside my head and I stop just in time, foot hovering above the chest of a slumped, snoring creature. It's one of the attendees of the Dreadful Banquet, gorged to oblivion on rook eggs and moon meat.

My eyes trace the hallway ahead, noticing what I failed

to see before: multiple slumped beasts scattered at intervals, sleeping off the banquet's excesses.

I move as stealthily as possible, barely breathing, along the passageway, stepping over the sleeping forms, flinching at every movement in case one of them wakes up. I follow a stream of warm air and smells of baking, until a cavernous kitchen yawns open to the right, full of morning ritual. A great, bubbling cauldron of bone broth sits on a black iron stove.

I press myself flat against the wall, waiting for the right moment, and when the cooks' and servants' backs are turned, I reach around the wall and steal two plump little loaves and a clutch of boiled rook eggs from a basket, still warm.

I eat my thieved feast in the deep crook of a stairway, steeped in shadow, never taking my eyes off the steps on either side of me, or the balcony above.

Belly satisfied, I creep higher and tiptoe along the balcony, recognising the path to Flux's nest. I slip into the room. Flux is pacing restlessly across the floor.

'Things that hide in the darkness grow darker,' I say, permitting myself a small smile. I feel shadows gathering at my fingertips, remembering the bone structure of my panther, my dragon. Any creature I might imagine could be summoned by my rage in this moment. The rage belonging to the betrayal of a potential friendship that would have been the first to be mine and mine alone.

'I was going to get you out,' Flux whispers, tears streaming.

'I was sick with fretting when I realised you'd vanished.'

'When you realised I wasn't caged where you'd left me, ready for the Hangman to harvest?'

'No,' they gurgle. They drop their voice to nothing but a brush against the morning. 'I didn't think the tales about the Underside were true, but when you vanished, I thought you must have got lost somewhere I'd never be able to find you.'

'I fell for your lies before,' I spit.

Then the Rookery quakes with the roaring of the Hangman. '*Shadow child!* Where is my grimoire?'

Flux flinches. 'It's over for me, Spel,' they whisper, quickly. 'I want to get out of here. My bones are calling me. They are barrow-weary.'

'Are you really ready to leave?' I ask.

Eyes watering, chin set, Flux nods. 'I will help you escape. But before the moons rise tonight, I want you to cut my tether.'

'Fine. But you're going to follow *my* lead, and I'm keeping my shadows close.'

I build a gathering of thick, plush shadows that take the form of the panther again. It snarls at Flux, and as we set off, it stays close to my side. Flux's feather cloak brushes the walls, sloughing off little shadows that dance around in pools of darkness by our feet.

Since we met, Flux has done things to help me – like when they helped me escape the Rook King, or when they showed me how to speak to Shranken Putch in the courtyard. But a lot of times they've tripped me up, or lied to my face, or slowed me down. They're not to be trusted, so I make sure not to be the one that's following.

We tiptoe through the echoing corridors, glued to the darkness, avoiding any pools of light. Faceless men troop past, full of exhaustion and streaked with blue blood, carrying a stretcher laden with dark blue moon meat. We leap into an adjoining room, hiding until they've passed.

This time when the wooden front doors appear, I rush up and pull them open before any bells can ring. When it's as safe as it's going to get, we slip outside, into a windy morning laced with brine. Another storm is kicking up. Rookery Hollows is waiting for daybreak, and in the distance the twin flames of Lych and Screech are ablaze.

The moons are a lick of ebony across the grey-blue sky. The thirteenth is bleeding thick black dust that falls like charred snow all around us. 'They've eaten so much of it,' says Flux, shuddering.

We move through the ancient streets, and shutters bang closed as we pass. Whispers die, doors slam shut, distant figures hurry away. 'The people here are frightened,' says Flux. 'The Hangman has become a tyrant, and won't stop destroying the wild things.'

'He's going to come after us,' I whisper, twisting to look behind us.

'I know.'

The sun is slowly climbing up from the sea, gilding the bone towers of the College of Macabre Arts in pink gold. People will be waking up, soon. As the light strengthens, it slices through my shadow panther.

A great, dark swirling cloud of rooks bursts away from the Rookery. A distant bellow shakes eggs loose from the sprawling nest covering its front.

'He knows we've gone,' I hiss, starting to run.

'We have to hurry,' says Flux, keeping pace. 'Let's take a bone glider as far as the Snags – we can land on them.'

We find racks of the white contraptions stacked against a wall, just beyond the Lych and Screech rook gates. The gliders

are skinny bones glued together into lightweight frames. 'This is supposed to support our weight?' I ask, doubtfully. 'In the sky?'

'Yep. Everyone uses them. If the storm were stronger it wouldn't be safe, but we should be all right at the moment.'

Flux takes hold of one and presses a button in the side. A canopy of stretched leather shoots out of an opening in the front, and I understand. *Now* it looks like a device made for flying.

We climb a circular metal staircase inside the Lych gate, which leads us out on to a rooftop, crunchy with ice. The rising wind snatches at our clothes. When I blink, ice crystals move in the corner of my vision. We move to the edge of the rooftop, and Flux tells me we have to jump, on their signal. 'Now!'

We hold on to the glider, and jump. We catch the current. My shadow creatures rides it with us. The Snags rise like multicoloured hills in the east, and we aim our glider towards them. While we're gliding, my eyelids grow sticky with ice.

We land on top of one of the giant snail shells and fold up our glider, storing it with the others that are already there. But when we climb down a metal staircase on the outside of the shell, and step on to the track that leads through the pines to where the portal is, a figure with long, bendy legs appears on the path in front of us.

It's a man wearing a wide-brimmed hat and a long beige coat. He's carrying a briefcase that knocks against his leg. And he's got no face.

'They've already caught up with us!' I yell, into the wind.

'Head for the train station!' Flux tugs my arm and we race away from the figure, making for the shelter of the squat building to our left.

A dark green, gleaming steam train is chugging towards the station. More faceless men appear from behind the trees, bendy legs streaking after us in pursuit.

The train slows down. The faceless agent closest behind us quickens their step. They begin to fumble with the catch on their briefcase.

'Do you remember those sugar tongs, up in the tower?' shouts Flux.

'Yes!' I yell, against the wind. The faceless agent has drawn something out of their briefcase. It gleams inside their fingers.

The train station is only yards away. Instead of stopping, the train begins to pull away, gathering speed. 'Jump on to the train!' bellows Flux.

'What? No way!'

'Remember that sugar lump?' Flux presses. Then they trip. Something buzzes over their head, narrowly missing my shoulder. It hits the sign swinging from metal loops on the wall of the train station, and the sign –

Pops into nowhere.

Other folds. That's what's in their cases. Those creepily calm objects, with the power to fling things – or people – across worlds.

My shadow panther growls. The faceless agent begins to keen. At first I can't understand what they're saying. Then the storm winds carry the words into my ears. 'Cunning Darlings,' they gargle. 'Cunning Darlings.'

Flux scrambles back to their feet. The train puffs closer. More faceless men have swarmed on to the path behind us, singing and muttering and whining the same words, over and over. *Cunning Darlings Cunning Darlings Cunning Darlings*.

They start to run towards us, clutching the hats on their faceless heads. The running is a horrendous sight. A scuttle.

When the train passes by, we leap on to it, grabbing the metal railing for dear life. I'm half aware of my own screaming.

A bell rings, and the train gathers pace.

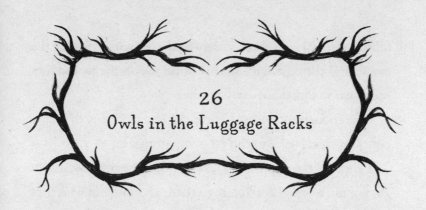

26
Owls in the Luggage Racks

The ground rushes underneath my kicking legs. My shadow panther dissipates into a mass of shadow pieces that whoosh back inside my fingertips. I summon all the strength my screaming muscles can muster, and haul myself up and over the railing. Flux is still hanging on, calling for help.

I shoot over to them and grab their arms, wrangling them over the side where they fall into a heap at my feet. A swarm of faceless agents are staring after the train. 'Come on!' I tell Flux, and we hurry through a door into a corridor that runs the length of the train. More doors in the corridor lead into compartments with seats, tables and luggage racks.

There are many different travellers on board – there are people in quivering, jelly-like forms, others covered in feathers or scales. One person reading a newspaper looks like a pile of rocks all glued together, with a pair of glasses at the top and boots at the bottom.

Some people have tiny animals sitting on their shoulders – black squirrels, grey mice or songbirds. We pass a compartment full of a family with great golden-feathered wings. Seeing the magic and the difference in this world makes me realise how much we've lost in my own.

The thought of failing to save the last wildness, there is a constant sickly ache in the pit of my stomach.

People watch inquisitively as we dash along the passageway. Part of me wishes I could talk to them and find out who they are and where they're going, and what magic they can work.

I watch snow-capped mountains through the windows. Forests and lakes stream past, filtered through the billowing steam from the front of the train. I pause for a moment, leaning my elbows on the cold brass railing running along the corridor. Then I see it.

Movement, like part of the mountain peeling away from itself. An icy limb of rock, streaking through the distance, making such an impact on the earth that the train rattles on the tracks as it passes.

Then, while I'm agog, we're past it and trees have crowded close, and all I can see of the mountains is the very peak.

'What *was* that?'

'Frost giants,' Flux replies. 'Keep going!'

We run most of the length of the train, and then I slide open the glass doors of a free compartment and fling myself inside, collapsing on to a green velvet seat. Flux stumbles in after me. Frost has skated across the window. However much I try to sit up straight I keep sliding towards it. The train curves through the landscape, leaning heavily to one side.

'Now what?' I hiss, balling up my fists and pressing them to my eyes. It's only now we've escaped the Hangman that I notice how, at some point, I must have been scared enough to bite my fingers – there are tooth marks around the knuckles.

'We have to find another portal,' says Flux. 'They're tucked away here and there, depending on where the Wayfaring Trees are.'

I stare at them, dully. I know it's because of them that we escaped the faceless men, but I still can't trust them.

'He promised true freedom,' says Flux, ashen-faced and not meeting my eye. 'After I trapped you in the mirror, I went to him and told him the deal was done. The grimoire had been found, after so much time. But he refused to honour the deal – I would never truly cheat death. I knew it, then. What I should have known all along. He was going to use me to plunder other worlds for the rest of time. None of it would ever stop.' Flux looks at me, then. Right into my eyes. 'When I've helped you find a portal, I'm going back. I'm going to find his Rook King's eye – the one that lets him see into all the worlds. The source of his power. And I'm going to destroy it.'

I don't really know what to say. 'If you can do that, maybe it'll stop your world turning into a drained one, like mine.' I stare around the compartment. From the luggage rack overhead, dozens of glowing eyes gaze back at me. My heart riots inside my ribs, until I realise they're owls, puffed up in the luggage rack, huddling together against the chill.

'Next stop, we get out,' says Flux. 'I know how to spot a portal. I've spent a very long time searching through them. *Don't* fall asleep.'

I glare. 'I don't think that's a risk!'

A lantern in the compartment squeals faintly as the train moves, and the owls resettle their feathers. Every time my eyelids grow heavy, I pinch my thigh.

I wake up sagged against the window, with a crick in my neck. Beyond the window is the glow of snow at dusk, the weight of watching trees. Remembering swoops over me like a bucket of blood from my head to my toes. Hideously, the train is not moving, and I have no idea how long we've been stopped here at a deserted train station in the middle of nowhere.

It's colder than ever. I tug my beanie lower over my ears and rub the tip of my frozen nose. The train is silent, and when I step out of the compartment to look, most of the other people have already left.

How could we have let ourselves fall asleep?

I nudge Flux and they wake up with a gasp, like returning

from death. When they look out of the window, they utter a curse. 'I'll be summoned when night falls. Quick!'

We step into the corridor and move towards the nearest exit. But a sound shifts into my awareness. The slightly dragging gait of someone walking along the floorboards behind us.

A voice is murmuring. When I turn to look, someone is standing in the middle of the passageway, a few compartments back. It's one of the faceless agents. They must have managed to jump on behind us.

Cunning Darlings, comes the whisper, laced with gruesome delight.

'Run!' I yell. We sprint for the door. A soft ruffle follows us as the owls in the luggage racks wake up and shake out their wings.

When I glance back, the faceless figure has reached out a hand and grabbed on to the back of Flux's cloak. 'Go!' they shout. 'Go, Spel!'

But I turn and scream at the faceless agent. 'Leave them alone!' I feel my shadows massing at my fingertips. I raise them at the agent and channel streams of shadow, until they take the shape of a screech owl.

My owl flies into the path of the faceless figure. Its wings brush the oval where their face should be, wingtips smearing away the blankness.

As the beginnings of a face emerge, the man sinks to his knees, uttering a hideous scream like a toad being tortured by a cat. From the feet up, he turns to a brittle red dust that blows out of the train door and dissipates.

'You freed him!' says Flux, voice full of wonder as they gape at me.

The train's engine begins to grumble, and a bell rings. The door shivers, then begins to close. 'Let's go!' I shout, jumping from the train on to the empty platform.

I blink. Snowflakes stud my eyelashes. Rays from an orange sunset filter across the tops of mountains in the distance. The train station canopy is festooned with rows of icicles that glitter like a jaw full of teeth. A huge, ancient yew tree stoops over the building.

Flux jumps from the train as the doors slam shut, trapping their cloak. I yank the feathers free, just as the train begins to chug away from the station, belching steam. We cross quickly through the station and cross the tracks.

'Where now?' I pant, as the sunlight fades from the sky and the moons set sail.

Flux smiles, pointing at what I thought was a puddle in the mud behind the station, reflecting the sky. Except it isn't reflecting the sky, because the sky is grey and the puddle is a brilliant, fresh blue. When I look at it – really look at it – there's also a barely perceptible shimmer. A membrane.

'Any portal will link to the Other Ways,' says Flux.

'Shadow, Bones, Flame, Frost, Fins,' I recite. 'And the Drained Place.'

Flux nods. They pull a small watch out of their pocket and flick the second hand backwards. The shimmer on the portal grows stronger.

'You've got a pocket watch, too!'

But instead of answering, they double over in pain. 'I'm summoned. Go! I'll search for the eye.'

'Good luck!' I call, and Flux flickers on and off like a light bulb in a storm, turns into an outline, then crackles out of the air right in front of me, leaving a faint smell of burning.

I'm left alone in the mud behind the train station, darkness unspooling like thick black ribbon around me. *Good luck.* What a daft thing to say. Apparently, even in times like this my social awkwardness is still a Thing.

I jump into the centre of the puddle. Time slows as I leap into the air, and the puddle expands as I fall towards it, edges spilling out to drink the world.

Then my feet sink through a cold, gelatinous blubber, and the earth gives way beneath me. The membrane slips over my face and I fall through a cave, walls woven through with bulbous tree roots.

Take me to the Drained Place, I think, keeping an image of my home locked firmly in my mind. I travel through twisting, twining, tumbling passageways, roots snaking through my hands and grasping across my skin. Memories spangle the backs of my eyes.

Bone gliders and bone broth, a storm in a tower. Diana adjusting my hat and miaowing into my face. The feeling of her spell threading through my mind. Egg eating noodles, laughing with her mouth full. Shranken Putch whispering that he's sorry.

I fall through the portal tunnel into a chamber with four glowing ovals on the wall. When I pick myself up off the muddy floor, I have to take gulps of air until the dizziness stops.

Then I scrabble for my pocket watch, flicking open the casing so hard that I rip my nail, and blood encrusts the glass face. I touch the second hand until it starts clicking backwards, and climb into the portal to reach home.

PART THREE:

UNRAVELLED

27
Hearse Music

I hang over the edge of the portal, calling for Grael. Nothing happens. My heart begins to thump too loudly in my ears. 'Grael?' Below me, the water is deep and thickened with soil, moss and slime. What if I'm already too late? Then the walls begin to vibrate, and the dragon shimmies through the water and rears up, eyes like shields and liquid gold.

I wriggle the rest of the way through, landing in a crumpled heap on her back.

'No time to explain,' I gasp. 'But I'm so glad to see you!'

Likewise, witch-ish one.

'Grael, stay away from the main well,' I tell her, urgently. 'Can you find a tunnel to hide in?'

Her teeth chatter, making a *click-purr-ripple* sound. *Yes. But should you need me, I will come.* She delivers me up to the top of the well and I climb the stone lip, dripping well water on to the floorboards.

Then I pause, jaw growing slack.

The basement is in ruins. The hole Sunken Putch came

out of has been dug outwards, until most of the floor is a mess of torn floorboards and splinters. He must still be looking for the ring. I pat my pocket, feeling the metal circle through the material.

I step cautiously through the ripped wood and clumps of plaster and general dirt and disarray. As I'm passing the main hole, I notice a thick vine that climbs out of the pit and stretches across the floor. I follow it out of the room and find Sunken Putch on the stairs that lead to the ground-floor hallway, snarling and scrabbling. He's started pulling up the floorboards out here, too.

'What're you doing?' I ask.

He jolts, turning to face me, skin taut with fury and urgency. 'You! Witch! Where is it?'

'You can't leave the place where you took root,' I tell him. 'Your tether won't let you. Not unless the pact is properly enacted. And it will not be.'

He snarls, straining against the vine that's plugged into his back, connecting him to the hole in the basement. The tether was invisible when he first appeared. I rush up the stairs two at a time, and he lunges for me, pulling me backwards by my sweatshirt. I scream, and a face appears at the top of the stairs.

'Spel!' Diana bursts into a cloud of vapour and gusts into the face of the Putch, making him screech and fall backwards. When his grip on me weakens, I'm propelled forward. I trip on the stairs, flying into the hallway above.

There's a tiny, metal clink.

I scramble on to my knees and stare down the stairs. The ring fell out of my pocket. It's lying on the second to last step, and Sunken Putch sees it at the same moment I do.

Diana solidifies again, crouched on the steps between us. I dart forward, and so does Sunken Putch, but Diana blocks him and I reach the ring first, snatching it into my fist.

Diana sweeps me backwards into the hallway and we watch as Sunken Putch hisses and wrings his hands, hurling all the curses under the sun.

'That behaviour won't help anyone,' chides Diana.

I put the ring back in my pocket and start to thank Diana when the whole parlour quakes, and plaster and horsehair rain down from the ceiling. 'No time, Spel!' she yells, diving into the sitting room.

Egg, Layla, Isla and Mariam stand in a circle with their backs pressed together, shouting commands to each other. 'Eleven o'clock!' yells Layla, and the whole circle rotates, each witch unleashing a bolt of power in whatever form they can – Isla releases a burst of flame, Mariam a strangling vine. Layla is obviously focusing her power on predicting where an attack will come from. Egg struggles under the weight of using her telekinetic power to shove the aircraft away from the parlour. Sweat pours down the sides of her face.

Directly outside the window, a crowd has gathered, bellowing for witch blood. I stare for a moment at the shining bone aircraft, knowing now that it started life in a room at the Hangman's Rookery, built by the faceless agents before being sent through the portal to spy on us.

Rats wriggle through holes in the walls, thunking to the floor. But the clews swoop around the room in several tower formations, screeching and chasing them.

'Annie and Jameela?' I ask, in a low voice, so as not to distract the others.

But Diana shakes her head. 'They've still not returned.'

I chew my lip, trying not to think too much about what that might mean, right now. 'I know how to stop all this,' I tell her. 'I have to get to Arundel Castle. It's where Shranken Putch is. If I give him the ring, he'll become the Putch again. And they won't be able to destroy this place if the pact is honoured.'

Diana looks impressed. 'That castle is not far away.'

'But it might already be too late,' I tell her, honestly.

'Don't think it, Spel. Just do. I will go with you.'

'You can't,' I tell her. 'You have to stay here and help the others.' But then I wonder. 'Unless . . .' I move to the middle of the sitting room, where the floral furniture is upended and the lampshade is spinning wildly.

'Spel?' shouts my sister. Her hair is stuck to her flushed cheeks, and her eyes are flashing bright. 'You're back! Did you find him?'

'Long story!' I shout back, over the noise of the aircraft

and the crowd beyond the window. 'There's more to do. But I want to try something first.' I think about the Hunt, and the Hangman, and their greed. I think about how we all spent so many years locked in a school for Wicked Girls, when all the while the Hunt planned to steal our magic for themselves. I think about the fact that years and years ago, a great forest grew on this spot, and many wondrous creatures lived here, before they were wiped out or displaced. The middle of my forehead burns. I let the pain strengthen me. I let it help me see.

I let it all fuel my rage. As my rage grows, the shadows swell, starting as a painful itch at my fingertips, and spreading outwards from my body, until a dense bulk of darkness hangs over my head and fills the space around and behind me.

'*What* is that?' Isla splutters. I almost laugh.

I lift my hands and charge my shadows at the windows, and imagine my power swirling all around the parlour, cloaking and concealing. Soon, we're wrapped in a silent cocoon. The wrathful noises from outside have been doused.

I whip round to face the others. 'It's only a plaster,' I tell them. 'It won't last. But I wanted to do something to help before I have to go again. I need to take Diana with me.'

Egg nods. 'I trust you, Spel. I know you can do whatever it is you have to do.'

Mariam grins. 'We'll be waiting. When they start breaking through again, we'll hold them off.'

Isla looks at me. Really looks, like maybe she never has before. 'You've changed, Spel.'

I shake my head. 'This was always me. I just needed to learn to believe in myself.'

Layla beams. 'And other people needed to learn to listen.'

'There's so much I have to tell you!' I yell, darting into the hallway with Diana. 'You won't believe any of it!'

Cloaked in shadow, I follow Diana out the back door and along to where the hearse is parked. From our right, the trees of the Ring bend towards us, more fruit ripening on their branches. Dredging up who-knows-what from the burial mound. Rain begins to fall. 'You can *drive?*' I splutter.

Diana narrows her eyes at me, and utters a small but distinct hiss. 'Of course I can drive. *That's* the skill you're most surprised by?'

Fair point. 'How are we going to get past them unseen?' I ask.

'We're not,' she tells me, wearing a resigned expression. 'If we don't succeed, staying hidden won't matter any more. And maybe we'll lead some of them away from the parlour.'

'What happened to *positive thoughts only?*'

She glowers at me, fires up the engine and sure enough, there are shouts of dismay and surprise. She takes the handbrake off and we bomb down the driveway and on to the path into the village, pursued by yelling villagers.

I watch in the wing mirror as the aircraft swivels in the air.

'We have to hurry! I think that thing is going to come after us.'

Diana drives us to Arundel in the hearse, through all the narrow back roads, trying to get there fast but throw off anything that might be following. We both know they will follow, though. The Hangman will realise I've escaped by now, so maybe he'll tell the Hunt what I am.

Diana's driving is awful. She hunches over the wheel, pushing her glasses up her nose. Thick rain. Smeary, creaking wipers. Freezing old car. Dark, dark roads. She presses a rectangle into a machine on the dashboard, and weird old chanting music flows out of two dusty speakers – who knew the hearse could play music?

It's a strange sort of choir music, haunting and monotonous. It loops round and round. 'How is it doing that?' I ask.

'It's a tape, Elspeth.' She glances sidelong at me. 'Putch likes Gregorian chant,' she tells me, as though that explains something.

'I have no idea what any of that means.'

'It's not really worth explaining.' She's sitting so close to the windscreen that her nose is almost pressed against the glass. 'Oh my god, I can hardly see a thing. And I'm still not used to having hands. Is your seat belt on?'

'That's reassuring.'

She grins, like a flash of light in the dark. Then, as the car rattles down country lanes, she begins to tell me the story of the Muddlewood demons.

The demons – once Muddlewood spirits – fought alongside the witches. When the Hunt prevailed they were forced to lie low, slipping in and out between the realms, lying panting beneath shrinking woodland and hedgerows. Trying to reach their kin, but not knowing how to begin. Where to look. Your father was one such being.

The bond was being stretched. But it could never be broken. The heartbreak waited in the way some witches began to forget. The ache came from witches always feeling like they'd forgotten something, on account of their stolen heritage.

It was like the rending of the forest again, when all the spritely creatures were forced into ditches and scattered loose on to towpaths and into the mist clinging to the underside of bridges. There is more than weather in those places.

The wild places shrank, and shrank.

We are all like two sides of the same coin. We cannot fully expand our lungs without the Others.

28
Only Witches and Demons

The journey to the castle is treacherous. We hurtle through the rain, the wipers groaning and the ancient heating system cranking out intermittent gusts of vaguely warm air. I pull a blanket from the back seat and swaddle myself in it.

Half an hour later, the hearse slides over a bridge and Arundel Castle is revealed to our right; golden grey and sprawling up and down the hills, crenellations like teeth in a dragon's jawbone.

Arundel is a small, sleepy town nestled among hills and woodland, and brushed through by a fast river. Diana parks the hearse at the bottom of the main street, and we fleet-foot up the hill towards the castle, through wreaths of mist and a fine drizzle. No one is around. The windows have lamps lit. 'Only witches and demons are abroad on nights like this,' murmurs Diana. 'And cats,' she adds, when a pair of eyes glow at us from the gutter.

I shiver. 'Just as well. I don't want any Unwicked to find us before we even get to the castle.'

Before we reach the top of the hill, my socks are wet and my hat is soaked. We pause in the doorway of a shuttered shop, staring up at the castle. It looks like a slumbering beast. 'They're in there, aren't they?' I whisper. 'The Hunt.'

Diana's nostrils flare. 'They are. They have held this seat for centuries, Elspeth.' She turns to me. 'You need to understand that if we enter that castle, we might not come out again.'

Fear grips me, but there's another feeling, too. A thing like relief. I know what to do, now. There's no going back. And if we fail, at least we'll have stood up for what's right. 'I know,' I tell her. 'But we have to try.'

Diana smiles, gently. 'We do.'

At the top of the hill, we pass through iron gates and into the castle grounds. We stick to the edges of a wide path that leads us closer, until the castle hulks above us, windows glittering.

'Portcullis is up,' muses Diana, sniffing the air. 'Drawbridge is down.'

'What does that mean?'

'Well, it means that technically we could stroll right in through the main entrance. But that doesn't seem right, does it?'

I see what she means. We pause, the trees in the castle grounds shivering around us. 'Why would the castle be lying open like this?'

'I don't know,' says Diana, taking another step forward, then halting again. 'But I don't like it.'

I nibble my lip. Maybe they're expecting someone.

'Come on,' says Diana, glancing behind us and then running down into a deep bowl that runs around the castle. 'Into the moat. Let's walk round to the back and find a subtler way in.'

As we steal along the moat bed, I notice a taint in the air. There's a cloud of malice hovering over the castle, like flies. 'There's something rotten here,' I whisper. 'I can feel it. It's horrible.' There's such a bad feeling in this place that a wave of anguish rolls through me.

'Yes, indeed there is,' says Diana, reaching out to place a steadying hand on my arm. 'You need to put up a defence against it, Spel. Try not to let it weaken you.'

I think of the cloaking spell and I think of my shadows, and take a deep breath before passing my hands in front of my face, clearing the air away and replacing it with a layer of magic. It makes me feel protected. The strength it gives me reminds me of what we're here to do.

We can't let them kill all the magic throughout the Ways.

Witches have a unique bond with the living world. It makes me rage to think of all the ways they've controlled us for so long.

Diana's silks stream in the mist, and she flows fluid as a ghoul that's been walking this moat for a thousand years. 'I could make a light,' she breathes, 'but I think it's safest not to.'

'I agree,' I mutter. So we inch forward in thick darkness, led by the faint shine of the castle's windows. The moon is a fingernail scratch in the velvet sky.

A tower erupts from the darkness to our right. Diana says it looks like the old castle keep. It has open, narrow windows she says are arrow-slits. We carry on, until Diana holds up a finger. 'I think we should leave the moat now,' she whispers.

The night is still. Mist clots the air, but the rain has stopped and there's no wind. We struggle up the steep moat side and trudge across the grass towards part of the castle that would be hidden from the front.

We crouch in a muddy ditch next to the enormous stone foundations. Up ahead is a wooden door in a wall lined with large windows. 'Where might someone be entombed?' I whisper.

'We need to find the oldest part of the castle,' Diana whispers. 'Now move like a shadow.'

'No problem,' I tell her, pushing a wave of shadow around us, which blends into the night. We use it as cover to streak across the ground towards the door.

It's locked. I glance around, then brew a curl of shadow on my fingertip and send it twining through the keyhole, grinning when it unlocks with a metal clunk.

'Show-off,' whispers Diana. She presses the iron handle, and the door whines open. We slip into a cold corridor.

We move through multiple dark rooms with shuttered windows and more closed doors, sitting rooms and bedrooms and dressing rooms, before emerging on to a landing. The stairs have suits of armour standing on them, and when we reach the lower floor, the walls are lined with tapestries. I hurry past them, shivering.

The stairs open on to a long, panelled passageway, which we follow until we reach another flight of stairs, into an armoury full of vicious-looking weapons: spears, longswords, more suits of armour, daggers, and shields. Diana reaches out and claims a dagger the colour of a storm cloud, twirling it in her fingers.

'Do you really need that?' I ask.

'It's pretty,' she replies, fangs hooking over her lip.

The next room is a long, lamplit library panelled in wood and furnished in crimson red. We whisk along it – and by now this place is really freaking me out, because not only is this a medieval castle at night but there is *no one here*.

I was expecting a fight. A struggle. Noise. Something.

We reach the other end of the library and pause on a short landing. Diana snatches a breath. 'Wait.'

'What is it?' I whisper.

Her limpid green eyes move to my face. 'Can't you hear that?'

There's a metal vent in the bottom of the wall to our left, and a thin sound is ebbing through it. I crouch and put my ear close to the wall. It's the sound of quiet weeping.

I put my mouth near the vent. Diana warns me with a

look, but I shake my head. This is something I have to do.

'Hello?' I call, into the metal slats. 'Who's there?'

The weeping pauses. Then sniffling, scratching, the sound of shifting limbs.

'Hello?' I say, again, frustration bubbling inside me. And fear.

There's a gasp. Then a startled voice floats out of the vent and into my ears.

'Spel?'

29
We Wunt Be Druv

'*Jameela?*' I hiss, hardly daring to believe.

Diana's mouth falls open. She drops into a crouch next to me.

'Spel!' floats Jameela's voice again. It's full of pain and horror. 'Spel, listen to me. You need to get out of this place.'

'No, I'm here to find Shranken Putch! I'm here with – um –' I pause, wondering how to explain.

Diana takes over. 'She's here with me, Diana, the demon formerly known as the cat, Artemis.'

Another pause. 'I've heard weirder things,' sniffles Jameela, through the vent. 'You should know – when they find you, they will make you suffer. Draining magic is a sport to them.'

'Where is Annie Turner?' asks Diana.

'I don't know,' drifts Jameela's exhausted voice. 'She was here, with me. But then they took her.'

'Listen,' I say, urgency flaring inside me. 'Where are you? We're going to find you and get you out of here.'

'Seriously, Spel, it's over –'

'Just tell me!' I bite my lip to keep my words from becoming a shriek. People need to stop telling me to give up.

'I'm in the dungeons,' whimpers Jam, voice wobbling, bravado melting away. 'Please come quickly!'

Diana decides that we need to get down to the very guts of the castle, and that there must be servants' stairs that we haven't found yet. We cross the landing and descend into the grandest room I've ever seen in my life. It's a long, elaborately decorated hall.

Two enormous hearths dominate the space, with rugs in front of them made from the skins of tigers. I shudder to see them, with their eternal snarls, their glassy eyes.

The ceiling is cavernous and hung with glass lanterns. The windows are arched and draped in voluminous silk. A banquet table stretches most of the length of the hall, set with shining silver platters and fine crystal glassware. And high on the far wall, heavy black curtains cling to the stone like a bat.

The curtains swing open, to reveal a tapestry. Diana hesitates, then presses forward. '*Hurry*, Spel.'

But the tapestry shows the inside of another hall, that's a lot like this one, except in the centre of the weaving is a black throne, with jagged edges made from bone and wing, feather and shell. A man sits on the throne, peering at us as though he's living.

I stop dead in the middle of the hall, breath tattered, wrapping my arms around myself. 'Diana,' I call out, feebly.

She's still striding on ahead.

'Diana!'

She stops, turns, gapes at me. 'What are you doing?'

'We shouldn't have come this way,' I protest, glancing around us. 'We're completely exposed.' I don't know what makes me say it. There's no one in here. But I know the man in that tapestry. Goosebumps spread across my skin.

This is all wrong.

'Don't worry,' whispers Diana, taking my arm to pull me along. 'Just be quick.'

But we're not quick enough.

Double doors snick open at the far end of the hall. A procession sweeps in two by two, stamping against the wooden floor. They're draped in long black or crimson robes, and the women wear high round bonnets, black as Other moons.

Mistresses, like the ones who ruled at the school for Wicked Girls, where my friends and I were lied to and made to believe we were sinful, just for existing. They truly believed in our Wickedness, too. But they also wanted to steal our magic for themselves.

The procession splits into two and fans out, surrounding us. Diana stands close to me, still gripping my arm.

At the end of the procession, two men are left in the doorway. They step forward, grinning sharply. Tobias Barrow the Witchfinder General, and the man with neatly parted red hair who came hunting for us at the tea shop in Knuckerhole village. The rat man.

'My, my,' calls Tobias, voice ringing with authority across the grand space. 'What a merry dance you lead us on, Elspeth Wrythe.' He gestures to the red-haired man. 'May I introduce my brother, James Barrow?'

'Charmed,' says James, cruel laughter playing around his mouth.

Diana squeezes my arm tighter. 'This place is coated in stolen magic,' she murmurs, close to my ear. I notice it almost at the same moment – the tapestry curtains opened by themselves, and behind the Barrow brothers, the doors swing shut without anyone moving.

'It's rude to whisper,' challenges Tobias. 'Demon.'

She pulls back her lips and hisses at him.

'Come now,' says James, malice carving his face into an imitation of delight. 'Let's be civilised.' He clicks his fingers, and two greasy black rats fall out of his pockets, racing along the floor. As they reach us, they turn into high-backed chairs. We topple backwards into them, straps binding themselves over our wrists. The arms of the chairs are slick with oily fur.

Tobias and James prowl towards us and take seats at the banquet table. Then Tobias smoothes his hands through the air, and the tapestry threads begin to twitch with life. 'This is my family's finest example of a fourteenth-century tapestry,' says Tobias, eyelids flickering.

'Elite witch-hunting families have been passing tapestries down, generation after generation, for centuries. Making sure they stay haunted with the spirits of their ancestors,' confides James, eyes misty.

'Making sure they keep stealing witches' power?' bites Diana.

'Sometimes,' says James, smirking. 'Other times they let us communicate in ways we never would have been able to before discovering how to steal magic.'

Tobias inhales deeply, as though smelling something delicious. 'It's incredible to think that once, people didn't really believe that witches had power. What a feat we Barrows have accomplished. Make everyone Unmagical believe witches are Wicked, while draining their magic for our own.'

The tapestry develops a waxy sheen. 'That's not something to be proud of!' I snap.

The brothers look at each other, then wrinkle their noses and begin to snicker.

The Hangman's rook throne squirms, broken feathers gleaming in the lantern light of another world. 'Witchfinder,' growls the Hangman.

'Yes, sire,' answers Tobias, standing and folding into a bow. 'Have you obtained the Shadow-Born?' he demands.

Beside him, the Rook King resettles his feathers.

'I have, sire,' confirms Tobias, nodding across to me. 'A slippery thing she proved to be, once again. But I have her. And my Huntsmen also continue to break through the defences at the Ring.'

The Hangman speaks. 'She is more than you know. She is a grimoire. Her blood sings with the power to create or destroy. It descends from the Muddlewood itself. Her marrow remembers the magic of that place. She is worth ten times any dragon. But remember – I am the one who discovered this. She belongs to me.'

Tobias and James peer across the table at me, and the silent Mistresses and Huntsmen around the hall begin to shift and whisper among themselves. I know they all want to crack my neck and sup the blood that wells there. The knowing makes my insides crawl.

The Hangman told them, because he knew I'd escaped him. He wanted to keep me for himself, but this way he can still control my fate and claim a portion of the magic in my bones.

'What of the witch you were having trouble with?' rasps the Hangman.

Tobias curls his lip. 'She's gone.' An unreadable expression crosses his face, before he composes it again. 'She won't be troubling us again.'

'Good,' says the Hangman, grimacing.

What witch? Does he mean Annie?

Diana mutters to me out of the corner of her mouth. 'Spel, I'm going to try something.' She begins to transform, body thinning to a waifish mist, but then – she solidifies again, abruptly, screaming in pain. A burnt, acrid smell filters through the air.

'Oh no, you're not!' says James, cheeks burning red with excitement.

Diana sags in her chair, whimpering.

'What did you do to her?' I yell. I lift a finger and channel a stream of shadow towards the Barrows. But in a blink the shadow is whipped back inside me with a pain like someone's taken a hammer and nail to my bare bones.

A howl of agony bursts from my lips.

'I wouldn't try anything else if I were you, little grimoire,' breathes Tobias, greedily. Then he turns his gaze back to the tapestry. 'We will drain the last witches in this world. We will take that dragon. We will break the pact, and then we will have so much more – we will access the Other Ways, and open trade with you, sire. We shall finally sit down to table together.'

The Hangman grunts his pleasure. 'Moon meat and more shall be yours to consume,' he gravels.

Tobias Barrow stands and walks slowly over to my chair. 'You brought it to me, didn't you, shadow child? You brought me the ring.'

He leans down and wrenches the pact ring from my pocket, and I catch the scrubbed lavender scent of him, underlaid with the rusty smell of old blood. 'No!' I scream.

Then he tosses the ring to James. 'Take it back to that wretched hovel, and finish what we started,' he snarls.

But there's a twist in the air that makes the room bend around us for a moment. It hurts my brain. Then the room relaxes and the ring flies out of James's fingers, pinging across the floorboards and landing near the hall doors.

'What's going on?' barks Tobias, balling his hands into fists.

Do not linger too long at the Liminal, witch-hunters, floats a voice.

I meet eyes with Diana. That was Annie's voice. But we can't see her.

'Are you scared yet?' I whisper up at the Witchfinder. Tobias blinks slowly, and then raises his hand to hit me. But I feel a sharp tug on the back of my chair.

I'm dragged backwards across the shiny floor, banging into the wall on the opposite side of the hall. Mistresses and Huntsmen yell, scattering out of the way.

Advanced craftiwork. It's like when Annie pulled me away from the Liminal, back at the Ring. How is she doing this? And – I feel a wild grin pull at my mouth – when can she teach me?

I glance around, but she's still hidden. Annie's voice

filters into my head. *Use your wits, Elspeth Wrythe.*
The straps covering my wrists slacken, and as I pull free, the
chair underneath me turns back into a rat.

The Liminal. She's here, somewhere. Behind a veil, like
the cloaking spell. When I was trapped in the Underside, the
Hangman said I was like a rat in the pipes.

That's what Annie's like now, in the castle.

Before I can draw another breath, Diana's chair is dragged
back from the table and her own binds have been undone.
She leaps up, rubbing her wrists and licking her teeth. 'You
have made a mistake toying with me,' she purrs, glaring at the
Barrows.

I scan the floor until I spot the quiet circle of gold and
bolt across to it, scooping the ring up and putting it back in
my pocket.

The brothers are glancing left and right, muttering things
to each other and cursing. I point at them. 'I thought you
didn't have to worry about that witch any more?' I mock.

Tobias takes a step towards me, and I notice the gleam of
something sharp in his palm. But then a gurgling sound of
distress throbs from inside the tapestry.

We watch the scene play out in agitated thread.

A troop of faceless agents emerges from the shadows
surrounding the Hangman. They advance, opening their
briefcases. He twitches, barking orders. But they're whispering
the words, over and over, that I never wanted to hear again.

Words that no one would ever want to hear.

Cunning Darlings. Cunning Darlings. Cunning Darlings.

'What are you doing?' he shouts, desperation creeping across his face.

Someone appears behind him.

'Flux!' I yell, unable to stop myself.

They hold something aloft. 'You'll never summon me, ever again!'

The Hangman goggles, flailing in his rook throne.

'Because look what I found,' says Flux. Inside their fist is an eyeball, dripping wet. 'Found it in the well water under the Wayfaring Tree.' Flux is triumphant, cheeks stung with glee. 'Your Rook King's eye! You can no longer see into Other worlds. Your power is *done*. Your agents will devour you! The raindrops have already fallen. Now you fall.'

The Rook King lifts off its pedestal and barrels for Flux, but they shoulder the great bird away, though it rakes their cloak into tatters. A mass of rooks circle over Flux and the Rook King. Flux holds a hand aloft, and the birds dive, attacking the eye.

They carry it away, pulling it to pieces between them.

The agent nearest the Hangman reaches into his case and brings out a shining object – a small, metal spring. Except I know better. I know it is only pretending to be that. It is a creepily calm object. A cunning darling. The agent flings it at the Hangman, and before he even has time to scream, he vanishes.

Crack. There one moment, the next, gone.

Then the agents disintegrate into piles of red dust that scatter into the air. And the tapestry begins to unravel.

'Do something!' screams James Barrow, to the rows of people around the walls.

The Huntsmen and the Mistresses begin to advance on us.

I send shadows crawling across the hall. I craft heavy paws for them; long, tapered claws, and jaws full of teeth. I make the shadows tower over everyone, and when I raise my hand and take a swipe, my shadow creatures do the same, knocking over a row of Hunters like they're skittles.

A rush of malignant energy, like a swarm of hornets, furies out of the hunting tapestry. The threads sag afterwards, empty, and it looks like what it should, finally – a centuries-old weaving, faded by light. It continues to unravel.

Diana bursts into a cloud of vapour and spirals through the hall, changing form long enough to win a fight and burst back to vapour again. She does this repeatedly. Finally, she bursts up to the ceiling like a flock of birds, and cuts one of the crystal lanterns away from its fitting. It crashes to the ground and sends people screaming away. Annie, the hidden witch, continues to fight as well.

'Show yourself!' screeches Tobias Barrow, but she does not obey.

She does, however, take a moment to appear behind me, whispering through a seam in the air. *I'll get Jameela.*

You find Putch. Look in the chapel, out in the grounds. I'll find you there.

As I'm sprinting back through the hall, cloaked in shadow, a group of people burst through the hall doors. I twist to look back, and let out a whoop of joy – it's the four sarcastic pallbearers and the coffin-makers who have worked with Putch for years, and a big group of villagers. The villagers are wearing the clothes of the Hunt, but they throw off their cloaks and bonnets as they cry the words my soul dances to hear.

'We wunt be druv!' call the people. 'We will no longer be bystanders to your tyranny!'

Not all Unwicked hate witches. Some of them have turned up to fight with us.

30
Stolen Magic Will Decay

The old chapel is flanked by yew trees. Ditchlings straggle across the ground towards me, groaning and reaching out with hands dripping in mud and slime.

I think they want to help me. I'm suddenly glad I never had a chance to ask Flux more about how to stop a haunting. 'Thank you!' I task them with patrolling the entrance to the chapel.

They stand guard while I race inside, past rows of tombs and statues of knights. My boots pound loudly over gravestones in the floor, and I keep stopping, heart in mouth, looking over my shoulder. But no one comes.

I stop at a tomb that is incomplete, but growing very, very slowly as I watch: grey stone knitting into place over the top of a person locked into the floor.

Being entombed.

His face is still and the skin is slack, his hair is wild and his eyebrows even wilder, and as I stand there, calling for him, his eyes snap open.

'Shranken Putch!' I kneel by his side, trying to dig the encroaching stone away from his cheeks, but it's no use.

'You really came looking for me,' he croaks, face a picture of amazement. He spits out a mouthful of grave dust and soil. 'No one has ever done that for a Putch. Most people forget about us.'

I laugh through my tears. Every moment with the grumpy old thorn filters through my mind. Hot chocolate in the kitchen. Weird odds-and-ends dinners. Spats with Artemis. Finding extra clothes and blankets for me and Egg, and teaching us everything he knows, and everything he knows about *us*. Hiding us from the Hunt even when his home and his dragon were at risk. He's as unique as an individual day or night, however many others there are. 'How could anyone forget you?'

I pull the ring from my pocket. A shine winks around its inside. Then I take Putch's hand, pushing the gold circle on to his finger. The entombment falls away like melting ice.

He stands, all limbs and eyebrows, and steps out of his tomb, quizzing me with his darkly silver eyes. 'I feel the Ring calling me,' he says.

But then a kid with a bundle of dark blonde hair and dusky blue eyes and a creature in their top pocket bounds between the tombs towards us. 'Flux!' I notice the scratches all over their face and neck, the bruises and the exhaustion as thick as their feather cloak.

Dawn light filters through the chapel windows. Shranken Putch turns his face to the warmth, a whiskery smile tracing his features.

But when Flux steps closer to me, I wish they hadn't come back. I remember when they told me they wanted me to cut their tether, and now that it's time I really wish I didn't have to.

'You told me you've never, ever met another Shadow-Born witch,' I whisper, around the lump in my throat. 'What if I never do, either? What if it's only ever going to be just us two?'

'If that's true,' they whisper, grinning, 'then wasn't it marvellous that we ever met at all?'

'It was,' I concede. 'You did an amazing thing back there, by the way. You found the courage to stop a cycle of hurt from going on and on.'

'And you saved so many magical beings from being drained. The barrow where you live will not be plundered now, either. It is where my ancient bones lay. It is where I will return, if you will help me.'

Diana drops into the air next to us, solidifying from a vapour as she does so. She stares from Shranken Putch and back to me, agog. 'You actually did it,' she whispers.

'Of course she did,' gruffs Putch. 'But she didn't tell me she'd taken the moon bind off. What menacing have you been up to, Diana of the Muddlewood?'

'Good to see you too, old thorn,' she replies, tartly.

Flux laughs. 'You have a good home to go back to, Spel.' They pull a small leather book out of their pocket, with browned, torn pages. 'Look – I found it, my Book of Shadows! I took it back!'

I meet Flux's eyes through a haze of tears. 'He never should have taken it. I'm so sorry you were trapped like that.'

'Cut the tether, Spel,' Flux breathes. 'Let me go to my grave, once and for all.'

Diana passes me a shining dagger. It's the one she took from the armoury. It glitters as the sunrise touches the stained glass, spilling rainbow gold across the hall.

I reach between Flux's shoulder blades and saw through the nub of tapestry thread that survives there. Within moments, I can see the floor through their limp body. They're fading so fast.

'Look around you,' whispers Flux, smiling gently as their shape disintegrates and scatters like dust. In the end, their voice is a half-heard trace on the air. *You are loved.*

Startled, I glance up and the truth of what they said hits me in the chest. Diana and Shranken Putch look back at me, worry moulded to their faces. Other people love me, too.

Who did Flux have?

I rock back on my heels, tears streaming. On the floor in front of me is a small pile of feathers, so old that when I pick one up, it falls apart. And buried among the feathers is the skeleton of a small creature. Grenwald, Flux's only friend, lost to time like so much else. But finally at rest.

'How very cosy.' Tobias Barrow limps along the rows of tombs and statues. But then he notices Shranken Putch, standing free of the tomb. Putch fixes Tobias with a silvery glare.

The Witchfinder stares around him, then shrieks as a grey calcification begins to crawl, slowly, along his arms.

'Stolen magic will decay, Tobias,' calls Putch, gravelly voice ringing out against the chapel's thick walls. 'There is a price. It is you who must pay.'

'No, no!' blurts the Witchfinder, eyes wild. 'This isn't how it was supposed to be!'

I think of all the witches tortured by him, all the magic leached away, used for evil.

All the betrayal. All the loss. All the pain, the fear, the deadening of feeling, the destruction of nature. All for their greed.

'Once, we were witches with roots in our soles, mud beneath our nails, songs imprinted on our hearts and mouths,' I tell him. 'Once, we were honoured for our knowledge and once we understood the voice of our homelands and the creatures dwelling there. Once, we shared kinship with peonies and owls, the muddy banks of rivers and the little crabs there, and the slow worms coiled in the earth.'

Shranken Putch takes up the incantation. 'Once, all the

other knuckerholes in Sussex weren't empty. Their water dragons dwelled there, and people paid their respects, sighing wishes and coins into well water.'

'The old Hunting families have hunted us for generations,' says Diana. 'But no longer.'

The grey scaly growth has spread all over Tobias Barrow, and now it slips up his neck and across his face, graceful as a thief. 'You'll be bound, now,' I tell him, as he staggers sideways, and the flagstones splinter and reach up to join the entombment. 'Never to do harm again.'

Outside the chapel in the early morning light, Annie hurries up to us, helping Jameela limp across the ground. Her head is lolled against Annie's shoulder.

'Will she be okay?' I ask.

'Course I will, Spel,' she grumps, and relief floods through me because she sounds exactly like her usual self. 'Can we just get out of here, please?'

'*Definitely*,' I reply.

We hobble down through Arundel and find the hearse, folding a shaky Shranken Putch into the front passenger seat. We help Jameela into the back, and pile them both with blankets.

Diana rootles around in the glovebox and finds a flask of

hot chocolate she made for him, spiced with nutmeg.

'When did you manage to do that?' I ask, astounded.

She pokes her tongue out. 'I'm a very good multitasker, Elspeth.'

Putch takes a sip, the tension easing from his expression. I watch as a small smile spreads across his face.

'This is a good recipe,' he murmurs. 'Who taught you to make it?'

'Oh, just this crotchety old undertaker I used to know,' she replies, clambering into the driver's seat. I climb into the back with Jam and Annie.

'Don't push your luck,' he tells her. But his eyes are twinkling. 'What of my dragon?'

'Grael is safe,' says Diana.

More of the tension leaves him at hearing that.

Annie leans across to me. 'Who *is* that?' she asks, nodding at Diana.

I bite my lip. 'She's, um . . . a very long story.'

'Why didn't she make more flasks of that hot chocolate?' grumbles Jameela.

During the ride home, we finally learn some of what happened when Putch disappeared from the parlour.

He tells us a twisting tale of being the last person in the

Drained Place to know a witch, and me and Egg being the first ones in a long while that he'd let know him, and not knowing if he regretted that, because it hurt. He tells of bidding goodbye to Artemis, and writing a hasty note to me, and being hauled to the castle in chains.

I gasp. 'What about Sunken Putch?'

Shranken Putch takes a sip of hot chocolate. 'He is receding,' he announces slowly, eyes glassing over. Then they focus again. 'Yes. He is reabsorbed. Returned to the soil.'

I watch his reflection in the car window as hot-chocolate steam slowly clouds the glass. Tears ache in my throat.

Then he ruins it all by turning to me and complaining in a gravelly voice, 'Hens living indoors and cats doing the driving, eh? Hellish thickets.'

Diana rolls her eyes.

Annie and Jameela both stare at the back of Diana's curly head, and at me, and back again. '*What* did he say?' yelps Jameela.

By way of explanation, I show them the moon collar, which is still fastened around my neck.

Diana meets my eyes in the rear-view mirror, and I fall into fits of helpless laughter.

Epilogue

I stand on a rooftop at night. The sea crashes against the foot of Skull Tower. The sky is big and wide and black, peppered with pinprick stars. Draped with a garland of thirteen moons, the thirteenth still flickering, its blue flesh half-eaten away. But it won't disappear completely. Perhaps it might even begin to heal.

Across the water the Rookery stands empty, overgrown with ivy and rook nests, a great tangled maze that still dislocates every hour, bone grumbling over stone. They say he vanished, the feared and hated Hangman, and his Rook King with him. They say he lost all his power the day a kid as old as lost civilisations fished the great rook's eyeball out of the sacred well waters that fed the roots of a tree between realms. The enchanted raindrops fell, and his faceless agents turned on him. Or so the stories say. The people of Rookery Hollows celebrated long into the night, and on into the summer.

The calling of the rooks is loud enough to send ripples across the sea. I watch them, black blots circling, and wonder at how Flux spent all those stolen years huddled under the eaves, tied to a haunted tapestry. Strangely enough, I miss them. Or at least, I miss what could have been – friendship with a fellow Shadow-Born, who understood true loneliness. My heart spasms against my ribs. I wish Flux and I could have had time to go adventuring together. I have no idea if I'll ever meet another witch that can step between the worlds, as long as I live. In my mind I see Flux's dusky blue eyes, flickering with reflected rooks.

Some adventures sound too wild to have been real. But the telltale signs are with me all the time. My shadow creatures are waiting in my blood and mind, ready to distil into the air when I need them. And here I am in another world, now that I'm free to explore them. The Way of Bones is a favourite of mine. I record everything I learn in my Book of Shadows.

The best thing about all of it, though, is that we changed the Ways for the better, together with Unwicked – or *Unmagical* – allies. The Crown and the scientific community were mostly horrified by what the Hunt was doing, as it turned out – so they issued prison sentences against them, for the first time. The Barrows – that ancient, powerful family that didn't want the witch hunt to end, ever, even if it meant tearing down the edges of this world – are finally gone.

The witchcraft laws have been reversed, by a progressive young monarch. The old king, who was in the pocket of the Hunt, was dethroned. The Ring is now a protected place, and wildness might just have a chance of thriving there again. The freak weather has calmed and the flooding has stopped, now that witches are free and showing people how to be in balance with nature.

By the time we returned from the castle, Sunken Putch had been reabsorbed back into the floor, down into his roots, waiting for the time when he will have to fulfil the next step in the Putch Pact. Sometime many, many years from now.

Egg, Layla, Isla and Mariam were all passed out snoring. We woke them up with a round of toast, and after the screeching and crying and hugging was done, they told us how my shadows had helped strengthen the cloaking spell for a while – and then suddenly, the aircraft had vanished and the people gathered outside the parlour had dissipated as though a spell had been broken.

Jameela was sent to bed and we all looked after her until her wounds healed. She's the most keen to practise her witchcraft now, because she wants to make up for the magic that was stolen from her.

Shranken Putch was extremely unhappy about the state of the parlour when he first saw it again (and nobody dared mention the hens) but even he admitted that we could hardly be held to blame, given that we'd been under attack. The clean-up operation was epic, but at least there were lots of pairs of hands to get the work done.

After that, we got back to the business of undertaking.

No more souls are becoming ditchlings – we are a fully functioning funeral parlour, with a blossoming business, helping each and every soul through the portal to the Shadow Way after death. Now, as well as using the death phone, people can come to call at the Ring and speak to us when someone passes. We take good care of the families as well as the deceased. It matters to me to do a good job, because the job really matters.

Diana, much to everyone's surprise, requested to wear the moon charm again. She said she found it *most discombobulating* to keep turning formless and to feel the pull of being a wandering spirit. *I want to feel grounded*, she said. *And I rather liked being Artemis. Lots of naps. Plus, the Ring is in want of a wake-cat, after all.*

I stand up and stretch, inhaling a lungful of sea-salted air.

There's so much room for me in my own world. And I do love it, and belong there. Egg's acceptance of my difference reminded me that I belong – with her, with the coven, in our world, with the animals and plants and witches that we've saved, in the safety that we've made. But I belong in Other worlds, too, even though she can't follow me there. I don't have to choose.

Back at the funeral parlour of the Ring, we settle into folding chairs in the back garden – Egg, Layla, Mariam, Jameela,

Isla, Annie and me. We cradle cups of hot chocolate, toast marshmallows on a fire and share bags of popcorn. Our fingers are snack-food greasy when we point out the stars to each other, calling them by name. Then we begin to fish, hauling a chosen star closer with a cord that shines between the sky and our eyes. A cord that only shows itself if you know how to look. A slight squint, a head tilt, patience. The cords appear like a tightrope stretching into the sky.

When the death phone rings I head inside to answer it, jotting the details of the death on to the little notepad we keep next to the phone. 'Thank you,' I tell the caller. 'We advise that you stop the clocks, cover the mirrors and turn down the photographs. We'll be with you shortly.'

Shranken Putch, Head Undertaker, appears almost instantly, already dressed in his top hat and black suit. Maybe he was sleeping in it.

Artemis pads out of the sitting room, yawning widely. She brushes against the doorframe, considering me. These days I feel like I can hear her thoughts, or at least imagine what she'd tell me if she could. *The Ring is in want of an undertaker, Elspeth Wrythe.* I reach down to scratch between her ears, and she rumbles a purr.

'Are you ready, deputy?' Putch asks me.

I nod. 'Let's go.'

As well as writing magical books for children, Sarah Driver is also a qualified nurse and midwife. She is a graduate of the Bath Spa Writing for Young People MA, during which she won the Most Promising Writer prize. She is the author of the critically-acclaimed fantasy adventure trilogy, The Huntress. When she's not writing, she can be found walking by the sea, reading or researching a story. She has learned that even horrifying bouts of sea-sickness make excellent research material.

Fabi Santiago is the author and illustrator of *Tiger in a Tutu*, which was shortlisted for the Waterstones Children's Book Prize. After studying art and design in São Paulo, Fabi graduated with an MA in Children's Book Illustration at the Cambridge School of Art. Fabi's illustrations are full of movement and bold limited colours, and her medium of choice is screen-printing. She lives in London and has three cats, Daisy, Bear and Pepper.

Acknowledgements

Huge thanks to everyone at Farshore for making this book shine. Liz Bankes – whenever I'm at risk of losing faith, you're there with calm encouragement, humour and utter belief in my stories. I've cut my teeth as an author with you, and I'll be forever grateful! Thanks to Asmaa Isse for your patience, level-headedness and support. Many thanks to Lucy Courtenay and Susila Baybars for a scrupulous copyedit. Thank you to Fabi Santiago for more gorgeous artwork that perfectly captures the Wrythe sisters and their world(s). I couldn't imagine a more perfect illustrator for these books. Thank you to the Farshore art and design team for putting together another beautifully packaged book.

Big thanks and love to Jodie Hodges for your expert guidance and endless wisdom. Five books!

Thank you to David for putting up with my painful bouts of self-doubt, and being so steadfastly reassuring. Also, for reading an early draft and totally understanding what I was aiming for despite the tangle.

An eternity of gratitude to all the readers and parents in the UK and beyond who write to tell me how much you've enjoyed one of my books – still the best feeling in the world, and the most surreal. Similar gratitude to librarians – and PLR! – and teachers. You are legends.

Thank you to Waterstones for your continued support and for featuring *Once We Were Witches* on various lists, you've made a lockdown book much more discoverable and I'll always be grateful for that. Massive thanks are also due to amazing indie bookshops like The Book Nook, Mr B's Emporium, and Bags of Books – always welcoming, always connecting young readers with fantastic books.

Thank you to bloggers and reviewers who have responded so enthusiastically to *Once We Were Witches* – you're the best! Special mention to Izzy of Feeling Rather Bookish, the teachers at River Reading, Fern of Bluebird Reviews, Belle's Middle Grade Library, Diverse Kids' Books, Fred's Teaching Reading, and Amy of Golden Books Girl.

Thanks also to *Stylist* magazine for featuring Witches in your Christmas gift buying guide. An awesome surprise.

Thanks, love, and respect to the incredibly supportive authors in the children's writing community. You are far too many to name, but special mentions go to Jasbinder Bilan, Pádraig Kenny, Sinéad O'Hart, Kieran Larwood, Emily Sharratt, Katharine Orton and Lu Hersey for quoting, reviewing and generally being lovely.

Thank you to Lily, Piggy and Barb, for catting in all the best ways. I couldn't have written Artemis without direct experience of cats. Barb actually did once fall asleep with her face inside my palm, leaving an indent from her tooth.

Thank you to the writers of children's fantasy, both classic and contemporary. Where would we be without you? This book was inspired by a lot of subconscious things but also a smattering of Terry Pratchett and Diana Wynne-Jones, a sprinkling of Neil Gaiman, Alan Garner and Susan Cooper, plus a pinch of Sussex folklore, Norse mythology and the history of witchcraft. Thank you to the unknown author/s of the Lyke-Wake Dirge, a fourteenth century funeral chant which informed the wake dirge (a perhaps more heathenish chant) sung by the witches in this book.

You can see tapestries including the Devonshire Hunting Tapestries at the Victoria and Albert museum in London. When faced with these huge, otherworldly depictions that once watched over the halls of medieval nobility, it's hard not to feel like the scenes might just twitch into life. It's a long time since I first visited the tapestries, but I always hoped to weave them into a story one day.

Discover the first
ENCHANTING and ELECTRIFYING
adventure...

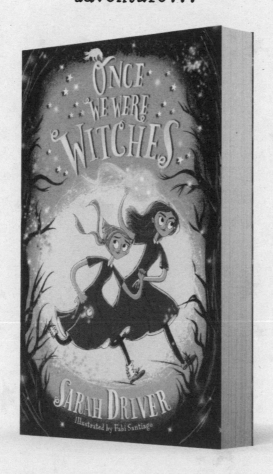